Escaping the Shadows

Aimee Blanc

Aimee Blanc

For my Gran and my Nana.
And for those who are missing their grandmothers.
Grandmothers are precious, hold on tight <3

Foreword

A LITTLE NOTE FROM AIMEE

I use historic Russian names of cities throughout this novel and change them to match the times in which the characters are living, so St Petersburg isn't St Petersburg, its Leningrad until the country changed the name. This happened quite a bit after the fall of the union so just something to bear in mind.

I will also note that the whole cult of personality thing is a wild ride, and if you think like the masses and think one person, such as a political leader, is the greatest thing ever, perhaps it's time to reevaluate your view. I do not prescribe to the view of my characters, nor their political beliefs. If something comes across as propaganda, its because that is genuinely what my character believed or was told by their state. As i said in the copyright statement, this is a work of fiction, and I take artistic license to parts of history.

While this is a work of fiction, I have done a heck of a lot of research into Soviet Russia, and perceptions at the time. But I am not perfect, I've not visited Russia (yes, I feel like a fraud, a euro trip is planned if this earns enough) so please take the history as I have written it with a grain of salt. Views and depictions of Soviet Russia and those in Russia at the time of the Soviet Union could be wildly wrong in my depiction. Again, I mean no offence, and I do not wish to insult anyone, I wanted to bring to life Anna's story in a timeline I know, in a countries rich history I'm inspired by (not its politicians though!)

I will note that this is **a work of fiction.** Espionage is a lot more complex and highly detailed than what I have depicted. I am aware, and honestly, my editor's brain has probably thrown all the insults you can think of at me

I still write in Australian English.

Mum and Gran, I learned my lesson.

Trigger warnings

This is a historically informed story, but a work of fiction and, as I am a westerner, there is a strong chance that I got some details wrong.

Also, there are a significant number of triggers in this one. I know some may see this as a shopping list, but please if any of the following is likely to cause you distress stop and consider what you're getting into. I may or may not have trauma dumped into this novel.

Grief (loss of a parent and a husband)

– Dementia

- Child loss (still birth and miscarriage)
- Emotional, verbal and physical abuse
- Suicidal ideation
- Ageism
- Family estrangement
- Illness and death
- Alcohol abuse
- Organised crime
- War (World War Two, Cold War and Hungarian revolution)

- Implied rape
- Homophobia
- Sexism
- Strong sense of imposters syndrome
- Cheating/ infidelity
- Financial strain/poverty
- Cultural differences/ prejudice
- Manipulation
- Secrets and lies

Please, please, please look after yourself, there is only one you and **you matter**.

November
1942

Anna, aged five | Gorky, Gorky Oblast , Russian Soviet Union

Anna was wide awake. Too awake for a five-year-old at ten pm.

She didn't want to be awake, she wished sleep would come, that she could feel safe enough to rest. Her mama had told her that she was safe, but she was scared. With the roar of the planes overhead, and the loud boom of guns.

Sleep would not be happening again tonight.

Anna clutched her itchy blanket tighter to her small chest. It made her feel safer, like it alone could keep all the bad things away.

The floor started to shake, like it did before.

Bombs, that's what her mama said. They left craters where Anna used to play with her father.

Before he left.

The feeling of grass beneath her toes, the way she would run away from her papa giggling after taping his side and yelling 'you're it!'

Memories of Papa would have usually made her sad to remember, because he wasn't there now, but this memory caused smile that lingered for only a moment before another boom followed by a series of sharp sounds brings Anna out of the calming moment.

She clamps her eyes shut, willing the world outside to be nothing more than a bad dream.

Why?

It was a question she asked often, her mother often scowling at her when she does. “Too many questions,” her mama said.

But why were the bad men in planes dropping bombs? What had the people of Gorky done to them?

Just for a moment, she wanted the world to stop and for there to be peace. She wanted to run and hide in a quiet place where the loud bangs couldn't get her.

Anna remembered the peaceful city she grew up in, with its rolling hills and the lazy Volga River taking its time flowing peacefully through the city. The memory of the river lapping against the riverbank to ease her frustrated tears. She wanted to live there if not wor the war.

All the fit young men, including teachers and her Papa, left the city to go and stop the Germans, the bad guys, her mama had said.

Mama said the Germans wanted some of Russia's land to become theirs, and that Papa and other Russian men couldn't allow that. Papa had to stop them. All the Russian men had to stop them.

Another bomb dropped nearby, the impact making the whole house shudder and the ceiling shower dust. This happens more often now. And that scares her, maybe the bombers don't realise only children and their mama's live here now. That maybe these men are cackling like witches in fairy tales as they drop their weapons from the sky. Or perhaps they don't have families of their own and don't know what it's like to lose someone.

It was cruel.

She burrowed deeper under the scratchy wool, a futile attempt to shield herself from the terror that lurked outside. The covers weren't keeping the heat in and the wool was uncomfortable, but Gorky was getting colder with winter drawing near.

The windows had thick black cloths over the glass, making the room so dark, darker than night, even when the moon was big outside. It felt like being shut in a box. Her mama had explained to her that light attracted the German Luftwaffe, the planes the bad men flew, like moths, and they were the ones that dropped the bombs that broke everything and made people die.

Maybe they could fly to the moon instead.

A few months after Anna's papa left to fight for Russia in The Great Patriotic War, it was what her mama and the men on the radio called it before the bombing started, explosives fell from the sky. Shaking the ground as if the land itself was revolting against the violence and destroying everything they landed near. Anna's mama covered the windows just before the sunset and told her to be quiet as a mouse. They couldn't risk their home becoming a target. They needed to stay alive for Anna's papa.

Anna could hear her mother getting up and creeping towards her room to check on her, the old wooden floorboards squeaking in protest. Anna screwed her eyes shut, knowing that if her mama knew Anna was scared, she would just worry more, and Anna didn't want to worry her mama more.

They would be okay.

Papa went to war so they would be.

The sirens started again, and the noise grated against Anna's senses. Mama promised this very school, the one Anna was meant to attend in a few years time, would be their safe place during the raids.

Their first practice run across the neighbourhood, was quick, but because Anna's legs were too short her mother told her she would need to be carried. She told Anna about sharp tiny pieces and invisible dust that made it hard to breathe when the bad sounds happened. She told her this as they walked back home.

“Anna!” Mama called, her voice loud like the scary sounds.

Anna squeezed her eyes shut for a moment, then opened them wide and ran. She crouched down low by the wall, right next to the special bags. She made herself small, like she was taught. The bags were heavy with clothes and bread, and her second-favourite doll. Not the best doll, but the second best.

The sirens were a noise that Anna hated. The sound of them seemed to wail incessantly, warning the residents of Gorky of an impending attack. She hated the fear, the pounding of her heart, and the tears they inspired.

The ground shuddered with another impact and Anna's mother dropped to the floor beside her.

“Do you remember what we have to do Sokolyonok[1] ?” her mama asked, leaning close and sweeping back a strand of hair wayward behind Anna's ear. She nodded, a tight, determlned bob of her head. Mama scooped her up, adjusting Anna on her back so the little girl clung on like a backpack, safe and secure.

Mama snatched the bags by the door and knocked twice on the frame – their secret signal. *Tap-tap!* It meant that when the droning of the bad planes faded, they would run, before the next wave arrived.

---

1. little bird

The heavy drone of the enemy planes finally receded after a few agonizing minutes.

Tap-tap!

Anna clung to Mama as tightly as she possibly could, burying her face in the familiar scent of her hair, trying to block out the lingering sounds of destruction.

Thankfully the run across the square to the school was short, and they filed into the building with the others.

They huddled with their neighbours, some of Anna's friends, and strangers. The ground around them trembled. A baby wailed. Someone screamed.

Anna hated being in that school. The air was thick and heavy, the smell... Anna wrinkled her nose. It was sweaty, and smelt bad.

December was one long, bleak blur spent more in the darkened school than in her own home. The whispers had started again, mama and the other women huddled together in tight circles, their faces serious.

From conversations the children pieced together, there was only one word they all seemed to agree they had heard: *Sverdlovsk*. One of the older children, who always knew everything, explained it was a city far to the east, protected by huge mountains. Anna asked her mama, who agreed with the child's explanation, her own eyes faraway.

“It's a long way to travel,” Mama had murmured later. “But the mountains will protect us.” It was the same promise she'd made about Gorky before they left their last home.

A cold dread settled in Anna's stomach. Leaving. Leaving the home where Anna expected to be found by her Papa after the war.

Sverdlovsk.

The word was a shiver down her spine.

Sverdlovsk.

It was scary.

Snow crunched under Anna's boots as she was finally able to leave the shelter, and the cold air bit at her exposed nose. She couldn't help but release a small shiver, before trying to pull the front of her jacket up further.

There was beauty in the cold, even Anna could admit that. But the cruel January temperatures and the falling snow were not ideal for going home after the sirens had finally ceased their wailing.

“Anna!” her mama called to her from Anna's bedroom.

Anna got up from her place on the living room floor and ran to her mama.

She had a suitcase out on the floor with Anna’s practical clothes packed in it. Not a single dress, or toy in sight.

Anna could feel her brows knitting together on her forehead, confused as to what her mother was doing.

“Sokolyonok, we need to pack. I didn't want to choose everything for you, so you can choose five things to bring with us.”

Anna went to work, pulling out every doll, dress and nursery rhyme book she had from her cupboard.

She knew she would have to leave some of it behind, but what? How could she choose?

Mama in the meantime had gotten up and stood in the doorway, her eyes glistening. She looked at the chaos surrounding Anna. Anna, surrounded by her belongings, looked back, her own eyes wide.

"Darling, we need to pack and get going," she eyes the open suitcase on the floor. The choices Anna was to make.

But how...? Anna thought, *how could she possibly fit everything*?

She picked up a doll, then another. *What if I don't come back?*

The thought made her stomach twist. Mama wouldn't be happy if she only packed toys. Her rhymes. Maybe the dresses. She chose a comfortable dress, her favourite, a warm one. One her papa told her she looked beautiful and like a tzarina in. She grabbed her favourite doll and tucked it next to the dress.

She looked up towards her mama who was nodding at her in approval, unshed tears in her eyes.

"Mama, why are you about to cry?" Anna asked her mother, still standing at the door, but now allowing those unshed tears to break free and make their way down her face.

"Sokolyonok," Mama said, her voice trembling, "I'm scared too. Even adults can be scared. But we must sometimes do the hard things to keep everyone safe."

Anna looked up at her mama and nodded, trusting mama knew best. She always did. She would keep them safe, until Papa came home.

December 1943

Anna, aged six | On the road to Sverdlovsk, Sverdlovsk Oblast, Russian Soviet Union

"One... Two... Five!" Anna was counting the cars that had been abandoned in the snowy landscape. The pristine snow contrasted with the stark reality that most of these families had to leave their vehicles for shelter. It made the war even more real, that the bad planes weren't just in Gorky but could come for them while they were on the road. The thought was a cold knot in her stomach and made her feel ill.

On the third day of travel, Anna found herself singing nursery rhymes to the younger children travelling with them until her mother shot her the *look* so she shut up and grabbed a book instead. She knew how to read, but the little words were hard to put together sometimes and some of them were super long. This book was one of her father's, Russian poetry.

Boring.

The jerky movements of the bus soon put a stop to her attempts at reading as the nausea set in. She spent the rest of that day, with her eyes shut, willing the journey to end soon.

Five days. Anna squirmed in her seat, the itchy wool coat a torment. She kicked at her mama's seat and wondered if she was uncomfortable too. She didn't want to leave Gorky.

Papa.

How would he find them?

The gentle rocking of the vehicle they were in eventually put Anna to sleep.

When she woke, the bus was still bumping. Mama had told her they couldn't go on the big noisy trains because the bad planes had broken the tracks, so they had to ride in a smelly cramped bus instead.

We must be close by now, Anna thought and asked in a small voice, "Are we there yet?" to the people in the front seat.

Anna heard her mama fail to smother a groan for asking such a question in an already stressful situation, then turned to say to her, "No little one, 40 minutes to go at least."

40 minutes? Anna thought, *that'll feel like forever!*

The wide snowy plains with the burnt-out cars began to turn into tall snow ladened trees and endless straight roads.

The car finally pulled to a stop in front of an old wooden house. Anna was out before her mama could even come around to open the door for her.

Anna raced up the steps to the front door, caution be damned as her mind was flying with a hundred unanswered questions.

"Mama?" Anna whined.

Her mama sighed. "Yes, little one?"

Anna's mama looked down; her green eyes shadowed. Anna saw the worry lines on her forehead, deeper than before. She'd heard mama whispering with the other women about empty fields. Scary stories. She pushed the thoughts away and came to her mothers side.

"Can I go inside and choose my room?"

"Little one, we need to share this space with those we travelled with. Wouldn't it be nice for the younger ones to choose where they sleep first? I know I taught you patience."

The other families piled out of the car, the steps Anna had just run up and down groaning under the added weight.

The wooden door let loose with an almighty squeak as another mama opened it for her children. The windows were dark from the outside, and her mama had mentioned they would be sharing a room as there were only two of them. Some of the families they had come with had six children, but Anna's Mama had said there would be enough space for everyone.

The house had a rustic feel, and because of its build, it would not have been out of place in a more rural location.

Anna's mama looked down at her daughter, and bent down to whisper in her ear "Go!"

Anna shot off giggling like a bullet into the house.

Inside, Anna tiptoed down the long hallway, peering into rooms in search of the perfect room for her and her mama. Too small. Too dark. She came to the last door of the hallway and peeked into the final room, still unclaimed by the other families. This one was small but not too small for her and her mama. It had a seat by the window and a view of the snowy backyard.

This is the one she thought.

It felt… safe.

July 1944

Anna, aged six | Sverdlovsk, Sverdlovsk Oblast, Russian Soviet Union

"Anna, it's time for school!" Her mama's voice emanated down the hallway and stirred Anna awake. She struggled to open her eyes, the hunger, the sleepless nights and the attempts at getting back to a sense of normalcy made all of Anna's limbs feel heavy.

She groaned as she got out of bed and put on the clothes she and her mama had chosen for the day.

Anna sometimes heard her mama crying and talking to herself at night, whispering her papa's name. The muffled sounds her mama made when she thought Anna was sleeping made Annas chest hurt for her.

Anna kept her worries to herself. Mama already looked tired; her brow always furrowed. She didn't want to add to her sadness, though she almost always looked worried, especially when she noticed how thin Anna had become.

Anna rolled out of bed. Her school clothes lay out ready for her.

It hadn't been long, maybe a few days before Anna found herself the subject to a group of boy's ire. They were bigger than her, and grabbed at her hair in the playground. Their laughter echoed around the play area. They called her names she didn't understand, but mama's face had gone white when Anna repeated them.

School was her own personal hell.

During the lunch hour, Anna learned to stay inside. The last time she dared venture out, the boys shoved her to the ground, boots connecting with her stomach and legs. She had curled up, trying to protect herself while they rifled through her bag. They took everything. Well, everything except for the books that they would have had for school too. Her empty stomach gnawed at itself, the hollow sensation where her tummy should be was uncomfortable and made her long for the days when her papa was home with them. She wasn't hungry when he was home.

So, Anna sat inside with the quiet nerdy types and learned to play chess. She always got to school early so she could make sure that she hid her lunch behind the teacher's desk.

“What are you doing, girl?” The teacher's voice boomed. Anna froze, her heart pounding. Isaievna Putina. The stern woman was more terrifying than the bullies. Her arms were crossed, her brow furrowed.

“Getting my lunch,” Anna whispered, shrinking back. She knew lying wasn't going to do her any good with this teacher. Even if she was hesitant to tell her why she hides her lunch away each day.

Isaievna raised an eyebrow. “Your lunch? Its behind my desk?”

Anna took a shaky breath. “I… I have to hide it.”

Isaievna's face softened slightly. She knelt, her eyes level with Anna's. “Why, little one?”

Anna's fingers twisted the edge of her skirt. “I… I don't want anyone to get in trouble.”

Isaievna frowned. “Is someone stealing your lunch?”

Anna's lips pressed together. She didn't answer.

“Is it the boys?” Isaievna asked gently.

Anna's eyes squeezed shut. A single tear escaped.

Isaievna sighed. “Anna,” she said softly. “You can tell me.”

“How long has this been going on?” The teacher's tone demands answers.

Anna put the floor board back and clutched her lunch to her chest. She didn't want to get the other children in trouble.

But they had been cruel.

“Anna?” Isaievna put on a stern, “you need to tell me.”

Anna looked down at the floor. She wasn't a huge fan of tattling, haunted by the memory of the boys circling their target. They had chanted 'snitches get stitches' in time with their kicks, while the small child curled into a ball on the ground, desperate for protection

Like Anna had.

"Please," Isaievna continued, "tell me what is happening. If you don't, I will have to call your mother."

No. Not mama, Anna thought, eyes widening and lower lip starting to tremble on its own. She was already so worried and Anna didn't want to add to her troubles.

Anna sniffed, feeling the tears starting to well in her eyes.

"They." Anna stops herself to take a deep breath.

"T-t-they take my lunch," she said quietly, her voice quivering.

"The boys?" Isaievna asked.

Anna nodded, tears welling up.

Isaievna stood. "Okay," she said. "You can eat your lunch by the window. Then, you can play. Inside or outside. It's up to you."

Isaievna turned and walked away.

Anna stayed on the floor, clutching her lunch. She savoured each bite, while also keeping her eyes open in case the boys decided to come in early. Would they notice? Either that she wasn't hungry during the second half of the day, or that her eyes were likely now red-rimmed and swollen from crying.

September 1945

Anna, aged eight | Sverdlovsk, Sverdlovsk Oblast, Russian Soviet Union

There was a loud thump on the front door, and it caused everyone home and around the table to jump, Anna, who was colouring with another child, included. It jolted Anna's heart, beating fast in her chest, like it was trying to escape.

"Come here child!"

The air was punctured with sharp, urgent whispers from the scared mamas as they got ready to scoop their children up and run away. Some even started to move until a couple of tentative knocks followed, causing the women to stop, children clasped tightly in their arms and look at the door.

The war was over. Mama had promised. And more than that, Mama had promised Papa would come home.

Anna knew him only from the faded sepia photograph on Mama's bedside table – a young, strong man with a wide, confident smile, standing beside a radiant Mama in her simple red coloured wedding dress. That picture was Papa.

“Katya? Sokolyonok[1] ?” a man called from the doorway. His voice sounded tired and gruff. Like he had been through hell and back. It didn't sound like the voice of her Papa she had in her head. She had distant memories of him singing to her before the war, the man at the door sounded like he had a cold or something. It didn't sound right.

Anna's mama started to cry when she heard the voice “Grisha?” she cried out, as the man stood in the doorway.

He was tall, taller than the women that Anna was used to being surrounded with. He was thin, much skinnier than he looked in the photo. He stiffened when her mama hugged him and his light eyes, which her mama had explained were the same colour as the ocean, looked more like storm clouds.

One of the women dropped a plate in the kitchen upon seeing the man, causing him to crumple in his wife's arms, both landing awkwardly on the floor by the door.

“Grigori?” Anna's mama was holding him and petting his hair while he cried out and eventually came back to the present moment. He stayed on the floor in the foetal position, his wife crouching down next to him rubbing his back soothingly and asking if he was okay.

---

1. Little bird

"Yes dearest, I'm sorry to scare you. I am fine."

And then it clicked.

Anna had heard the other mama's whisper quietly between themselves about the sickness. That some of the men around town had come back from the war with this sickness, called shell shock, and that most of them used strong adult drinks to help them feel better.

Anna considered the man on the floor, while she remained still as a statue in her seat. The way her mama was holding him and telling him he was safe, the way the man dropped to the floor like there was gunfire when it was just a plate being dropped.

Her papa.

How bad was it?

March 1947

Anna aged nine | Kazan, Tatar Soviet Republic, Union of Soviet Republics

Anna's eyes felt heavy keeping them closed as her mama called up to her while she slept in. The bed was comfortable, the blanket was warm, and she was stubborn enough not to go to school.

That was until she heard her mama come up the stairs. She was relentless in her mission to make sure Anna had a good education.

She groaned as she sat up, her mama bursting through the door.

"Why are you not dressed child!" she said, before closing the door again and allowing Anna to get up, at a much more hurried pace, on her own.

She had started the all-girls school only a few weeks ago, coming from Sverdlovsk She had been pre-emptively warned by the other girls not to trust any of the city girls.

Her parents had decided she was going to boarding school after the summer. Mama called it "next year," but Anna knew it was just a few months away. She just had to survive this school until then. Papa said she *had* to go. He wasn't home much anyway, always working long hours, his car leaving before sunrise and returning long after dark. That left their big, wooden house on the edge of the city empty all day, except for Mama. Anna knew Mama spent her days scrubbing floors until her back ached, getting meals ready, and trying to make the house feel like a home again.

The wooden house, tall and two-storied with a swirly staircase, felt strange to Anna, even though they'd lived here before. The familiar tiny nicks from her own growth spurts were still there on the doorframes, but now there were new ones too, carved by a family who had stayed there while they were gone. Mama always sighed about them, complaining they hadn't taken care of *their* house, hadn't kept it tidy enough.

The kitchen was the same though, smelling of faint spices and old wood. The lounge however, was bare. Most of Papa's thick literature novels were gone, and even the big bookcase had vanished. Anna guessed they probably used the books for the stove, to keep them warm during the coldest parts of the war. She shivered a little at the thought.

Anna stood at the top of the spiral staircase, clutching the banister. Ever since a slip on the slick wood two weeks ago, her aching ankle had been reminding her to take every step with care. By the time she made it down, her mama was already in the kitchen laying out breakfast.

"Now, I know that this school isn't ideal, but you only need to get through to the summer Sokolyonok[1] , then we can get you off to a boarding school." She said to Anna as she placed a plate of oatmeal with the familiar pinch of sugar on top in front of Anna.

Anna rolled her eyes at her mama, who had turned away to gently cough into a handkerchief.

Anna wasn't a fan of school. Her love of art, the way a paint brush felt in her hand as paint glided on a canvas, had waned because of the war, and supplies were difficult to come by.

Her new school, a sprawling building filled with girls who didn't know her and teachers who, with their kind but distant smiles, treated her simply as a child, was the perfect, unassuming stage. Here, she could stay in plain sight, a quiet observer, watching them all.

From the small unassuming girl clutching her backpack in front of her as she walked through the main doors, her body told a silent story of previously being bullied or perhaps scarcity of supplies that affected so many during the war.

To the teacher at the front of the class, who drawled out a lesson in a monotone. That suggested to Anna that they didn't want to be here, or perhaps

1. Little bird

they had seen horrors of war that had stolen their humanity.

While Anna wasn't a fan of school, the art of reading people, and subtly finding what influences them, became one of her new favourite past times.

July 1950

Anna, aged twelve | Moscow, Moscow Oblast, Russian Soviet Federative Socialist Republic

"Hi," came a quiet voice from the bed next to Anna's. It took Anna by surprise, she wasn't expecting anyone else in the dormitory, and the usual creak of the bedsprings didn't provide the typical alert to another's presence.

The room was filled with beds, a big open style dormitory. Not allowing any form of privacy, secrets or escape when one of the girls started snoring during the night.

Anna looked over at the slight girl sitting on the once empty bed, her uniform loosely hanging off her frame.

She looked thin, like the children Anna had seen in Sverdlovsk. Gaunt, like she was starved during the war, that perhaps the ration cards never made it to her family. Or the rations she was meant to be allocated were stolen.

Anna raised her eyebrow at the girl, wondering what the newcomer might want with her.

It was Anna's second year in a boarding school in Moscow. Anna kept to herself, watching, wary. Never again a target. Never again.

"Um," the girl sputtered under Anna's intense gaze, "I'm Darya Volkova, your classmate? I'm new to this school"

Darya held out a hand, a hesitant offering. Anna took it, a limp handshake, gave it a firm two shakes, then released.

"So, you're Anna, right? Kira was talking about you."

Anna raised her other eyebrow in surprise and then was a touch concerned. Kira wasn't known for her flattering descriptions of the teenage girls in her care, so what had she told this girl? Anna had on more than one occasion heard Kira complaining about the girls, complaining about who ate too much, who didn't eat enough and who ought to have learned basic cleaning when they lived at home.

"And what did Kira have to say about me?"

The question, though obvious, seemed to take Darya off guard.

"Oh, um, that you were quiet, maybe a bit aloof but nice enough."

That made Anna laugh. Once people got to know her, she couldn't be deemed as quiet, and while she hung back more often than not, she wouldn't deem herself as aloof or shy. It showed how much the people running this school paid attention. Or not as the case might be.

"Alright," Anna responded. The silence between the two girls stretched on for what felt like forever.

The hesitant girl stared back at Anna, not unlike a deer stuck in headlights.

"So Darya, tell me about yourself," Anna said leaning herself back against the wall on her bed.

"If we're going to live together, and Kira has already disclosed all my secrets, I think it's fair I learn something more about you right?"

The girls talked until dinner time. About their upbringing, that Darya was from a fishing village up near the white sea and was sent to boarding school because there was no other option for her in her family's rural location.

The girl was smart as a whip and didn't want to follow in her family's footsteps of working on fishing boats or in that industry. She was drawn to science and the space race that was currently occurring between Russia and the United States. Anna didn't understand the appeal of space. It seemed too vast, too dangerous, and for what? She preferred her feet to be solidly on the ground. At least then, she could keep an eye on people, especially those in power.

The two girls walked down the stairs to join the crowd wandering into the dining room to have dinner, and Anna brought Darya over to a table where a bigger girl sat.

The girl at the table wasn't fat, or even overweight. She was however very solidly built. Not someone that you'd want to argue with as her scarred knuckles told stories to anyone who dared to look.

"Hi, Sef!" Anna said to the girl as she sat down at the table.

The girl, Sef, just looked at both girls before returning to her meal.

Darya shot Anna a concerned look, to which Anna just shrugged her shoulders and started on her meal, a stew of some sort with bread on the side. God only knows what meat the stew was made from, but it would get them through the night and into another day.

"I bet her mama was a whore during the war. Allowing herself to be open for both the Germans and the Finnish, and she takes after her, I mean look at her," the girls snickered as they looked towards the front of the classroom, where Anna was focusing on getting her schoolwork done.

Anna was sitting alone in the near-empty room so it wasn't like the toxic nasty words and taunts could have been aimed at anyone else.

Anna rolled her eyes and tried to focus back down on her work. She learned the hard way, during her formative years in Sverdlovsk, that the best way to deal with bullies was to ignore them completely.

They weren't worth the effort of expelling more anger into the world. There was already enough of that. Anna rolled her shoulders, allowing their words to fall away as she focused back on her schoolwork.

"Actually, I bet she's a charity case, didn't you notice how skinny she was when she started here, and how fat she is now?"

Undernourished is not the same thing as thin, healthy is not the same as full bodied, Anna reminded herself. She was like most people and had issues with how she looked. But it wasn't her fault.

The girls continued their murmurings, the head matron Kira actively ignoring them so that she didn't have to report the issue to any caregivers. Not that much care was given here.

Sef walked into the room and sat next to Anna, which prompted the girls to turn their nasty words into an effort to degrade the both of them.

"Oh look, guys! It's the kolobo[1] girls!" the girls erupting into a fit of giggles, proud of their 'original' insult.

Sef shoots them a glare that shuts their mouths so quickly, the snap of their jaws so sudden you could hear their teeth clicking together. The other girls seem to be highly interested and highly engrossed in their schoolwork. Their heads were dipped, eyes glued the pages.

---

1. round bread roll

"How do you do that?" Anna whispered to the girl next to her.

Sef looked at Anna, who was staring at the girl, a mixture of apprehension, fear and awe painted across her delicate features. Her pupils blown so wide that only a thin line of green could be seen.

"I don't," Sef answers curtly. "My papa does for me."

Anna gulps at that.

As young as she was, she knew that being able to shut down bullies like that must mean that Sef was from a particularly dangerous family. A family that with the right strings could cause the family of the girls' immeasurable grief.

"What does your family do?"

Sef looks back at her schoolwork, dismissing Anna, only to whisper,

"I like you, Anna but this conversation cannot take place in front of people."

And with that, Anna's imagination ran wild.

Was Sef's papa a spy for the union? Was he a politician? Was he a criminal? The possibilities were endless.

And terrifying.

"I can see you thinking there, Anna. I will tell you. Just not right now," Sef mutters under her breath to Anna.

Upon the end of the hour-long class, which felt like an eternity, Sef pulled Anna aside as everyone else left the room.

December
1950

Anna, aged thirteen | Moscow, Moscow Oblast, Russian Soviet Federative Socialist Republic

The rain pitter-pattered against the window, and the heavy grey clouds that the water fell from added to the melancholic mood for Anna. It was cold again too, adding to her disdain.

Her papa had been quiet during the last couple of months, no phone calls, no letters.

The last call she had from him had caused her to need to visit the front desk of the boarding school, in October, and the call...

It felt strange.

"Anna?" the gruff masculine voice of her papa came down the line. It had been a while since she had heard it, and while it was nice to hear from him, he was a strange to her after the war. Even before the war, But perhaps with him calling he would pass the phone over to her mama. She was who Anna missed.

"Papa?" She replied.

"Anna, I need to be quick here."

Hearing that, Anna's heart dropped. A quick call meant she wouldn't speak to her mama.

"I just want to confirm that your marks are up to par?"

"Yes papa," Anna answered automatically. She wasn't sure if he really did care about her academic progress or not, or if it was an excuse.

"Okay. Also, just before you go. You are not to contact your mama. To do so would make things difficult. Difficult for you, for your mama and me."

"Papa!" Anna cried down the line, surely the bitter man wasn't doing what she suspected he was doing.

"No arguments. This is for your own good. And hers," He stated and hung up the phone.

Fat ugly tears trailed down Anna's face as she clung to the receiver, praying to whomever would listen that he'd call back and say it was a hoax.

His order isolated her. Made her feel lonely despite being surrounded by dozens of teenage girls constantly. Her very soul yearned for the soft comfort of her mama's arms wrapped around her shoulders in a tight hug.

She had spent the last two months wondering why he'd forbidden her from calling home. But as she walked toward the office, she was hopeful; maybe the restriction was over. Maybe it was her mama calling at last…

"I am sorry to break this news to you, Anna," Kira starts, pointing Anna towards a comfy-looking seat across from Kira's desk.

Anna felt a sense of uneasiness, worry tinging the air, and she wasn't looking forward to what Kira had to say to her.

Kira was looking morose, formal. Not that the woman was known for being highly gleeful, but she felt colder than normal. Like someone had forgotten to turn on the heating.

She slowly lowered herself into the chair, which felt like a hug. Her slow movements gave away her sense of unease.

“Your mother passed away last night. She died of a suspected tuberculosis infection in her lungs and later complications. Your father is on his way to come and collect you.”

Anna missed the last part of the conversation and slid off the chair onto the floor in a flood of tears.

Sobbing loudly, she thought about the unfair situation. How she hadn't spoken to her mama in months, since she came back to school in September.

Her chest heaved with each sob, a physical manifestation of the grief and shock clawing at her heart. Tears streamed down her face, hot and stinging, blurring her vision as her shoulders shook uncontrollably. Her throat constricted, making it difficult to breathe.

She was excited to head home and spend a cosy Christmas with her mama. Fireside hot chocolates, traditional tea and classic Russian treats or baking. She wanted to surprise her mama with some poetry she wrote as part of her literature lessons. Her papa seemed to be missing from many of her daydreams of him, perhaps because of his absence while she was growing up.

She was due to gift her mama a necklace and pendant she had spent hours pouring over and making.

And now…

For what?

The pain was sharp, like a thousand tiny cuts, as if her heart were shattering into a million pieces.

Unrepairable, broken beyond belief, shattered into miniature pieces.

Kira looked down at the sobbing, blubbering mess of a girl on the floor and barked, "Anna, you need to get a handle on yourself. Your papa will be here within the next few hours, you will be heading home with him and not returning until the Christmas break is over."

The growled order from the headmistress snapped Anna out of her sobbing, and she looked up to her through her lashes, which tears still clung onto stubbornly.

"Okay. I need to go and pack," she said emotionlessly. Numbness crept up from her feet and swept up over her body, cold and heavy until it settled in her chest.

Nothing would be the same. Her mother's warm nature would be missed in the household and her papa would likely run a tight ship.

He was as cold as the white sea and at least her mama's warm nature meant the house was lukewarm rather than frosty like she knew to expect. When it was just her and her mama, the house was warm. Perhaps filled with more people, but the mood was warmer. Comfort was provided.

Back in the room, Anna grabbed her things, shoving them into a bag. No order to it. She just knew her mama was gone.

“Anna, are you okay?” asked a still very shy Darya to Anna's back.

Anna turned around; it was clear that she had been crying recently. Her eyes, rimmed with red, were swollen and puffy, and her cracked lips were dry and chapped.

“Anna?” Darya asked, in a more worried tone. Anna had been careful not to show any kind of weakness or distress in front of Darya for the short time she had been at the school. Until now. She was sure that Darya caught the usually stoic Anna in a moment of weakness.

"I need to pack, Darya," Anna managed, the words catching in her throat. Even her own voice felt alien, thin and trembling, nothing like the strong, assertive tone she usually commanded. The effort to even speak felt immense, the words feeling like sandpaper on her tongue.

Anna felt empty, like a shadow of herself, and every little noise made her jump. Her usual strength had evaporated, leaving her exposed and raw. She just wanted to disappear. Her very soul yearned for the soft comfort of mama’s arms, for the familiar scent of her hair, for a tight hug that could somehow put her back together.

Darya, bless her, didn't ask questions. She just started gathering Anna's scattered belongings, her movements gentle, efficient. She helped Anna stuff things into a small bag, then guided her, almost physically, down the quiet hall and to the visitor's area of the boarding school. The cold air outside bit at Anna's chapped lips.

"Will you be okay, Anna?" Darya's voice was low, filled with an empathy that made Anna's chest ache. Anna knew Darya was worried, that she saw how utterly shattered she was. Anna hoped she would be okay too, hoped this wasn't something that would stick with her forever.

"Maybe," Anna whispered, the single word feeling heavy, definitive. A dark car waited outside, and an older man Anna recognized as her papa stood beside it, his face grim. Anna didn't look back at Darya as she got in.

The door shut with a soft click, sealing her away from everything that had been her life just hours before.

January 1951

Anna, aged thirteen | Kazan, Tatar Autonomous Soviet Socialist Republic, Union of Soviet Socialist Republics

White rose petals drifted over the casket, settling against the wood as it was lowered into the earth.

Her mama's ultimate resting place.

Everything was monochrome, like the color had been sapped from the world with the death of her mama. Only the black of the mourners' coats and the stark white of the earth remained.

Anna watched her tears hit the ground, carving tiny, jagged holes into the fresh powder.

While Anna was inconsolable, her papa was a statue. He remained perfectly still, offering stiff handshakes to 'friends' he had never met, his face as frozen as the earth beneath them.

Did her mama's death not affect him? Did he lose his humanity in the war?

The news travelled fast once Anna made it home. The girls had made quite a few friends during his time at war. There was a network of women, a lot of them now widows, who all supported each other when times were getting tough. People travelled from Gorky and Sverdlovsk to celebrate her mama's life, short as it ended up being.

Anna was still withdrawn and sullen. She didn't understand why her Papa had become so cold, and why her mama never said goodbye.

They had a few days left until New Year's, and even if her own Babushka on her Papa's side was visiting, she wasn't in a festive mood. She didn't even want to be around her family. She was numb.

And she wasn't sure if she would ever feel again. What's the point? She thought.

Feelings just lead to heartbreak and disappointment.

She found the letter on her last day in Kazan before coming back to school.

She had an inkling to check the old hiding spot she and her mama kept secret in the house in case something happened and they needed to come back for money and identification.

Just behind the spiral staircase was a loose floorboard. It was unassuming, but the only floorboard that was unblemished by knots or scuff marks.

Anna lent down and got her finger nails between the boards and started to move them to get a purchase on the board. Anna's mama had cleared out everything from underneath there after the war was finished and they moved home again.

The board finally flexed and *Success!* The floor board came free.

Anna wasn't expecting anything to come of her brief trip down memory lane, but inside she found a folded piece of paper.

It was addressed to her, in her mother's cursive.

And while that was a surprise, more so was the fine mist of dried blood on the outside of the envelope.

"Anna?" her papa's voice came from the living room. He hadn't moved from 'his' seat in there for the past week. Since they had buried her mama.

The only useful thing he had done was keep the stove running.

"Bring me another bottle, would you?"

He wasn't coping with the loss well. Anna had started switching some of the older bottles of vodka out with water so he wouldn't put himself in an early grave.

Anna quickly put the letter in her pocket and shimmied the floorboard back into place, before getting off the floor to fetch her father a bottle of clear liquid.

"Anna?" Darya gently elbowed her in the ribs, her voice loud enough to cut through the haze Anna was lost in.

Anna barely registered the nudge. Her eyes were fixed on the crumpled envelope in her hands, with handwriting Darya hadn't seen before.

To Anna, it felt like if she blinked or breathed too hard it'd disappear. The words would vanish. It was precious.

She didn't want to open it in her father's home. If he had found it, he would have thrown it on the stove and watched it, her mama's last words to her daughter, burn.

Anna hid it in her suitcase and only got back to the boarding house twenty minutes ago.

The light of my life.

I have a feeling your papa hasn't shared the other note I wrote before, so I wanted to write you another one.

Just for you.

I love you.

I loved you from the moment I felt you flutter in my belly; I loved you when you kick at my ribs and pushed against my organs from inside my stomach.

I loved you even when you don't let me or your papa sleep for weeks on end because you are a colicky newborn.

I loved you when you wanted to pack all your dolls when we escape, Gorky.

I love you, Anna. I loved you then and even now I am gone I love you still.

I am sorry I am not strong enough to beat this illness. I want to live to see you graduate, find a husband (who better treat you right) and produce beautiful children.

I know you are going to live a long, beautiful full life Anna, and I want you to please not let my passing affect this. I know it hurts right now, dear child, but this pain will pass. Or at the very least, it becomes bearable.

Please look after your papa. I think the war broke his spirit and he needs love too, even if he seems too gruff or cold to receive it.

I look forward to seeing all your achievements from the afterlife, dear girl.

Love you forever,

Your Mama.

Tears silently streamed down Anna's face, the salt leaving her lips stinging, and her eyes burning. She couldn't stop the torrent of tears or the overwhelming emotions that reading the letter for the first time bought on.

She read it again, trying to seek comfort in the words from her mama. Her final words to her.

Seeing her reaction to the note, a startled Sef gently removed it from her hands, placing it carefully on the bed beside them so Anna wouldn't cry on it and ruin the precious paper.

"Anna?" Darya's voice was a quiet question, a hesitant sound, and Anna felt the unspoken confusion from her friend.

The girls sat with Anna while she let her emotions out, keeping the matrons at bay as they did the rounds to check the girls were studying. There is no chance that Anna would be able to focus on anything beyond her grief in that moment.

Left to deal with her deep grief.

April 1951

Anna, aged thirteen | Moscow, Moscow Oblast, Russian Soviet Federative Socialist Republic

The old floorboards of Anna's room knew the rhythm of her grief by heart. Each evening, after the last echoes of dinner conversation faded, she began her restless pacing. Back and forth, back and forth. She was pretty sure her friends were being too polite to say anything, but the constant creak in the floorboards she treaded every evening must have been driving them crazy.

"Think, Anna, think. How can I feel better?"

The whispered question tasted unpleasant, a futile plea against the crushing sense of gloom. As if one could overcome four months of dulled, morose, and overwhelming sadness with the magical click of fingers. Her mama's very breath had been one of Anna's own reasons to live, and now... now there was only this hollow ache in the centre of her chest. Anna just wanted to feel alive again, to claw her way out of the darkness in her mind that had claimed her since the funeral.

Then it hit her. A bolt of an idea, reckless in its nature, but more than just a thought. It was a jolt of electricity, a raw, desperate strand of something that promised to pierce through the numbness. Something that could, finally, make her feel truly alive again.

She turned to her friends, who were chatting a few beds down from where she paced.

"Sef, Darya! Let's go for a walk down the Moskva River! I want to escape this place and feel the breeze of the city coming off the river. I want to live again and explore. Let's go!"

Darya's eyes widened while Sef shifted uncomfortably from her position, sitting on the edge of Darya's bed, a frown creasing her brow.

The river wasn't an especially safe place for a group of 13-year-old girls to be walking at nighttime. But they also didn't want to let Anna go on her own, if her papa ever found out, the hell he would rain down on them would be the least of their problems.

Such as disappearing or being forced to live in isolation in Siberia would probably be the result of that kind of action. Something not even Sef's family could prevent with the absolute power Anna's father held as a legitimate top businessman within the union.

"Anna," Darya started gently, "we can do this during the day?"

Anna shook her head, feeling a pull and need for a rush now.

She needed the adrenaline.

"Okay, how about we chat through this plan a little more then, come up with some better ideas than just going? We can go on a night where there's live music playing somewhere or when someone from Sef's family could go with us?" Darya continued.

Anna knew of Sef's family, the thieves-in-law who managed to escape to Spain during the war, only to come back and take over the territory again.

Anna shook her head again, making both of the girls wonder if their friend was suicidal. Because her plan was.

Both of their eyes widened, and Anna grinned wider at their dismay.

"Seriously guys, what's the worse that can happen?"

Sef was the first to answered, "We could be kidnapped, tortured and ransomed".

"We could be trafficked as sex slaves," Darya piped up.

Anna took her turn to shake her head at the girls.

"Well, if you guys don't want to come, I guess I can go by myself," she said resulting in her friends screaming "NO!" at her.

Anna chuckled at her friends as she popped up to her room to get ready to sneak out.

The boarding school had one entrance and one exit, all through the same set of old creaky doors.

However, because it was an older building, some of the ancient windows' latches weren't what they were previously.

The girls got into warmer clothing, and quietly made their way down the stairs to the ground floor.

Keeping themselves in the shadows, they made their way down to the common room keeping an ear out for the elderly man who patrols the grounds after dark.

Mr Utkina was fond of his nightly routine, Anna had figured out what time he took his smoke breaks, by the smell of smoke wafting from the street level. She heard the crunch of gravel as he walked past, the familiar glow of the cigarette hanging out of the right corner of his mouth as he walked past the girls, shrouded in the shadows inside.

"We have five minutes." Anna declared in a hushed command.

She got to work on the window latch, the one that took her eye a week or so ago as she was walking down to dinner. That day it was blowing a gale, and the window rattled with the force of the wind. Anna was making the bet that no one had bothered to fix the issue yet, or knew it was an issue to begin with, and it was this weakness she would use to her own benefit.

Anna quickly tested the window sash, and like she had thought, the top screws were loose. She fished out a 5 kopeck coin from her pocket and while the other girls whispered at her to hurry up before Mr Utkina came back, Anna carefully twisted the loose screws until she could feel the screw was no longer gripping into the wood.

Just as she managed to get the first screw loose, and was half way through the second, she heard the telltale noise of stone crunching under foot, Mr Utkina was coming back from his cigarette break.

"Anna!" Sef whisper yelled from behind her, and dragged her back into the shadows to wait for the man to walk past.

Anna released a breathe. She had been concentrating hard to get the screws loose, it required the right pressure, the right speed of turn and she wanted to make sure it hadn't looked like it had been tampered with. She slumped back against the wall as the other two girls admonished her for her stupidity.

But the night wasn't over yet.

A few minutes passed and she heard the outer door open, and the watch man came inside the building and headed towards the downstairs lavatory.

This was a short break, Anna was sure of that, but it meant she had the time to be able to get the final part of the screw loose and the girls could be free.

Anna ran back to the window, much to the disappointment of the other girls, who were furiously cursing and asking Anna where her common sense was.

One, downward pressure, slight turn to the left, two turns, three and it was free. The screws were loose. Anna lifted the window open enough to get out of and motioned for the girls to follow her.

The cool night air kissed Anna's skin as she sunk down onto the ground outside the window and held it up for the other two girls to also come through.

As Darya, the last of the three, made it through the window, a flush came from the hallway down which Mr Utkina had been.

Darya's eyes widened as she tumbled out of the window, and Anna gently lowered the glass, careful not to make a sound.

"To the grass, and we run!" she hissed at the other girls. There was a risk of being chased by the old man. And she wasn't all that keen on starting her night off with a run.

The girls, donned in black clothing to blend in with the darkened streets, made their way into the heart of the city.

The faint scent of wood smoke carried on the light breeze and filled the girl's nostrils as the cold of the night seeped through their thin jackets and chilled them to the bone. Anna sped up to make sure they all stayed warm, much to the annoyance of both Darya and Sef who really just wanted to get back to their warm beds.

The cobblestone streets weren't well-lit, but the full moon helped guide the girls around the once majestic city.

Anna could have sworn she could hear the faint sound of construction, but shook her head and dismissed the thought, thinking instead that everyone would be in their own warm beds at this time of night.

Darya quietly commented about how some of the buildings were still standing despite being riddled with bullet holes and the building next to it being a bombed site.

A sharp bark pierced the quiet, making them all flinch. Stray dogs. Creatures with empty bellies and suspicious eyes, who'd been abandoned when the city emptied out during the big retreat, when the Germans were so close you could practically hear their boots. Their owners never came back for them. Anna quickened her pace, and the other girls followed her into the streets next to the Moskva River.

Moonlight glittered off the river, with a breeze following the river movements, bringing with it the sharp scent of metal work occurring upriver.

The girls walked for an hour or so around the city, stretching their legs, hiding when they heard others not wanting to be caught by the secret police, and running at sounds that don't feel like they match what they were meant to be, like dog barks, the hiss of cats and car horns honking.

They returned as the church bell rang out a mournful single chime, letting them know they had been out for a couple of hours.

Tired, they ambled back to the boarding house, carefully climbed back through the open window and crept back in. Being very careful not to allow any loud creaks or groans in the old building to emanate from the door or surrounding floor.

The girls softly padded upstairs, leaving the key in the door for the matron to find again the next morning and allowed the adrenaline of the evening to wear off in their beds.

It wasn't long before sleep took them under.

March 1953

Anna, aged fifteen | Moscow, Moscow Oblast, Russian Soviet Federative Socialist Republic

Kira's loud bell rang out by the doorway, waking all the girls in the long hallway filled with beds.

It was brash and jarring, and the groans of the girls waking up echoed throughout the space.

Anna wasn't a fan of the bell, but regardless, rolled out of her bed, put on her uniform and ambled down to the cafeteria for breakfast.

They served the usual thin porridge to the girls, with the choice of an apple slice on the side.

Anna thought the soggy meal wasn't all that best for growing girls, but who was she to complain?

Her voicing the concern wouldn't make a difference, and the oats provided sustenance. It reminded her of some meals her mama made her during the war, scraping everything they could together so they could survive.

Especially on the days when the lines for the rations were too long, but the cupboards were not quite bare enough yet to cause alarm.

The room was quietly buzzing with the sound of over a hundred girls babbling away over their breakfast. Sunlight streamed through the large windows, illuminating dust motes dancing in the air. Chatter and the clatter of silverware filled the room, a warm, communal feeling.

She sat with Sef and Darya, both of whom were nattering away in German, undoubtedly because of the test coming up. Anna didn't like the sound of the language, harsh and guttural, almost sounding like the speaker had a cold. She preferred English. It would be a useful language, undoubtedly serving her in whatever she wants to do after her school years.

She left for her first class, social sciences, as a younger student came running into the class, panting and puffing, holding out a note for the teacher, who promptly read it and dismissed the child.

"Class," the older man bellowed from the front of the room. Any nattering away from any of the girls stopped in a flash, and all eyes converged on the front.

"The rest of this class is cancelled. You must go to the hall for an emergency assembly." He announced.

Confused murmurs filled the room before the teacher snapped at the class, "That means now, girls, MOVE."

His booming tenor caused every girl to stand at attention and move to leave the classroom.

Anna fought her way to the already-packed assembly, the heat of so many bodies palpable; the low hum of chatter making it hard to hear herself think as she looked for a spot near her friends.

A wave of silent judgment washed over her as she sat down between two girls who she wasn't friendly with; their upturned noses and narrowed eyes spoke volumes.

"Dirty whore," the whispers slithered over Anna, each word laced with venom.

"Idiots," Anna snapped, the sharp word a sting in the quiet anticipation before the assembly started, silencing the girls' petty plans to report her.

The principal, an older man with a broom for a moustache and a body that his clothes struggled to contain, came ambling up to the front of the stage. He stared until, one by one, the rows of girls in the hall, all seven hundred of them, hushed to allow the man to speak.

“Thank you for coming today, girls,” he started, as if any of them actually had a choice in the matter.

“We've had some news from the head of the union.”

Anna's head started spinning. Stalin had sent a message to the school?

The man had a cult-like following. He was everywhere. In the streets, on posters, on their stamps when they sent letters. He was the father of the nation, what would he want to do with an all-girls school in Moscow?

Some students, Anna thought, must be from working-class backgrounds and knew that they would have likely died from starvation or execution if Stalin and his Red Army hadn't defeated the Germans on the Eastern Front.

The man was someone to look up to.

Some boys wanted to be him.

Girls saw him as a protective father figure.

"Joseph Vissarionovich Stalin passed away late last night after a short illness, I will now read the statement from the USSR Council of Ministers and Presidium of USSR Supreme Soviet.

Dear Comrades and Friends: The Central Committee of the Communist Party of the Soviet Union, the USSR Council of Ministers and the Presidium of the USSR Supreme Soviet announce with profound sorrow to the Party and all working people of the Soviet Union that at 9:50 p.m. 5 March, Iosif Vissarionovich STALIN, Chairman of the USSR Council of Ministers and Secretary of the Central Committee of the Communist Party of the Soviet Union, died after a grave illness.

The heart of Lenin's comrade-in-arms and the inspired continuer of Lenin's cause, the wise leader and teacher of the Communist Party and the Soviet people, to Joseph Vissarionovich Stalin; has stopped beating."

The speech went on for over five minutes, and Anna knew she wasn't the only one in shock.

What was also interesting was the feeling of worry Anna had, the apprehension of what the future might hold. Stalin had ruled the union for thirty-one years. The idea of anyone else taking on the rule, outside of the dead tzars, for that amount of time felt absurd to Anna.

“We will now hold a minute of silence for our fallen comrade.” The principal said as the room hushed.

Anna counted the seconds in her head, and as she got to fifty a girl two rows back from her coughed.

Bad move.

The girl was dragged from the room, the teacher's hand clamped over her mouth to silence her racking coughs, the silent judgment of her peers heavy in the air.

March
1953

Anna, aged fifteen | Moscow, Moscow Oblast, Russian Soviet Federative Socialist Republic

The leader laid in state for a full three days, and all the girls were expected to go and pay their final respects. Anna wasn't sure how she felt about visiting the dead body of the great man, but because it was expected of her, and her Papa also made the order for her to go, so she went.

"Sef!" She hollered down the dormitory hallway, "Sef, we need to get going! Or we will miss out!" That wasn't strictly true, but Anna was keen to get the visit over and done with. Since her mother's death, she always seemed to think about how she never could say a proper goodbye, and how pale she had looked, pale and almost sleeping in her coffin. Death itself unsettled her, having someone without a pulse just lying there, displayed. Looking like they're sleeping when they're actually actively decomposing in front of people in anticipation of becoming fertiliser.

The line to view Stalin was long. It felt like they were waiting for ages, the chilly air only dispelled by the sheer number of people lining the streets with them.

It was more people than Anna had ever seen, there was almost a line from the street outside the boarding school leading to the Hall of Columns. It was like the entire Soviet Union was coming out to mourn their leader. There were quiet murmurs, shoulder to shoulder with people as the girls made their way. It took an age, but everyone was respectful, coughing from where the cool air hit lungs was stifled. Handkerchiefs given by strangers to those who were silently crying. It felt like it wasn't just Moscow mourning, but the entire country. Perhaps even the entire world as far as Anna was concerned.

The girls waited in line for hours before they got in the room, each got their moment with the leader and was then ushered out of the room quickly.

It wasn't until Monday morning after Kira's bell had tolled a little later, due to the national day of mourning and the girls wore black to show respect that Anna found out only hours after they had left Stalin's side, that a crush event had occurred. That they were in the eye of a chaotic storm. They were just rumours, but rumours that had basis in fact.

Sef and Darya joined Anna in the common room, waiting to hear what will happen next. Kira addressed the room, "Hello everyone, today we will listen. We will mourn. First we will have breakfast, but I expect everyone back here in 20 minutes sharp. Stragglers will be on chores for the rest of the week."

The girls burst into action, going for breakfast, aiming to be the first to eat, slurp up the sad excuse for oats, then head back into the common room so they didn't get put on chores. Cleaning up after the other girls wasn't a punishment dealt out often, but when it was, the ladies who usually cleaned got a paid day off.

Anna finished her meal in record time before making it back to the common room, and was quickly joined by Darya and Sef.

"Did you hear what Darya said at breakfast?" Darya whispered to Sef, who was sitting stoically. Sef raised her eyebrow at the girl before she disclosed the gossip.

"Last night, Darya said that there was a crush event just before they closed up the viewing of the leader in state. Her lad said hundreds were either hurt or died because so many people didn't want to miss out on seeing the leader." Darya's eyes were wide as she relayed the gossip, and Anna overheard, feeling shocked.

Darya didn't know loss, not really. How could she? Her life was neat - a mum, dad and a family home. She didn't know how it feels to have the world shift in a moment.

"What's wrong?" Darya asked, her voice dropping to a whisper as she crouched beside Anna, a gentle hand settling on Anna's shoulder.

Anna shrugged off the hand, the touch of a feather where she needed a rock. The very thought of how close a call last night was put a boulder in the pit of her stomach and caused her to start to feel unwell.

“The crush. It was hours after Sef and I visited the Hall of Columns. I’m just… processing how close we got to death.”

Sef snorted, a sharp, quick sound that always grated on Darya. Darya’s head snapped up, her eyes narrowing into a dark, dirty look aimed squarely at Sef.

“Guess the devil isn’t ready for us yet, hey Anna?” Sef said, her voice rough, but something like a grin playing on her lips.

Anna looked up at her friend. *Why the devil?* Her gaze drifted down to Sef’s hands, those teenage hands that looked anything but. They were poxy with tiny, angry scars where cigarettes had been put out, and her knuckles were not smooth or clear like a fifteen-year-old girl's should be.

No, they were lumps of old scar tissue, testament to too many bare-knuckle fights. It made Anna sad, a hollow ache in her chest, to think that Sef truly believed she wasn't redeemable, that the devil *would* be waiting for her.

But then, a strange, dark comfort settled over Anna. If she ever ends up burning in hell, at least she’d be in very, very good company.

August
1954

Anna, aged seventeen | Moscow, Moscow Oblast, Russian Soviet Federative Socialist Republic

Anna,

Congratulations on reaching your 17th birthday. Your Mama would, I expect, be satisfied with your progress as you near adulthood.

However, you've got one year until you come of age. I have an expectation of you.

This year, on top of focusing on your schoolwork, I want you to also focus on securing a beneficial marriage. Someone who will enrich your life, can pay for any lifestyle you want, and someone who can carry on our family legacy. Someone who will be proper.

It was also part of your mother's wishes for you, so you need to have found someone you wish to wed before your next birthday.

Yours,

Papa

September
1954

Anna, aged seventeen | Moscow Oblast, Russian Soviet Federative Socialist Republic

Anna looked at herself in the mirror, her blue eyes sparkling with excitement, her dark locks pinned back and a red ribbon helped to keep it in place. Her dress, a deep shade of plum, made of a simple polished cotton, had a flared knee length skirt that she couldn't help but twirl in. The sleeves were capped, the neck line rounded and modest and the look was topped off with her freshly shined black shoes. Anna was excited to get to the dance. The first one her papa had allowed her to attend after her birthday.

Her Babushka had come to the city so they could go out and shop for "the perfect dress to find a husband" in. Of course, Anna blushed at the idea. It wasn't like a click of the fingers could summon the man she would fall in love with and marry.

Anna was excited, and Sef and Darya were also coming, this wasn't just a dance with the brother school, where nothing could ever occur under the watchful eyes of their teachers, it was one that boys from around the city could attend.

She was free from the prying eyes but shackled by family expectations.

At seventeen, she was keen to meet boys and follow in the footsteps of her friends, who had already found themselves in whirlwind romances with men who seemed to treat them like tzarinas.

Darya and Sef burst into the washroom, where Anna was using the mirror to put finishing touches on her hair.

"Hurry, Anna, or we'll miss all the best ones!" Darya chirped, already smoothing down her own skirt. She leaned closer, her voice dropping to a conspiratorial whisper. "My cousin Anya said the university students are going to be there tonight. They're supposed to be so mature and smart."

Sef, ever the pragmatist, leaned against the doorframe, pushing a stray lock of hair off her forehead. "Mature and probably looking for a quick twirl, not a lifelong commitment, Darya. Remember Lydia last month? Stood by the wall for three hours because she was too fussy about accepting dances."

Darya giggled, nudging Anna. "Well, you won't be fussy, will you, Anna?" she winked, "what if there's a new cadet from the Academy? Or a strapping young scholar from the university? My cousin said they're *dreamy*."

"Dreamy and probably looking for a wife, not just a quick twirl around a dance floor," Sef retorted, but her eyes held a similar glint.

Anna smiled, trying to quash the blush that threatened to rise. Her friends talked of boys and dances with such easy confidence, like solving a simple equation. For her, it felt like navigating a minefield. She adjusted a stray dark lock, the red ribbon a bright spot against her hair. Her friends' whirlwind romances seemed to happen with such ease, while her own foray into "relationships and stuff" was less about dreaminess and more about duty.

The girls signed out of boarding school in a fit of excited giggles, and got into the first tram that was heading towards the hall the dance was being held in.

The air coming off the Moskva River caused Anna to shiver, and she wrapped the shawl she had bought with her more tightly over her shoulders. There was only a couple of blocks they needed to walk in order to get to the venue, and they did so as one of the few clear days of the month faded, the setting sun bathing the pavement in golden light.

The girls rounded the final corner to the venue, and Anna knew she was in the right place by the big banner stating 'GLORY TO THE MOTHERLAND'. The doors were swung wide open, with other girls and young men milling around the entrance.

The music was typical for these kinds of affairs, a band was playing folk music as Anna came in, but as couples gathered over the hour Anna stuck to the wall, they transitioned to waltzes.

It was after Sef, who seemed to only entertain men as a duty, left Anna by the wall, being dragged on the floor by a young man who had no idea what he was getting himself into.

Anna, moving awkwardly side to side felt very much like an outlier while couples dances and twisted in front of her.

Her hopes were diminishing, it wasn't the done thing to ask a boy to ask. And no one seemed interested in her.

Until, a couple in front of her twisted around and a young man emerged from the dance floor, offering his hand to her. His presence drew her in. Almost like a spotlight had been set on him, and

He was taller than most, his dark hair neatly cropped and his shirt freshly pressed, as if he'd stepped from Anna's own dreams. He hesitated as he asked, hand perhaps not quiet as steady as he was hoping he was portraying. His nerves were plainly painted on his expression, though Anna wondered why? Why would this kind of man feel nervous approaching her?

He cleared his throat, cheeks coloring, and continued to hold his hand out. "Hi, I'm Vladimir Zaitsev and I was wondering if would you honor me with this dance?"

Anna could feel the blush heat her cheeks, honour was perhaps a strong word to place on dancing with her. He may be lucky to have any untrod-upon toes by the end of the night.

As he moved, taking her hand and beginning to guide her towards the dance floor, Anna felt an almost disorienting shift.

The nervous boy was still there in her mind, but another, more potent impression began to form. His whiskey-coloured eyes, deep and knowing, no longer held a hint of shyness, instead they seemed to peer right through her, past her polite smile, and into a future she hadn't dared to imagine. They spoke of sinful times ahead, not of petty mischief, but of a profound, intoxicating thrill that vibrated with the dangerous pull of the forbidden, promising a world of desire and trouble she knew nothing about.

He pulled her onto the floor and pulled her into a waltz pose. Anna followed along with the moves as she had been taught years ago. Remembering the steps that her mother taught her in Sverdlovsk in the evening after dinner had been made. Vladimir was making it easy enough to follow though. His toes were being spared because he led well enough Anna could just follow along.

The way he waltzed with her, with an almost predatory grace that belied his earlier bashfulness, conveyed an irresistible, dangerous allure. It was a silent, confident promise that simmered beneath his bashful facade, drawing her in with a magnetic pull she was powerless to resist. Every controlled movement, every subtle shift of his weight, seemed to speak to a profound certainty, a silent command that had her instinctively following his lead even before they reached the dance floor.

"So, what brought you here?" he asked, looking into Anna's pretty face while they swung around the dance floor with grace. He wasn't just looking into her face; his eyes held her gaze with an intense, unwavering focus that made her feel, for the first time tonight, truly seen. It was as if no one else in the crowded hall existed. He smiled then, a slow, disarming curve of his lips that melted away any lingering impression of nervousness.

"Uh. I'm here because I don't get to hang out with boys very often and wanted to see what my friends were on about. Like relationships and stuff." Anna mumbled she couldn't very well come out and said that she'd been told she had to find a husband from tonight. That her father had barred her from attending until she came of marrying age.

Vladimir chuckled hearing her nerves taint her voice.

"So, you're here for a husband huh?" he asked in a teasing tone.

Anna was at a loss for words, so Vladimir spun her and brought her close before dipping her.

Anna stared up into his eyes, full of sinful thoughts and desire. She gulped. She didn't realise how confronting and close they would be doing a waltz, but the thought only lasted a moment. Before she could catch her breath, she was back on her two feet,

Vladimir bowing before her. In his arms, spinning through the hall, a part of her felt like she was exactly where she was meant to be, a feeling utterly foreign and utterly exhilarating.

"Thank you for the dance, I hope to see you again." And with that, he walked away from her.

Anna could see his broad shoulders, and how from a distance he shrugged on a formal jacket before exiting the premises.

The encounter was much too brief for Anna. She wanted to follow the boy out of the dance hall and find out what kind of sin his whiskey eyes hinted at. But she remained. A wallflower, sitting against the cool plaster of the wall where his jacket had recently held his warmth.

The echo of his grip on her hand has he led her around the floor still lingering on her soft skin.

Back in the quiet of her dormitory days later, Anna couldn't stop the smile that tugged at her lips. She spun a little circle in the empty room, a lightness bubbling in her chest. The encounter has been far too short for her liking.

Darya's bed lay empty, and Sef was probably out with her bodyguard, Aleksandr, who had also become her lover following a questionable night in Moscow.

So, Anna had no one to talk to about the encounter with this beautiful boy. So instead, she did what her mama had taught her to do, and wrote a note for him, hoping that maybe at the next dance, she could hand it to him.

Vladimir,

It was incredible meeting you and dancing with you. I'm sorry I was a little awkward. I'm not usually like this but I haven't really been around boys before, and I just wasn't sure how to act. Maybe you could teach me?

Let's meet up outside one of these dances, or if you're like me and prefer to write, my address is at the bottom of this letter.

I now also realise, with much embarrassment, that I never told you my name.

I'm Anna Sokolova and I come from Gorky before the war, Sverdlovsk during the war and lived in Kazan before I came through boarding school in Moscow.

Perhaps you also moved around a lot during the war too.

I look forward to spending more time with you and hopefully getting to know you a bit better.

Anna folded up the note and put it on the hanger with the dress she had picked out for the next dance in a month or so hoping that he was going to attend the next dance.

July 1955

Anna, aged seventeen | Moscow, Moscow Oblast, Russian Soviet Federative Socialist Republic

Her final year's expectations weren't just a mental weight; they were also of a physical nature, in the form of the heavy textbooks sitting by her bed.

She was expected to do well, to be one of the best in her class while also making sure she found time to court a boy was bearing down on her, causing a bone-deep exhaustion. The night of the dance she was looking forward to had come and gone, Anna was found the next morning with her face plastered against a worn copy of *War and Peace* by Sef. She hadn't been awake when the others had gotten ready to go.

Another dance was a light on the horizon of test dates and exams for Anna. Boys from a neighbouring school were descending on the school hall, all nervous cocky grins, hair recently cropped close to most of the boy's skulls. Ties would likely adorn their necks, and Anna wondered if that felt like a noose of expectations from this dance, like Anna would if she was forced to wear a tie.

Marriage, and all that entailed, was the only goal for some of the girls in the same year as Anna, a husband to provide, while they provided their husbands with a life filled with domestication and children. Anna thought this was unusual, and lacked any real drive for their futures, but some wanted nothing more. Anna wanted to make a difference in this world, and while she wanted children, it wasn't all she wanted. Each to their own, Anna guessed.

Children was not a draw card for marriage for Anna, the chaos of it was incredibly off putting. Her thoughts drifted back to the Red Banner Institute, which she intended to attend once she had finished secondary school. She had a knack for watching people. Understanding their drives, and intentions, and sometimes before they even realise it. She was good at remaining in the background and people innately trusted her with things they proud ought not to. The idea of working for the KGB and passing on information that helped the nation… held great appeal.

Sef was going to join her family's business – a vague chain of 'small goods' stores in her hometown. Anna had her theories, and everyone did. The scars and pockmarks that decorated Sef's knuckles, the authority she demanded simply with her presence and the way she walked. She wasn't a criminal empire princess. She had to fight and fight hard for her position. To prove herself, not only to the men but to everyone in her family that she belonged.

Darya was also following a family pathway. She always spoke of how proud she was of her mama and babushka for being nurses and caring for those who couldn't care for themselves. The appeal of sciences and space diminished when Darya explained the kind of course work it would entail to get there, falling back onto nursing. The profession was admirable, but the idea of Anna ever doing it caused her to shudder. Anna strongly thought that the fluids Darya would be dealing with, bile, blood and bowel movements, are best kept inside one's body, or at the very least kept private and not shared with someone. Surely.

Yes, working as a spy, or helping decode American messages sounded like a clever idea to Anna. More her speed. She knew there would be times where it wouldn't be pretty or clean, but again, sounds better than dealing with vomit or blood every day.

It was the night of the conjoint dance between the two schools, and Anna pulled the dress she was going to wear to the state dance, out of the back of her wardrobe, spying the note as it floated off the dress and to the floor of her bedroom.

Bending down to the old worn hardwood floor, Anna picked up the note and read it back.

Anticipation filled her, and she had that strange fluttering feeling deep in her belly again. Was that lust? Was she scared? She couldn't place the feeling though it wasn't negative.

She put up her long dark hair into a complicated braid that allowed some of the length to flow and curl down her back. She also grabbed some of the makeup her mama had and used that to line and make her eyes stand out even more. The dress she wore was flattering, light pink in colour and it flared out from her petite waist, as was fashionable for the time. She knew she looked good, she only hoped that Vladimir was there and thought the same.

October 1955

Vladimir, aged eighteen | Moscow, Moscow Oblast, Russian Soviet Federative Socialist Republic

Vladimir walked down the cobbled street, his jacket slung over his shoulder. He was dressed in his usual shirt and dress pants for a dance at the local Palace of Pioneers.

His papa's words still echoed in his ears: *Find a wife.* And then, the less subtle nudge: *That Sokolova girl.* Enchanting, Papa had called her. Vladimir remembered the faint scent of jasmine and plum that clung to her, the surprised wideness of her forest green eyes when he dipped her, and the slight parting of her perfectly plump lips as he bowed and left her on the dance floor.

It felt as if he hadn't been to a dance in months. The family business had demanded all of his time. Smuggling. American cash, Western luxuries – nothing as sordid as people, which wasn't uncommon in similar family businesses. Anti-Russian, maybe, but the rubles flowed freely, and Vladimir wasn't about to dam that stream.

He hoped she would be there. He craved the feel of her small body against his, the surprised little gasps she'd let out when he led a spin and the way her slight curves felt pressed against delicious parts of him. The almost worshipful way she'd looked up at him with those vast green eyes as if he hung the moon in the evening just for her.

She made him, for that one short dance, feel important. Special. And it had been a long time since anyone had made him feel much more than contempt.

October 1955

Anna, aged eighteen | Moscow, Moscow Oblast, Russian Soviet Federative Socialist Republic

Anna managed to get her letter to Vladimir at the dance. Even though the dance was called off early as some of the boys were caught in compromising positions with some girls in the bathrooms and the teachers were aghast at the behaviour of the boys who were older than the girls and should have known better.

Anna didn't even manage to kiss the boy. She handed him the letter when she saw him, and they came together for a dance. Halfway through, as she whispered things to him like her name and nonsense small talk, the teachers cut the music and yelled at the top of their lungs for the girls to head back to the dormitories.

Anna found Sef quickly, with her lipstick smudged. Anna raised a brow at the woman, who hadn't really shown an interest in anyone before.

"Seffy?" Anna started and received a glare for making Sef's name 'cuter'.

"Have you seen Darya? Was she with you this evening?" Anna asked as Sef's eyebrow rose, and she looked away as she thought.

"No, we split up pretty quickly when you saw your lover boy." Sef replied.

Anna could feel a flush creeping up her neck thinking of the boy, Vladimir, becoming her lover properly. The way his body could fit against hers, without the barrier of clothing.

"Oh." Sef exclaimed, "Did something good happen? Spill the gossip, Anna!"

Anna was now tomato red and had the distinct need to run the hell away from the conversation with Sef. She hadn't had 'relations' with anyone before and wasn't about to figure out that side of it. She hadn't even had her first kiss and the idea of.

Well.

That.

Freaked her out a bit and caused a bit of anxiety to settle deep in her stomach. She wasn't sure of how they could kiss without bumping noises, and what if he wanted to kiss and stick his tongue in her mouth!

"Nothing happened," Anna snapped at Sef, "I gave him his letter, and we got in half a dance before those horny boys were found defiling those girls."

Sef would have pushed Anna further if Darya hadn't suddenly appeared in front of them, coming from either a side path or out of the bushes lining the path. She looked thoroughly debauched. Her usually sleek dark hair was ruffled and tangled like it would be if someone had been holding it. She was flushed, and the back of her skirt had a tell-tell grass stain on the back of it. She was also puffed, like she had run a marathon but the hall they were holding the dance in wasn't that far from the boarding premises.

"Darya! What in the hell have you been up to??"

Darya turned quickly and spotted them, and you could see the guilt that painted her expression. Both of the girls sniggered at the look. Darya fell into step with the girls as Sef elbowed the girl, "So Darya, what have you been doing?"

Darya blushes deeply and sported a sly grin. "Wouldn't you like to know?" she asked them both. "A lady doesn't kiss and tell." She states as the other two girls jostled her for information on the deeds she did that night.

October 1955

Vladimir, aged eighteen | USSR Post, Moscow, Moscow Oblast, Russian Soviet Federative Socialist Republic

Anna,

I am glad we meet again. And this time I have a way of contacting you.

It was unfortunate our time was cut short. Some of the boys from my school, being their usual selves, got into some trouble with the girls. They were caught, of course, and now they're busy cleaning classrooms One would think they'd know better than to get caught. It's a simple risk of conducting themselves like that.

Enough about others.

I moved around a bit during the war. I hail from Leningrad, and while there are good schools up there, my Papa had us move down to Moscow after the war. We left Leningrad for a few weeks in the lead-up to the occupation, but I cannot for the life of me remember the name of the small town we stayed in. I prefer the city, more to do and less manure based smells.

I graduate school this year, and I'm not entirely sure what I want to do. I'll probably end up in a trade school, but I don't know what trade I'll do. Not farming is probably the strongest suggestion I can give at this moment in time. Perhaps I'll be drafted like others were in wars gone past. I do not wish to be a solider, but will do so if it means I serve my country with honour.

If you want to write back my address is below.

Yours,

Vladimir Zaitsev.

March
1956

Anna, aged eighteen | Moscow, Moscow Oblast, Russian Soviet Federative Socialist Republic

Letters from Vladimir, explaining his attraction to her, and how much he's looking forward to seeing her, were a constant surprise in the shared boarding home mailbox. They had decreased in frequency as of late but regardless the simple Cyrillic print on the lined paper, distinctly his style, made Annas friends jealous, resulting in much teasing at Anna's old fashioned love. She was the only one receiving letters, the others having the joy of meeting up with their lovers at a nearby park.

Anna daydreamed about the way it felt to be in his arms, swaying to the beat of the music playing at the state sponsored dance. Just allowing herself to melt into Vladmir's presence, he holds her while she allows herself to be vulnerable with him. No toes had been harmed in their time together and the fact that Vladimir can dance well, lead her around the dance floor in time to the music, was another part of him that made Anna fall even further in love with him.

It was safe to say she loved being in his company. And she liked herself in his company, more happy and content with the world. She felt safe in his presence, like a warm blanket being wrapped around her on a cold day.

Anna was finally graduating from secondary school and had sent off an application to the Red Banner Institute, the soviet spy school. The prospect of being out in the world on her own, dealing with money, food and everything else that comes with being an adult.

The three girls were set to be separated. Sef had talked about going to a technical school, wanting to get some practical skills before she inherits her family business. What that was, she had never disclosed, but Darya and Anna had heard other girls whisper about 'Sef's papa' as if they were afraid to name him fully. The whispers were of illegal activities under soviet law, and men who weren't afraid to hurt others in order to get their own way.

Cups of tea warmed their hands while they chatted about their futures together on a cold Moscow evening. Darya was moving away, continuing a family tradition. She's going to the Stalingrad Nursing school. She's moving into an apartment with her boyfriend, the same boy she was discovered to be in a compromising position with at that dance. It was heart-warming to see the two of them together still, especially after Darya's pregnancy scare. Thankfully it was just that, rather than cutting Darya's dreams of being a third-generation nurse short. The scare was a good reminder for all of the girls to be careful when it comes to having intimate relations with boys.

The idea of having to be an functioning adult without the watchful eye of a matron or family overwhelmed Anna, causing her to be unable to concentrate through her last few classes and seemingly being unable to sit still. A heady mix of anxiety and excitement. She would need to learn to cook.

The thought caused a tidal wave of grief to wash over her. Her mama would have made sure she could cook. Memories of a small Anna standing in the kitchen with her mama during primary school holidays, making some Persiki because they were Annas favorites. The peach shaped cookies complete with a delicious caramel and peach filling were mouth watering and only for special occasions. The favours still invoke a sense of deep sadness at the loss of her mama. The grief never truly left her, a constant companion in her day to day life. It always felt sharper when it came to big events, events that her mama would have cherished.

The noise was hushed as Anna's mind whirled, coming back to the moment. She was in a line, with others the same age as her awaiting their turn to shake a hand and get a certificate declaring they had passed secondary school. She had survived boarding school - no small feat, and had made a couple of close friends who would undoubtedly be with her for life.

But there was the next stage of line too, the thoughts of that rushing past at an almost dizzying speed.

Only a couple of people were ahead of her currently. She wanted to just rush up, grab the paper, and get back to her row so she could sit and stew about the future. Would she be one of those who dropped out of the institute? Then what? Would she resign to becoming a housewife? She shook her head at that thought. She would figure something out. She wanted to be with Vladimir, and she wanted to work for the KGB. The two ideas weren't conflicting.

Vladimir may not be the only love she has in her life, but he would have the title of her first love.

Anna wasn't going to have the chance for too many intimate relations with her Vladimir for the next three years. The both of them had discussed their futures in a series of letters. Anna's intention of heading to the Red Banner Institute for three years. Unlikely to get much in the way of 'time off' to visit her beloved. He knew how dedicated she is to getting this education. One that few were given to this level. He was excited about his future too. He decided he was going to learn how to fix things, namely machines. His family did some importing of cars and the likes and he thought it would be useful for him to learn the skills that could further his families empire building goals.

My dear,

These next few years will be tough. The summons arrived this evening. My service to the Motherland is required, and I must report in a week's time.

I will not pretend this is an easy thing. The time ahead will be difficult, but it is my duty. Have faith dearest. I will return to you, perhaps changed, but still your Vladimir.

We will write to each other often, yes? I don't know how much I'll be able to say, or you able to say about your own schooling, but with the nature of the world currently, I think even writing of the mundane would bring light to my eyes.

You can always tell me how you're feeling, if you need to unburden your heart or anything I am only a postage stamp and a couple of pieces of paper away.

Yours,

Vladimir

November

1956

Vladimir, aged eighteen | Soviet Field Post, Kecskemét, Bács-Kiskun, Hungarian People's Republic

Anna,

It has been eight months since I was last able to write to you. In eight months, I have been well indoctrinated into the Soviet Military way of life. I learned things that my Mama taught me, but that I never did well. Its highlighting how much she cared, and those moments are more precious than ever. We are no longer children.

There is no easement of rules here, for one slip could result in death. A snap of a twig could be the only warning one gets here. A late reaction to this could end with a bullet piercing something vital.

The front has been a place of pain and noise, constant noise. There are people like you, like your papa that I see daily. I do my duty. But I sincerely hope you are safe and well. I hope you are still able to find the quiet peace you always held while you're studying.

Yours,
Vladimir.

He carefully folded up the letter, sealed the envelope and placed it on the bedside table next to his bunk.

"Yours," it felt false, a bit of a lie. He wasn't hers. He wasn't even his own person anymore. He did miss Anna and her incredible body. But the other men around here had reminded him that girls liked to be reassured that their 'soldier' was still faithful while away. Honestly, Vladimir didn't understand it. Like yes, no sex before marriage but he was a man, and he had urges. Anna had said it was okay, and what's one little white lie?

He had been a child, a rifle shoved into his arms and expected to fight in a war he had little understanding of. He still vividly remembered the day he got into Budapest with the other soviet soldiers.

The clack clack clack of the train coming into the countryside of Hungary, followed by the sight of burnt out tanks was his first sign he wasn't in Russia any more.

The train was packed with men and smelt like sweat and grease. There were aged faces, often with scowls and hardened eyes, but most were like Vladimir. Bright eyes, posture perfected, and ready to serve in any way they can for the union.

The night before everyone piled into the lorries making their way towards the capital of Hungary w as... Some of the men didn't sleep at all. A few were on watches, others bent over lights writing notes they hoped to send home. Others, like Vladimir were lying on their backs, some softly snoring. Vladimir couldn't sleep.

He wasn't sure if he wanted to. The stories the older men had told were the cause of his nightmares. That and the threat of being shot while sleep walking was real.

Vladmir was exhausted when the men loaded up onto the lorry leading towards the capital. His eyes drooped of their own accord, the movements of the truck lulling him into a false sense of safety that allowed him to sleep.

It was less than a week, and in that time he was ordered to kill anyone seen to be a dissident. Anyone talking of democracy, and most importantly, anyone pointing a weapon at him. He wasn't fighting soldiers. There was one woman's face that haunted him. She wore her hair in waves, like his Anna had and was wearing a civilian jacket. For a split second he hesitated, and almost lost his life for it as she pointed her rifle at him. Except the man beside him saved his life. Vladmir dldn't even know his name. It was harrowing and not something he liked to think about.

He had come into this war expecting it to be like the Great Patriotic War, to help protect borders or kill Nazis. That was not his reality.

The death, the smells. All of it made Vladimir shudder as he remembered everything, his senses overwhelmed. It caused a bolt of nausea to hit him, and he had to struggle not to retch.

But now he was here. In a quiet outpost of a city. Surrounded by people who wanted to kill him. And so he occupied the space he was meant to, and waited.

And watched.

Vladimir wasn't sure if it was worth it any more, the duty to his country. But saying that out loud, writing it down, even admitting to himself was treasonous.

He flopped back onto his bunk, attempting to get rest. He had been on a night shift, jumping at every leaf rustle, door slam and twig snapping. He was on edge, unable to relax.

He was off duty tonight however and while he lay in his bunk, wondered how he might swing a clandestine liaison with a local woman to try and take some of the edge off his mental spiralling.

He and Anna had planned the engagement, and Vladimir was a 'good' boy and made sure he kept up his family's part of the deal by keeping Anna on the hook. But that didn't mean that he had to stay celibate while they were both getting ready to spend their lives together. He hadn't wed her, or even asked her for her hand yet.

He justified it to himself as needing to take off the edge. If he didn't he was scared of who he might become.

December 1956

Anna, aged nineteen | Moscow, Moscow Oblast, Russian Soviet Federative Socialist Republic

Anna groaned as the piercing alarm came through the apartment she shared with two other girls. It was five thirty, on the forty-fifth day in the first year of the institute.

She knew she had to get up quickly if she wanted to get a decent breakfast and hopefully a good warm cup of tea, with the others in the institute thinking the same thing as her. Her thoughts were often solidified, either by her missing out on the best kind of food, and often seeing other weary souls leaving their rooms at the same time.

The air in the mess hall already buzzed with a subtle tension, even before the first student grabbed a tray, the entire place was built on being a competition, one that no one would afford to lose. Anna had witnessed it in the past few weeks: the almost imperceptible surge forward in the queue, the carefully placed elbow to gain an inch, the way some students would pair up, one distracting the server while the other snagged an extra piece of bread. It was a silent understanding, a daily game played out over lukewarm porridge and watery tea. Missed your chance, hesitated for too long, and you'd be facing a morning of demanding drills on a rumbling stomach.

Anna groaned and stretched as she rolled out of the uncomfortable bed. She tossed on some clothes and kept her long hair in the braid she slept in. She knew she could outrun some of these cadets. She sprinted down the hallways, before she made it to the mess hall, only a dozen or so first-years like her lined up already. Not bad. Though one of these days she wanted to be first, not thirteenth.

“Anna!” A voice behind her yelled. It was her roommate Nika.

She raced up behind Anna and panted behind her in the breakfast line. Obviously also having the same idea about needing to do one heck of a sprint in order to get enough food to survive what was already shaping up to be a gruelling day.

“Anna,” she panted, hands on her knees trying to catch her breath from the last burst of speed to catch up to Anna but a laugh dancing behind her eyes. “You realise your clothes are inside out?”

Anna could feel the blush creeping up her face, the utter mortification of rushing and making a mistake in running out the door that morning.

Mortification was nothing compared to the niggly feeling of being hungry halfway through the day like she would have been if she took the time to be more careful.

Anna shrugged at Nika, "Beats being hungry though."

Both girls went and grabbed their food and sat down at a table.

"What classes do you have today?" Anna asked the girl next to her, who was slowly chewing away at her dry toast.

"Um, this morning after the run, I've got Fundamentals of Counterintelligence followed by Small Arms Proficiency and finishing the day with Hand-to-Hand practice."

Nika's enthusiasm bubbled as she recounted her counterintelligence class, a stark contrast to the quiet satisfaction Anna felt when piecing together fragments of overheard conversations in the mess hall later. While Nika seemed energized by the idea of uncovering hidden motives and reporting suspicious behavior, Anna found a different kind of focus in observing, listening, and storing away details that might prove useful down the line.

Given a choice, Anna would always gravitate towards a quiet corner to watch people rather than navigating a crowded social gathering. However, she had learned the value of a well-placed smile and a carefully chosen word, skills she occasionally deployed when trying to glean information from a reticent classmate or smooth over a minor infraction with a stern instructor.

The thought of the afternoon's hand-to-hand combat drills brought a knot to Anna's stomach. While she diligently practiced the judo throws and takedowns, the instructor's stark pronouncements about incapacitating or even eliminating an opponent left her feeling uneasy. Yet, a flicker of grim determination always followed. She remembered her father's stories from the war, the stark choices he had faced. If cornered, she knew instinct would override any reluctance.

Tomorrow would bring the weapons familiarization session, a class Anna approached with a distinct lack of enthusiasm. The cold weight of the practice pistol in her hand felt alien, and a persistent thought echoed in her mind: wasn't there a more skilful way than relying on such a blunt instrument? Still, the instructors drilled them relentlessly on disarming techniques, a skill Anna attacked with focused intensity. The risks of her chosen path were becoming increasingly clear, yet the potential to contribute to something larger than herself kept her grounded.

The predawn runs were a constant trial. Each inhale burned in Anna's lungs as her muscles screamed in protest against the relentless rhythm. This was a far cry from leisurely strolls. Yet, as she caught sight of a taller cadet, one rumored to be destined for the police academy, just a few strides ahead, a familiar spark ignited within her. Her pace quickened, a silent challenge issued with each determined footfall.

History of Spycraft was a favorite. It offered a blueprint of the past, showing her exactly which shadows to walk in and which traps to avoid in her own career.

During their rigorous drills, the tutors' voices, sharp and unwavering, often echoed across the training grounds. “You will face the unexpected,” one had barked during a particularly grueling obstacle course. “Hesitation is failure. Adapt. Survive.” Their lessons, whether in the classroom or the field, consistently emphasized self-reliance and the ability to overcome any adversity, a silent promise of preparedness for the unpredictable realities that lay ahead, both within the shadows and in the light.

Anna kept eating her apple and spiced porridge thankful for the meal still being warm and filling. She could remember times during the war when she and her mama only had one meal a day because of the scarcity of food.

A familiar ache tightened in Anna's chest as she finished her porridge, the warmth a fleeting echo of her mama's comforting presence. But she quickly straightened her shoulders, her gaze sharpening as she observed a group of upperclassmen boasting loudly about their latest training exercise. A wry smile touched her lips. Sentimentality was a weakness here. Instead, she met their confident stares with a cool, unwavering look of her own, a silent challenge daring them to underestimate her. A small voice in the back of her mind whispered her mama's worried pronouncements during the war, the fear of losing another loved one to the country's demands. Papa's quiet nods of understanding, a shared history of sacrifice, offered a different kind of solace, a silent acknowledgment of a path chosen with conviction, despite the potential cost.

Vladimir,

My world feels darker without your presence. I hadn't had the perspective to see exactly how much you had changed my life in the last couple of months. I feel more complete around you, and I need that feeling to anchor me now.

Yes, we will write. I'm afraid everything here is run by the State's own rigid clock, so forgive me if my letters are sometimes brief. My official address is below, but I doubt you'll find it on a public map.

I know you understand the meaning of silence better than I do right now, and I must learn that discipline quickly. I can tell you that the lessons here are not what I expected. My mind is being pushed and filled with information I never thought I would hear. I'm just trying to remember everything so I can be the best student for the Motherland—and for our future.

What is certain is that they expect absolute endurance. What is surprising is the amount of physical exercise we're expected to do as part of our classes;

they tell us our minds are only as strong as our bodies. We only got here a couple of weeks ago, and I don't know in what world I am going to get used to the five-thirty wake-up. Only a year ago I was convinced that this hour didn't exist for normal people. I am sure you are well aware of it now where you are.

I miss you so much, my V. We aren't allowed to travel home for the first six months, which they insist is necessary for focus. I miss your strength, your comforting touch, and your gentle words. I send you all my love, and I will be looking at the calendar until the day I can see you again.

You are my world, Vladimir, and my days are emptier without you in them. Be careful. Be well.

X

AS.

January
1957

Anna, aged nineteen | Moscow, Moscow Oblast, Russian Soviet Federative Socialist Republic

V,

Your letters always manage to bring a real smile to my face the moment I see your handwriting on the envelope. It's funny how hearing about the ordinary things – what you ate for breakfast, some trouble you had with a stubborn soldier– feels like a little piece of you when everything here is so... regimented. It soothes something deep down. Even if the letters are few and far between. My papa mentioned that during service sending letters is difficult.

Have you been working on anything interesting lately? Any particular drill or exercise that's caught your attention? Or is it mostly just the same thing day in and day out? I always imagine you surrounded by others, enjoying the comradery of your fellow men, or hunched over your weapon, cleaning out each part in quiet concentration.

Things here are intense, but good. You remember Nika, my roommate? We've become such good friends. This morning, Nika even left me an extra piece of bread because she knows I struggle with the early starts. She's a morning person, it's a different world for her at five-thirty!

Speaking of which, you wouldn't believe the chaos of trying to get breakfast. If you're not sprinting, all that's left is cold porridge. Yesterday, I was so rushed I didn't even notice my shirt was inside out until Nika pointed it out in the queue!

The days are long – that ten-kilometer run before classes really wakes you up, and then it's lectures and drills until evening. I definitely feel different in my clothes these days; all that running and combat training has changed things. I sometimes wonder how it would feel to dance with you now. Probably less... yielding.

Anyway, I miss you, VZ. It feels like time is crawling, but I keep looking at the calendar. Not much longer now.

Thinking of you,

AS.

Anna gently folded the letter and slipped it into the envelope, before grabbing his latest letter to her and placing it in her cupboard with all the others he had sent her, she was sending more to him than he sent her way. She planned to send it tomorrow morning after the mad rush for breakfast but before the gruelling run, she had come to use it as a mediation time of sorts, a chance to get out of her mind and focus on her breathing, and the sound of her feet hitting the ground.

Other men around had shown interest in Anna, but she wanted to make sure that any kind of relationship she partook in was for the right reasons and with the right person. Vladimir felt like the right kind of person. He was her calm. Her safe harbour. He was her person as far as she was concerned. Even if everything between them had been talk, letters and plans. No ring, no wedding ceremony yet. But that would come.

She could wait.

August 1957

Anna, aged nineteen | Moscow, Moscow Oblast, Russian Soviet Federative Socialist Republic

It was the start of Anna's second year at the institute. She had survived, a quiet satisfaction warming her from the inside out, a feeling as profound as the landscape she runs through in the mornings, pushing past the point when her mind tells her she's done enough and going into a semi-euphoric state. Thinking about it never failed to bring a slight smile to Anna's face. The admission to get into the school was already tough, and Anna knew this program wasn't for the weak, a shudder immediately shaking her at the thought of the admission process. The tests, the being watched for weeks, all to make sure someone was worthy of the institute.

The warnings about the dropout rate proved chillingly accurate. Each week seemed to bring news of another student gone, unable to withstand the brutal combination of nine-hour study days, gruelling physical training, and the scant reprieve of a single day off. Often gone can mean being moved into another 'area' of the service. But if the worst cases would mean complete disappearance, a one-way ticket to Siberia.

Anna felt the constant pull herself, the way exhaustion clung to her muscles and a dull ache throbbed behind her eyes. This wasn't just about intelligence; it was a test of endurance, of sheer will.

Anna was up at 5.30 am, the sun pouring through the sheer curtains. At least she thought it was the sun. It may well have been a plane-spotting spotlight on the rooms from outside in order to wake them early. Anna quickly got dressed, checking for outside seams to make sure she was correctly dressed, wanting to avoid the same mistake as she had made in her first year, where she had a few mornings showing up with her garments inside out, and headed down to the mess hall. She preferred to get there as the staff were serving up the food so she could eat in peace. No rush for the last bits of food, no constant chatter and gossip. Just Anna, the sounds of the food being plated and the shuffle of the few other early risers' feet as they moved up the line.

This year she was especially looking forward to learning more about the psychology of people, and how to read them. She wanted to master the understated skill of being a wallflower, someone who could absorb everything by watching and listening, only speaking when required, and otherwise remaining silent and observant. She enjoyed being underestimated and proving people wrong. The idea that people who are just milling about and minding their own business aren't listening in and making mental notes of what's happening is just one example of such an underestimation. It's in those moments where being unassuming, small and female worked so well to Anna's advantage.

She was just as capable as the rest of them when it came to charming and schmoozing, able to smoothly navigate tense and difficult social situations. But the energy it required felt like a drain, a performance rather than an authentic expression. It simply wasn't her way. She was more awkward naturally, but knew how to slip a mask on when it truly mattered.

A quick final swallow, and Anna was done. The clatter of distant cutlery on metal trays echoed faintly in the sparsely populated mess hall; the air hung heavy with the lingering smell of burnt oats. Her corner table felt cold and oddly vast, the absence of her roommates leaving a hollow ache in the silence. Their day, a whirlwind of hushed whispers and intense scrutiny, would begin soon enough. She knew it, the stark reality a cold contrast to the quiet calm she currently sought.

Anna jogged back to her room, and stretched for a minute before she set off down the track, a full five kilometres. Running through forestry, then out into farmland, before making it to the end. The turning point was always the old oak, its bark smooth and worn from countless touches. every student touched it, a small, silent plea for good fortune before facing the return leg. It was part of a tale the tutors had told at the beginning of the year – that the one time a student hadn't tapped the old oak, they didn't survive the run back. Apparently being attacked by something, or someone. Anna wouldn't put this school past something like making sure some of the wives' tales told stuck. Anna reached out as she approached, tapping the bark lightly before turning to run back, a brief connection to the shared experience of all who ran this track.

The rhythm of her breath, synchronized with the steady *thump-thump-thump* of her shoes on the path, became a form of meditation. A quiet settling within. She couldn't quite reconcile this feeling with the dread that had once clung to these early morning runs. Ten kilometres had seemed insurmountable then, a punishment. She used to dread the run as she laced up her shoes, but now that she had the fitness, it became second nature. The stillness of the morning, being one of the first that she knew to experience the new day, was her solace. Almost a form of control.

She thought about her summer break, as short as it was.

She could spend more time with Vladimir, and she had to admit she really liked him.

Their letters had chronicled their separate paths. Vladimir's consumed thoughts of coming home to her, what he can tell her about where he is and how long it'll be before he was back in her arms. He was hers and she his, and that's what mattered, the realization of that warming her from within.

Anna jogged the last part of the run, there was no point in rushing it. She got back to her room, stripped off for a shower and allowed the warm steam to wash away the sweat and stresses of the past day.

July 1958

Anna, aged twenty | Makhachkala, Dagestan Autonomous Soviet Socialist Republic

Summertime in Russia wasn't exactly known for being warm, the temperature in the capital getting to around 20 degrees rather than other balmier places in Europe, though in their little part of the Caspian coast they were able to bask in some of the warmest temperatures Russia had to offer. Anna was just pleased to get away from the hustle and bustle of Moscow City for a little break, there was only so much hustle and bustle one could take between school and city life. The sunshine and sea was exactly what she needed. What they both needed.

Vladimir and Anna were down at Anna's family dachas, a little cottage on the Caspian Sea that had been in her family for generations. Anna learned from the stories her mama told her during the war that one of her mama's papa's Dedushka's was gifted it from the Tzars before the revolution. Four generations, and when her mama passed, it went to Anna's papa until Anna marries.

Vladimir was a few steps in front of Anna on the path down to the sandy beach, somewhere that held precious memories for Anna. They couldn't wait to sink their feet into the warm sand and swim in the sea. Memories of running through the sun warmed sand, being chased by her mama, laughing together after the war allowed a small smile to grace Anna's face as she followed Vladimir into the shallows of the water.

They frolicked in the water, splashing each other as if they were ten years their junior before finally coming to rest on the sun-warmed sand that lined the shore.

"This is bliss," Anna said to Vladimir, wiggling her toes in the warm sand, the sun a comforting weight on her skin. Vladimir murmured his agreement, a relaxed smile on his face. She was glad he seemed to be enjoying himself so much here. The Caspian Sea differed from the northern waters he was used to; he'd mentioned the beaches on the shores of the White Sea were rockier, the sand coarser, water too frigid to swim in. She hoped this felt like a proper holiday for him, a proper escape. A chance to properly relax. She could only imagine the horrors he had seen, or not seen while he'd been conscribed and forced into the Red Army.

The silence between them was easy and unhurried. Away from the rigid walls of the institute, Anna felt a rare warmth blooming in her chest. Her skin, still cool from the water, hummed under the afternoon sun. Beside Vladimir, the world felt steady enough that she considered closing her eyes and actually letting go.

"We should probably get up Vladimir, I don't want my Papa to find me out here with you alone," Anna said, rolling over on the towel below her to face him.

He looked good in his dark swim trunks, the fabric clinging to his lightly dusted with hair thighs. She remembered the curve of his shoulders as he swam in the sea earlier, the way the sunlight caught in his hair as he flipped it, trying to dry it off a little before coming to shore. There was a strength about him that she found undeniably attractive. Was it the training he had done as a soldier? Was it the mental strength? It didn't matter. As long as it was him.

Warmth bloomed in her chest as she looked at him, a desire to reach out and touch his arm. The sun had brought out freckles she hadn't noticed before across the bridge of his nose.

"I'm sure he's been far too busy to notice our absence, Anna," Vladimir said, his voice a low murmur. She noticed the way his gaze flickered down for a moment before returning to her face, a slight tension in his jaw.

It was as if he could feel Anna staring at his cock, and he raised an eyebrow at her ogling. "Have you seen one before? Touched one?" Obviously talking about his ever-growing appendage. Anna, not taking her eye off his swim shorts, shook her head delicately. She felt bashful about the subject. Was she meant to before now? She hadn't really been around many men or boys…

"Do you want to?" he asked, bring her out of her overthinking and back into this moment with him. With her staring at his hard cock through his swim shorts, asking her if she would like to see it in all its glory. On a very public, albeit empty currently, beach.

A sudden boldness washed over her. She wanted him. The heat of the sun on her skin seemed to mirror a growing warmth deep within her. His eyes were blown out with lust, though there were other obvious indicators of his attraction to her.

He was all she desired in that moment. She was sure he knew she was still a virgin, they hadn't really talked about it and they hadn't done anything that had lead to him ever getting any other impression. Despite the heat and the sea, she felt a moistness gathering for him between her thighs, causing her to tighten them together. A desperate tremor ran through her, her body sending out a plea for something, anything, to alleviate the agonizing need clawing at her core.

Vladimir started to lower the waistband of his swim trunks a fraction, and her breath hitched. Then, a sharp, familiar voice cut through the quiet.

"Anna! Vladimir!" a man's deep tenor bellowed from the lawn in front of the beachside property.

Vladimir quickly pulled his swim trunks back up, his eyes wide as he looked at her, a silent plea in their depths.

Ignore him his eyes seemed to say. Her Papa's voice had definitely startled her, the sudden intrusion breaking the spell of the moment. A wave of embarrassment washed over her, she was almost caught with a boy. And while Vladimir and she were adults, her Papa catching her... The thought was mortifying.

Thankfully, the large beach umbrella was positioned between them and the lawn where her Papa was walking down towards the beach. She took a deep breath, trying to compose herself, knowing her Papa's disappointed frown was likely to follow. She heard Vladimir quietly murmuring curses, eyes closed, as they both composed themselves.

The sound of her Papa calling them back to the house definitely brought her back to reality, the earlier heat now replaced with a flush of embarrassment. She hoped Vladimir was managing his own... reaction. The thought of her getting pregnant before finishing her studies sent a shiver of panic through her.

As they both composed themselves after their heated moment was interrupted, they also started to pack up the bits and pieces, including the towels and umbrella, before they both trudged up the beach back to the dachas.

July 1959

Anna, aged twenty-one | Moscow, Moscow Oblast, Russian Soviet Federative Socialist Republic

The next eighteen months became a relentless grind for Anna. She faced interrogations that stretched her mental limits, endured gruelling physical trials that pushed her body to its breaking point, and navigated complex strategic simulations that demanded every ounce of her intellect. All of it culminated in this final, unsettling assignment: being snatched off the Moscow streets.

There was to be no warning, no way of knowing when the final test would occur or how it would happen. She had been given an identity, a secret code word she had to keep to her self. She was expecting the worse. She had seen people crumble, not so much from the actual test itself but the waiting. The waiting and knowing something bad was going to happen. People who despite all their training weren't cut out for this life.

She was walking down Bolshoy Kamenny Bridge, heading away from the golden spires of the church. It was late evening, and she had indulged a friends need to meet up. It had been short and unremarkable, hoping that maybe this 'friend' had insights as to what the trials were, but not even liquor was loosening their tongue. Anna knew that being out this late, by herself was asking for trouble. She backed herself against most people though. Even those bigger than her may find themselves in a spot of trouble if they tried to fight with her.

Anna had seen the perpetrator a split second before she was grabbed, which gave her a moment to consider her options. She allowed herself to be caught, she knew that she would be no match for the man who grabbed her, at almost two meters tall the man was solidly built, and she wouldn't have been effective in fighting him off, being just shy of 160cm. She was roughly handled, in a way that was likely to leave bruises and thrown back against a hard cold brick wall. The man looked her up and down and tried to nudge her legs apart.

Hell no. Anna was not allowing this creep, an alumnus of the course she had no doubt, to touch her like that, she was not in the mood to add attempted rape to her tertiary educational experience.

"I would think twice if I were you, I bite, and I will torture you to the point you will want to cut off your own cock." Anna spat towards the man.

He stopped the movements to try and pry her legs apart and looked down at her.

With a smirk she added, "I might even let you cut it off."

"Bitch." He spat at her, before hoisting her over his shoulder and started striding away, with Anna kicking, as hard as she possibly could, against his chest. She was tired, but was still trying to find purchase with her sore leg muscles, feeling her toes dig into his firm flesh through his clothing.

She landed a blow against his spine with a well aimed closed fist, and heard him grunt before he released her, dropping her like a sack of potatoes onto the cold cobblestones lining the streets. *That hurt,* Anna thought. Being dropped wasn't part of her plan, and she winced a little as she started to get back to her feet.

A second shadow appeared from beyond the where the lights decorating the bridge shone, and Anna knew then that this was it for her.

Fuck.

Before she had time to scramble up she was being dragged by her long hair, and Anna cursed herself for plaiting it before heading out tonight, she had wanted to keep the damned locks out of the way but she had figured out that perhaps that wasn't her brightest idea. Her scalp burned from the pull and she grabbed the hands pulling her hair to reduce some of the strain on her scalp.

She had seen her classmates go through this already though they refused to say anything about what had happened. Still, it wasn't hard to guess that a fight had occurred. They often came home with black eyes and slung arms.

The second man hissed at her, “Do not make this harder than it has to be bitch, just do as I ask.” While the first came up behind them both.

Anna knew better than that. Anyone who fell for that kind of line wasn't worthy of being in this course.

Anna threw all her weight backwards against him and heard the familiar satisfying crack of a nose being broken as the back of her skull hit him. Her hair was immediately released, and she stared down at the man, who was trying to stop the blood that was pouring out of his nose and drenching his shirt.

She stepped back., admiring her handy work. As she turned to walk away from the man now crumpled on the ground a fist flew at her face, too fast for her to react. She had forgotten about the second guy in her moment of smugness! She shouldn’t have underestimated them both.

Her vision swam, the blow feeling like it hit something important.

That was her final thought as her feet dropped out from underneath her and she crumpled onto the brick path below.

July 1959

Anna, aged twenty-one | Moscow, Moscow Oblast, Russian Soviet Federative Socialist Republic

White.

That's all she could see, all she could hear when she woke up. She was tied to a chair, probably white, with harsh lighting overhead making the room devoid of shadows.

This was a deprivation room. Something she had been taught about, something she had hoped to never experience.

This must have been an extended part of her final test. She scanned her body – her head throbbed, but that may have been from the lighting. She moved down her body, tilting her neck side to side to make sure that was working. She moved her fingers, tied behind her back, making the position uncomfortable but not impossible to escape from.

Her clothes had been changed from what she had been wearing when she caught up with her friend now she was donned in white. Her ankles had also been tied to the chair, but she was able to wiggle them to make sure her heels and feet weren't compromised.

She was physically fine. Sore jaw, and one hell of a headache but otherwise fine. Now she had to figure a way out of here, lest she become a temptation to torture.

She felt for the material of her ties and groaned when she couldn't.

Its okay. She thought. *They would come for her. There's no way they would leave a recruit in here long enough to be declared insane.*

She quickly ran though what she needed to remember. She was Rosa Kuzmina, the daughter of a previously well known general in the Red Army. She was 25 years of age, and completed university. The code word she needed to remember was D'yavol, Devil.

The door opened and Anna opened her eyes to the men who came in. They too wore white. Likely another tactic to try and make sure that she didn't get her hopes up by seeing colour any time soon.

"Hello Rosa," the first man greeted.

They had pulled chairs in with them, and sat in front of her bound form.

"Aren't you going to talk to us? You left quite an impression on a few of our comrades with your fighting attempts on the bridge."

Anna just continued to stare at the men. Unimpressed with their attempts thus far.

"Rosa," the second man began.

“My name is Anna.” She stated. She was to burn her own identity to keep ‘Rosa’ safe.

“Rosa,” the first man purred. “We’ve met before and I never forget a pretty face.” He stood up at that and walked towards Anna, stroking down the side of her face in a manner that she supposed would have been tender if they were lovers, but was a thinly veiled threat.

“I’m sorry, you must have been mistaken. But I’ll take the compliment.” Anna said back to him, voice low so only he could hear.

The man grabbed her jaw, seeming to dig a thumb into what she knew could be a burgeoning bruise from her fight.

“Give me the code word.” He hissed into her ear.

She turned and smiled sweetly at him.

“Please?” She asked. “That’s what my mama said was always a magic word.”

The man was angered by her attempt at humour and slapped her across her cheek, causing her to spit out blood. The other man was trying, and failing, to hide a snigger.

“Comrade, you know we aren’t to leave marks.” He said trying to hide his evident joy at Anna’s teasing of the big man.

“Our boss wouldn’t be happy to see Rosa all torn up.”

“Anna.” She stated once more, for the man at the back.

"My name, hopefully for the last time, is Anna Sokolova. I was coming back from visiting a friend before your men jumped on me, and attempted to take something that wasn't theirs to take." Anna spat the words with venom. Remembering the one man who had tried to weasel his way between her legs, into a place only she had touched.

"Okay." Said the first man, backing away from Anna like she was a cornered cat. "If you're not going to talk then we should just leave you in this room. I hope you don't need to piss, because soiling yourself is the only option."

And with that they left the room.

Anna had survived the first test.

A few hours later, though Anna wasn't aware of time passing, only closing her eyes to attempt to rest her body and mind before the next and final test of this assignment, a woman walked though.

She had not taken the same approach as the men. She worn all black, except for her sharp red lipstick. She exuded power.

"Rosa." She stated, as she went behind Anna and leant to whisper in her ear. "Will you be civilised if I untie your wrists?"

Her voice was soft, but laced with force. She was a woman used to getting her own way, and Anna had to admit, despite it all she kind of wanted to be like this woman one day. With power and authority radiating out of ever pore.

Anna beared her teeth at the woman, showing her just how uncivilised she could be.

"My," Anna started, struggling through ropes binding her, "name is ANNA!" she yelled at the woman.

The woman stood and watched as Anna struggled in her binds.

"You know how to stop this Rosa." She stated, all pretence of pleasantries having left the room on a seemly cold breeze.

Anna shuddered at the change in the room.

"Ah, Rosa, we can do more than sensory torture. We could perhaps see what you think of water, the cold or even seeing those you love being hurt."

"I love no one." Anna stated. Her cover hadn't said that, but she was working with what she had at this point.

"No one? What about that soldier?"

Anna struggled to keep her face impassive, but could feel the jolt of fear rush through her system.

"Bingo. I found your weak point." The lady said with a chuckle.

"No!" Anna screamed. Had she failed? She had a real life weakness for the man who was fighting for the motherland. Who was hers. Her Vladimir.

“I know you’re not Rosa, I know what you’ve been told to keep secret. But this isn’t recorded. Unlike what your beloved did. Do you know what he’s doing in Hungary?”

Lies. They’re just lies.

“He was part of the front line that kept the Hungarians from overturning communism. And he’s there still. Waiting for the day when a housewife of a fallen Hungarian soldier, or professor or just general civilian, gets fed up and stabs him to death.”

Breathe, one two… Anna counted in her mind as she breathed deeply, reducing her heart rate and trying to bring her mind back to the present rather than the "what if’s" that this vile woman was projecting onto her mind.

“It's rumoured that he killed a couple of comrades during the fighting. Is that who you’re involved with? A traitor?”

Anna released a deep breath, one of the ones she was meant to release as part of her calming exercise, but red was painting her vision. How dare this stranger, this unknown person, insinuate something so vile about her Vladimir.

“No.” Anna released the word through a gritted jaw. Teeth clenched tight enough that Anna was mildly concerned she might break a tooth.

“Are you defending his honour? The indefensible actions he took?” The woman asked with an eyebrow cocked, coming in front of Anna’s face, close enough she could smell the woman's perfume. Meaning she was rich. Which wasn't common in the union.

Anna took a deep breath in, and came up with her argument.

"Are you meant to be in here?" Anna asked the woman.

The woman stepped back from anna, looking affronted.

"Excuse me? I'm asking questions you insolent little girl." She stated, raising her palm to Annas face until she remembered herself.

"Yes Anna. I am meant to be here. I am to break you."

"I only ask because its obvious you're a wealthy woman, and doing men's work just feels... wrong. You should be home with your husband, cooking for him, spreading your legs for him and giving him good little soviet babies."

The woman's face started to redden at Anna's statement.

"All good soviet citizens have a contribution to make. And this is mine." The woman stated.

Anna didn't think so, she was onto something with this woman, the perfume, the lack of a ring. Perhaps she couldn't bag a husband? Or she was a lover of a rich man. She wasn't meant to be here, and Anna was going to make her leave.

"Well, to be fair, I see no ring. So perhaps you're just a high end lover for another. Not good enough to marry and produce his heirs…" Annas sentence was cut off as the woman slapped her.

Hard.

Anna took the hit, nails scraping down her cheek after the slap, likely leaving a mark.

"You said this wasn't recorded. The men before said I couldn't be marked. Let me loose, and I will not tell my mentors of your actions."

The woman had back away from Anna after she hit her, face blanching.

She moved and left the room, leaving Anna, her face stinging alone in the white room.

She wasn't there for more than a couple of minutes, until the head of her program came in.

"Congrats Anna. The devil knows we're proud of your reversal of roles here." He clicked his fingers and two boys came and unbound her.

"Is that all sir?" Anna asked.

"Da," came his response over his shoulder as he left the room.

She had done it, and the very thought lifted a weight off her shoulders.

She hadn't broken.

But at what cost.

April 1960

Anna, aged twenty-two | Leningrad, Leningrad Oblast, Russian Soviet Federative Socialist Republic

Even months after the abduction assignment, Anna still produced a small smile every time she remembered that she had done it. She had survived and passed the final, brutal test.

There was something sweet about the sheer mental triumph of her mental fortitude, and how she managed to subvert the test. It was a smug memory, a comfort and something that she knew she could rely on. She had finished formal education and could now go and finally join the workforce. Walking out of the building of the school for the last time had made her feel lighter, both physically and mentally, because the gruelling task of being educated as a KGB asset was done.

Anna felt the need to escape the bustle of Moscow, and Vladimir had provided her the perfect excuse.

I think I need to spend some time in a city I know well. Can you set us up in Leningrad and I'll meet you there as soon as I'm out of mandatory service?

Anna had chosen her new location carefully: a small, temporary apartment in central Leningrad. She had lived there through one hellishly frigid winter, nesting alone in the tiny space, and was looking forward to warmer weather, more privacy, and just getting to be an adult, even if that adulthood was currently spent in a limitless limbo.

Officially, she was in active service, but the work that came her way was still somewhat ad hoc. They didn't seem to trust the new recruits with anything major until they had earned their keep. Her current assignment was a clerical post at a state-run housing bureau, A boring, bureaucratic, and maddeningly beneath her training kind of job. It felt like a punishment for passing the test, an exile of competence, just because she was fastest, and smarter rather than working harder than her male counterparts...

She could read the most closed off people and from their reactions and micro expressions break them or expose their deepest secrets, yet she spent her days processing paperwork for apartment transfers.

Anna was lonely. The thrill of her professional victory had faded into the silence of her tiny boxy apartment.

She took walks during her lunchtime, needing the bustle of the city to remind her that the world was still alive. One day, on a street corner dense with foot traffic, she ran right into someone.

The person was bored, and captured her in their arms easily, stopping them both from tumbling out onto the street.

The body she ran into was clad in a polo shirt and jeans, looking remarkably out of place in the crowd. Also it was a him.

“Excuse me,” he said as he let go of her and made sure she was upright and standing on the footpath.

He was American. Anna hadn’t heard the accent in person, but had heard enough about it in her studies and could pick it out of a crowd.

Americans weren't common in Leningrad, or in Russia as a whole. At this stage of the war, they were the enemy. The Cold War was in full swing, and there was very much an us versus them mentality.

She eyed him warily, looking him up and down. He wasn’t all that tall, but was solidly built. His facial hair was non existent, giving him a youthful look. Perhaps in his mid twenties.

What is he doing in Leningrad? Anna thought.

The ingrained lessons about Americans surfaced in Anna's mind. Capitalists obsessed with personal gain at the expense of the collective. Their foreign policy, a series of aggressive interventions masked as righteous crusades. Their society, driven by a relentless hunger for material possessions, seemingly blind to the human cost. In Russia, they prided themselves on equality and a supposed higher moral ground.

Yet there he was, a piece of the enemy ideology, looking like a lost puppy while the city's foot traffic bustled around him.

“Are you lost?” Anna asked in clipped English. It had been a while since she used the language, but she was fluent, and it was a useful part of her secondary and tertiary educational experience.

He glanced back at her, his eyes reflecting shock and fear. Anna hadn't seen fear in someone's eyes for a very long time.

“Uh yes, ma'am. You speak English?” he asked shyly, quietly, suspicious of a Russian woman speaking English. He had the right to be concerned; it wasn't a common language in Russia, spoken only by diplomats, academics, and spies. He was undoubtedly trying to figure out which one of those Anna was.

Anna nodded. “Are you looking for the embassy? Because you're in the wrong city for that. It's about 700 kilometres south east of here.”

The man chuckled, slowly letting down some of his walls. “No ma'am. I'm here to soak in Leningrad before I head back down to Moscow to start a job at the Embassy. I was told Leningrad was the more artistic city, and well, that it’s tourist friendly.” He suddenly became flustered.

“As tourist friendly as this country gets, I guess.”

Anna offered a small smile at that. Russians as a general rule were a friendly people, especially if they were hosting someone, but they were distrustful of anyone who spoke English, especially if they spoke with the accent of Eisenhower or the newest American president, Kennedy.

All of that aside, she was drawn to this man. She liked his reserved attitude, yet he wasn't scared off by the fact that she was very Russian. He made her feel seen. Vladimir was months away and only available to her via delayed letters and monitored correspondence. In the meantime, Anna's days were spent in bureaucratic silence and her evenings were spent re-reading old letters, because that was the only thing that made her feel closer to him. It was that or wait at the post office for more to arrive.

This man offered a spark she hadn't realized she missed, she liked the curious nature of it all.

He cleared his throat, bringing Anna out of her momentary dreary daydream. She knew better than that, damn it. No distractions.

“So, what's good to see around here? Can you recommend much for an American to do?”

Anna raised her eyebrow at him. Like, sure, there was plenty to do around the city, but not much of it would be accessible to this man...

Unless...

More things would open up to him if Anna went along and showed him around town. As long as the KGB didn't get wind of this.

“Looking for a tour guide?” Anna asked, eyebrow still raised.

“If the lady insists,” the man responded with a wink.

“I need to know your name first; I don't believe it's safe for any woman to walk away with a man she doesn't know.”

He chuckled softly, sticking out his hand towards her. “Hello, I'm sorry, I'm Charlie Rodin.”

Anna took his hand and shook it efficiently. “Hi Charlie, I'm Anna.” She wasn't about to give a stranger her surname, but her first name was common enough that it shouldn't be an issue.

“Okay, Anna, so what are we doing today if I can persuade you to be my guide for the day?”

Anna provided a tour of the city's sights, discussing the galleries and the historical landmarks, including those from more recent times, ultimately ending their evening together at a restaurant where they enjoyed a glass of wine.

Charlie had offered to walk her to her front door, and she knew that was dangerous for several reasons. Firstly, she couldn't have her neighbours see her with a strange man, let alone an American, not that he looked any different but the moment the man opened his mouth it was obvious he was different.

It was a security and political risk she shouldn't be taking. Also, she had left the office for the afternoon, and if her superiors found out it wasn't for a medical appointment or a legitimate errand, they would be furious with her.

So, she had Charlie walk her close by, a few streets away from her actual apartment but close enough that he wouldn't be able to figure out exactly where she lived.

"Thank you for a fantastic day," he said as they stopped on the sidewalk.

She nodded efficiently; it had been a good day.

He leaned in to kiss her, flustering Anna. She instantly spat out, "I have a fiancée!" before he got too close to her.

While not strictly true, she felt like her and Vladimir were fated. They had talked extensively in their letters about marriage and what being each others wife and husband might be like. He was just away in the army at the moment, so she didn't have a ring yet.

He pulled back suddenly, embarrassment painting his face a bright red colour. He started sputtering apologies and pointing at her right hand, speaking fast in a deep Southern American accent that Anna couldn't understand at the high speed he was speaking.

"It's okay, Charlie. The cultural differences between our countries are vast. I wouldn't expect you to pick up on every nuance," Anna said, softening her voice slightly, then making it firm. "But I can't risk this. I'm committed to my husband to be. He is coming home very soon."

She stuck her hand out to him again, a sign of good faith and that nothing was fundamentally wrong, but a curt way of acknowledging that they were on different pages and should leave as acquaintances, if not strangers.

He shook her hand, then melted into the night in the opposite direction to Anna and the short couple of blocks she needed to walk before she got back to the empty home she was preparing for Vladimir.

July 1960

Anna, aged twenty-two | Leningrad, Leningrad Oblast, Russian Soviet Federative Socialist Republic

The previous three months had been defined by a relentless grey feeling, the sky match her mood. Her work was an insult to her training. Her evenings in the small Leningrad apartment were spent in silence, interrupted only occasionally by the familiar comfort of Vladimir's delayed correspondence. Yet, cutting through the endless dreariness, was the memory of that single, vibrant afternoon. Anna found herself feeling guilty every time she thought back to it, but it seemed she could not help herself.

The American, Charlie. He was a brief, reckless flash of colour in a world built on regulation. He was a lightning flash in her dull grey skies. He was also risk she had taken - a flirtation she had cut off before it could even start – though it was now a secret she felt hanging over her, like a guillotine swinging on a tenuous rope above her head.

Charlies laugh, the surprise in his eyes at her offering to show him around the city, the almost kiss, so close she could feel his sharp intake of breath as she declined his affections… It was a bright, tempting and so very dangerous alternative to the predictable course of her life. The schooling, contribution to the state, marriage, children and then what?

The distraction was over now.

Vladimir's last letter from wherever he had been stationed arrived, devoid of any kind of poetic flourish or romance, and stark in its command.

I'm coming home with the train due in on Tuesday evening, Anna. Meet me at the station, then we will go to the home you've prepared. We must settle down, and soon.

Settled. It was a word that grounded her, the stable future she had earned through years of gruelling dedication. She chose security. She choose safety.

Vladimir met her at the station, his presence hitting her like a sudden, physical shock after four years of absence punctuated by carefully curated correspondence. He was not the boy she had waved goodbye to, he wasn't even the gangly young man she played in the Caspian sea with. His uniform was crisp, his posture rigid, and his gaze, though seeking her out, was intense and practical, carrying the heavy look of a man who had seen too much. He reminded Anna of her father. She lightly shook her head at the thought. This was Vladimir. Her father was Grigori. Two very different men.

"Anna," he said, his voice deeper, flatter without any kind of intonation, than that she remembered. He took her hand immediately, but the touch felt like a claiming, not a gentle embrace of a lover. Its caused her gut to attempt to warn her of danger, but she ignored it. It's Vladimir. Not a danger.

"It is good you are here. We need to leave the city, somewhere quiet. We have something to do before we return to our home."

He led her not to a private car, but immediately into the bustling crowd, navigating them efficiently to the nearest street corner. Within minutes, a dark green state-run taxi pulled over. Vladimir opened the back door with an economical movement.

"Kamenny Island," he instructed the driver in a clipped, formal tone.

Anna sat in the cab, the silence punctuated only by the rumble of the engine, and she could feel his unfamiliar stiffness. Something was up with him. Anna had to scold herself when she started to analyse his movements, or lack of. He is her boyfriend, not a mark.

He didn't ask about her job, her life, or her loneliness. He focused his plan, whatever that may be.

He was guarded, distant, and the man beside her felt like a well-trained stranger.

A stranger.

Her heart hammered with a sudden, fresh fear. Her secret afternoon felt insignificant compared to the change in him.

What happened to have him acting this way?

When they stopped, Vladimir pulled her into a secluded spot near the water, framed by trees and the quiet lapping of the Neva River. There was a prepared blanket and Vladimir gave a nod over his shoulder to a man who was obviously watching the set-up for him.

He turned, his eyes fixed on her as he lowered himself.

"I need us to start on the right footing, as a couple," he stated, his voice a low rumble as he made it onto a single knee.

Anna nodded, her own professional demeanor clicking into place. She squeezed his hand, a gesture of affection, yes, but also a silent promise of partnership.

"Anna Sokolova, would you do me the honour of becoming my wife, and allow me to love and adore you every single day?" He asked, eyes looking up at her.

The beauty of the endless dusk of the white evenings of the Leningrad summer, the gentle air mirroring the burgeoning warmth in their relationship, brought tears to Anna's eyes. She was safe.

She was finally safe.

"Anna, I could use an answer," Vladimir said nervously. Anna laughed, hiccupped out a yes and Vladimir jumped up to squeeze his new fiancée into a big hug.

There were claps in the background, but Anna was only aware of the feeling of her now intended arms wrapped around her. The simple smell of him coming from the spot behind his ear. She nuzzled herself deeper into his neck, soaking his formal uniform shirt in the process with her happy tears.

He pulled back to look at her and asked, "Do you want the ring or..."

Anna was nodding vigorously as Vladimir pulled a solitaire emerald ring surrounded by *diamonds from a little box he had been keeping in his jacket's front pocket.*

How the hell could he have afforded something like this?

"This had been my mother's," he whispered in her ear as he slipped it onto her right-hand ring finger.

"It's beautiful," Anna whispered back to him. It was a stunning but simple ring and being a family heirloom made it all the more special.

November

1960

Anna, aged twenty-three | Leningrad, Leningrad Oblast, Russian Soviet Federative Socialist Republic

Thoughts flew through Anna's mind at a dizzying speed as she looked at herself in a full-length mirror, in a flowing simple white gown. The silk was cool on her skin, clinging to her on the warm, endless afternoon of the 'White Nights'.

The emerald ring on her right-hand finger was solid, a solid weight she had only just become accustomed to... It brought her back to the present moment, anchoring her away from the rush of pleasant memories: Vladimir's tight hug and relief when she said yes on Kamenny Island just a few short months ago, how he held her during that first dance and the sudden, gentle chuckle of a nervous American.

Woah, where did that thought come from?

She had said yes to him. And in a few brief hours, she would become his wife. The thought sent a fresh flutter of anticipation through her, a feeling equally thrilling and daunting. Was she, in essence, transferring ownership of herself to him? Was she now a possession of Vladimir's? The question was sharp, yet she pushed it down. She had chosen security. Safety.

Her courtship felt enchanted, a magical mix of stolen moments across dance halls and the thrill of dangerous correspondence. Her breath hitched as she recalled the letter, the scent of the library's old books battling the chilling reminder of his previous absence.

"I am safe, my Anna, and soon I will be home. I hold the thought of your smile like a treasure against the noise. Wait for me. I will be home soon. We will be together soon."

Her heart fluttered with the warmth of his words, the image of his smile before he went to war, filling her with joy as she imagined their life together. She was sure he would smile like that again. She just needed to give him time and unconditional love.

She stood, still looking at herself in the mirror and steeled herself against one part of the evening she was curious, but also a little scared of.

Tonight, their intimacy would move beyond the gentle hand held across a table. Marital duties. The phrase echoed in her mind, a cold, clinical reminder of what was expected of her. Would it hurt? Would he hate her if for some reason she didn't bleed?

During the ceremony earlier in the day, when the official registrar had called them forward, Vladimir had leaned in and whispered his intentions for the evening. A warmth bloomed in her chest, not from the words, but from the sudden, powerful timbre that made her spine tingle, the playful tone of their past life. The words stole her breath, causing a low, conflicted heat to blossom in her belly. She was both drawn to and deeply afraid of the hardened stranger she was about to take as her husband.

Draped in white, the woman staring back from the mirror was on the edge of a new identity. Her gaze drifted to the empty space beside her in the reflection, the space where her mother should have been. A sudden, sharp pang of loss hit Anna in her chest. The white dress felt like her: simple, elegant, unburdened by the expectations that her mother's traditional red gown would have carried. White whispered of the clean future she was building.

"Anna!" A deep, booming, bassy voice laced with impatient affection echoed through the hallway. Her father, Grigori, breaking her out of her moment of mourning. Of course it would be him. Ready to take her to the next stage of her journey of becoming a Zaitsev.

The walk from the dressing room to the central hall was short but felt endless. The building on the embankment was built of cold marble, grand and imposing. Less a place for romance and more a testament to Soviet permanence. The interior hall, where the formal ceremony was held, was overly warm, the air thick with the perfume of flowers and the stale scent of aged velvet.

Anna was guided by her father into the room. At the center stood a stern, stout woman in a dark uniform, the official Registrar. She stood behind a massive wooden desk, upon which lay their marriage papers.

The Registrar didn't smile. She read from a prepared text, her voice a flat monotone.

"Citizens Anna Sokolova and Vladimir Zaitsev, you stand here before the Soviet State to register your union. Marriage is not merely a private affair; it is a profound commitment to the collective, a pledge to mutually contribute to the building of our glorious future..."

Anna's eyes flickered to Vladimir. He stood beside her, utterly still, his posture perfect. He wasn't looking at her; he was looking at the Registrar, acknowledging the State. He looked less like a groom and more like a soldier reporting for duty. The contrast between the bitter words of duty and the heavy presence of the emerald ring on her finger made her feel increasingly small.

The official eventually reached the core questions, stripping away the political preamble. "Citizen Anna Sokolova, do you freely and without coercion agree to enter into the bonds of marriage with Vladimir Zaitsev?"

Anna's mouth was dry. She looked at the polished marble floor, thinking of Charlie's genuine smile, then at the ring—her promise of security. "Da," she managed, her voice barely a whisper.

The Registrar's eyes snapped to Vladimir. Vladimir Zaitsev, do you freely and without coercion agree to enter into the bonds of marriage with Anna Sokolova?"

"Da," Vladimir returned. His voice was loud, clear, and utterly devoid of emotion, sealing the contract with the decisive finality of a lock clicking shut.

Vladimir placed a small, silver pin onto Anna's dress—a meaningless tradition, overshadowed by the weight of the state's pronouncements. The official produced the final certificate.

"You may now exchange a kiss," the Registrar instructed.

Vladimir turned to her. There was no tenderness, no passion, only possessiveness in his eyes. He leaned in, his lips cold and brief against hers—a quick, official stamp on the transfer of ownership Anna had feared. The applause that followed felt forced, dutiful, and strangely loud in the cavernous hall.

Her fate was signed.

December 1960

Anna, aged twenty-three | Sevastopol, Crimean Oblast, Ukrainian Soviet Socialist Republic.

People's smiles, the scent of champagne, and the sheer joy that filled the room the couple had just been in—all of it left the moment the door of their suite clicked shut. Their wedding had been a joyful affair, but the couple felt the exhaustion like a physical blow.

Now, a profound stillness filled the cabin, mirroring the sudden draining of Anna's own reserves. She and Vladimir lay side-by-side on the tiny bed, stiff as a board, the silence punctuated only by their breathing and the rattle of the train as it hurtled southbound.

The consummation didn't happen in the warmth of their own bed, but aboard the southbound train in the soft class carriage, a gift from her papa. Anna lay beside Vladimir afterwards, a sense of anticlimax settled over her. He had been…

Considerate, she supposed, but his eagerness had felt abrupt, almost mechanical, driven by a need to complete a task. Her body had responded with resistance. There had been no prior warning, no attempt at warming her up to the task, just the shedding of his clothes and his rutting into her core until it gave way painfully. The sight of blood blooming from her core on the sheets seemed to snap something in Vladimir. His movements became more insistent, his breath quickening in a way that felt less like passion and more like a singular, almost unsettling focus on the physical act.

A wave of surprise, bordering on disbelief, washed over Anna. This was it? This was the celebrated intimacy of a honeymoon? She had been promised pleasure, and instead was left in pain and with an uneasy feeling in the pit of her stomach. His seed dripping from her wetting between her thighs, mixing with the blood that was slowly drying.

Darya had gone into great depth about how sex was a mind-blowing and highly enjoyable encounter; Anna wasn't sure what she was doing wrong. She felt cheated by the experience.

The next day, the long journey continued. They transferred to a car for the final hour long drive down through the Ukrainian SSR. The endless fields had slowly given way to the rugged hills of the Crimea, and finally, to the deep blue water of Sevastopol.

The heavy, salty air of the Black Sea coast filtered through the open window of their hotel suite. It was the morning after their arrival, and the start of their official honeymoon after their long journey to get there.

Anna woke early the next day to an empty bed, it wasn't warm, and the sheets were rumpled, indicating that Vladimir had gotten up a while ago. Stretching out like a lazy cat she called out to where she thought Vladimir might be, in the adjoining kitchen. "Darling, what's the plan today?" Vladimir didn't answer. She would have thought if he wasn't next to her then he might have been in the kitchenette, preparing his morning tea. A sense of unease settled deep in her stomach, different from the passionate kisses and heat that, although short-lived, blossomed last night. He had been much more gentle the second time around, seeming to understand she had been in pain after that first time, he claimed he couldn't see her face when he caused her pain.

Anna got up off the wonderfully comfortable and soft mattress, and padded out of the bedroom into the small kitchen area. Vladimir wasn't there either. No note was on the table, though his shoes weren't at the door.

The water she was meant to drink before bed last night, the water she saw Vladimir pour for her, sat on the counter still. Upon smelling a faint, bitter chemical scent in it, she quickly tossed the contents down the sink not wanting to risk the water making her ill on her honeymoon.

She waited…

Why was the smell of the water wrong? And where the hell was her husband? What kind of man skips out on the honeymoon with their wife?

Not a good one. Had Anna made a major mistake?

Forty-five minutes after Anna had gotten up, Vladimir burst through the door in a rush and was visibly shocked to see Anna awake, sitting at the table, arms crossed, waiting for him.

"Honey, I thought you would prefer a sleep-in. I went to the uh..." As he paused, Anna's concerns grew, the tension palpable in the room. He was about to lie to her, his gaze darting away from hers.

"I went to the seafood market down by the docks, but the haul wasn't up to standard. We leave now for Leningrad. Everything is better in Russia proper."

He fast-walked into the bedroom, noticeably out of sorts.

Her instincts, honed by years of specialised education in human behaviour, screamed that Vladimir wasn't telling the truth. Why the hurried excuse? Why the fear of her being awake?

"Honey?" he called out from their suite, breaking her line of thought.

She went to him and helped him pack up their bags. She grabbed their luggage and started packing them into the state car that had brought them from the train station.

"Vladimir?" Anna asked as she slipped into the passenger seat, "Is everything okay? You look like you just ran from the police."

Vladimir's jaw tightened almost imperceptibly as he avoided her gaze, his movements while packing jerky and hurried.

Something definitely happened this morning, Anna thought, an icy knot forming in the pit of her stomach. An unpleasant encounter at a dockside market didn't explain this palpable tension.

"Yes, my love, I'm just eager to get home and have some proper food. The Black Sea fish tasted too salty for my palate."

The long train ride back to Leningrad began, punctuated by overnight stops in various towns for food. But despite the change of scenery and the new tastes, a subtle tension hung in the air between Anna and Vladimir, a silent acknowledgment that their idyllic honeymoon had been abruptly cut short.

The feeling of safety had vanished, replaced by a sense of unease.

January
1961

Anna, aged twenty-three | Leningrad, Leningrad Oblast, Russian Soviet Federative Socialist Republic

They were finally settled in Leningrad, the city Anna had prepared for their new life. The warm memory of her graduation from the Red Banner Institute contrasted sharply with the stale reality of their marriage. Vladimir, having completed his military service, hadn't been to school; his education had been immediate and practical: assuming control of his father's 'business'.

He had promptly picked up the mantle from his father in, what Anna understood to be, their less than legal operations. Vladimir's talk of learning a trade now echoed in Anna's mind with a sinister undertone – it had all been deception. Anna refused to accept this conclusion, however. She had chosen stability, and stability meant Vladimir was legitimate. He had to be.

The Union's attention, vast and cold, was wholly consumed by the threat of American aggression and the treacherous whisper of domestic opposition. It made Vladimir's petty dealings in banned Western goods beneath the state's majestic contempt. Making it outside of Anna's remit. Even if she was an active agent. Yet, his desperate, deep dive into the destructive legacy of his father's black-market network instantly transformed him into a profound, existential threat. She couldn't ever admit to knowing who or what he did. She refused to shatter the precious, fragile illusion of their marriage.

Leningrad felt like a different world from Moscow, and opportunities for Anna were suddenly scarce.

She took the job of manning the reception at his mechanics business, a position she insisted upon, hoping to impose normalcy for them as a newly married couple. It certainly felt like a farce. Few vehicles actually came through, but the influx of cash was constant. Anna allowed herself to suspect this was money laundering, but she did not let herself *know* it. She focused instead on her job, processing the endless stream of funds while diligently recording the few legitimate repairs they performed. Like any good, determined wife, she overlooked the obvious discrepancies. The veil was well and truly pulled over her eyes and she couldn't afford to lift it.

"Anna?" Vladimir called from under a car in the garage, expecting Anna to get up from where she was sitting in the reception area and walk over to him as he slid out from underneath a car.

She wasn't really in the mood for a fight, the idea of it draining her further. Though she knew she could easily cause him to fall foul of the KGB through the institute, she still had connections back to the government even though the previous contacts were cold.

Cold, but not frozen.

His money laundering and racketeering weren't as lucrative as they expected them to be. They were poor, and she was sick of it. Sick of not being able to get a new pair of shoes, or a good cut of meat for dinner.

She ambled her way over to him, for him to roll out from under a car. As she watched Vladimir slide out from under the chassis, a fleeting, morbid image of the car crashing down flashed through Anna's mind, quickly suppressed, though she wasn't entirely displeased by the thought.

“Where did you go yesterday?”

“I went for a long walk. You didn't have customers booked in. We don't do walk-ins, so I left for a few hours to clear my head.”

He scoffed and got up off the trolley that allowed him to glide under the cars he pretended to work on to stand in front of Anna. He was filthy, grease-stained overalls, and his short blonde hair slicked with black grease. Highlighting the time he spent here working on his cars, and hiding items in them where they shouldn't be hidden, instead of being with her. Anna realised at that moment she was lonely.

That wasn't a good realisation.

“Do not do that again.”

Anna raised an eyebrow. Don't walk?

“I think we should have children,” he then started.

Anna gasped at his sudden demand and replied, “Dearest husband, you do realise what goes into making a child right? And with your work, do you think we have the time to have a child?”

Anna knew this was one way he wanted to exert some control over her, forcing her to stay home to look after their child, especially while he was in the criminal world.

“Of course, I know how children are made Anna.” He replied incredulously.

In the first few months of their marriage, she made sure she methodically worshipped his body and brought him pleasure.

One of those evenings, Anna risked a direct request. She asked him to return the favour, to make her feel good, too. He laughed at her - a harsh, dismissive sound.

"Sex isn't about a woman's pleasure, Anna. It's purely for procreation," he told her, the words a cold slap.

"It just so happens I enjoy the feeling of your tight, wet heat grasping me as I release my seed deep inside you.”

The memory flashed across her mind, the feeling of being denied the chance to enjoy things that other friends said they had experienced tangled up between the sheets with their husbands… it stung.

Anna scoffed at the memory and how she reduced her worship. He could have fooled her just by how often he came to visit her in bed. His touch was a ghost. Rumoured but with no actual proof.

“We will do a schedule. Every second night until you're pregnant with my heir.

Anna was shocked by his brazen attitude to having children, but it wasn't out of character for him. Just another part of her he wanted control over. His complete disregard for how she might feel about the situation. It was her body that would grow and stretch to support this new life.

His heir. Not Anna’s child. Not their baby. His.

“Okay my love, we can have children, but we will need to move back to Moscow in order to bring them up. I want my Papa close, and I want my children to grow up with parents who are able to work. I would want to work for a year or two, not in the 'family' business but on my own merit.”

Vladimir nodded along, seeming to agree with what she was saying. An unusually easy agreement. Suspicion clouded Anna's mind. *What angle is he playing at?*

It was as if he were allowing her this small victory, knowing it would ultimately serve his own purpose.

Did he believe that a move to Moscow and her father's presence would somehow benefit him?

She couldn't shake the feeling that he saw her father's connections in the capital as something he could exploit, perhaps even a way to shed his criminal skin.

And wouldn't that be a dream?

July 1962

Anna, aged twenty-four | Moscow, Moscow Oblast, Russian Soviet Federative Socialist Republic

Time seemed to drag as Vladimir got his affairs in order, and himself 'transferred' down to Moscow. The physical job of packing their belongings fell on Anna's shoulders, and she thought that if she saw another box for her to pack it would be too soon in this lifetime. The noise of her packing, the clatter of plates and other kitchenware being wrapped lovingly in newsprint, the feeling of sealing the box shut felt like the end of a chapter.

They had help to move down to Moscow, with Vladimir's family only helping on the proviso that they were to be the first to meet any of his future offspring.

Vladimir's nod at his sister's request was quick, and the look he shot Anna's way made her bite her tongue. Seemed she was going to be used as a pawn in this relationship. Her lack of response was taken as approval of the idea, a quiet concession of her own making when she wed this man.

Their Moscow home was beautiful, and while it might take a little while for Anna to find the work she needs to feel whole and like herself again, being in Moscow felt right.

The first weeks while Vladimir settled into his role as a mechanic's apprentice in Moscow, a job given to him thankfully by one of his old soldier friends he had served with, Anna was tasked with the house and home. The mundane tasks gave her a chance to leave the house however, and she could overhear conversations.

Those quiet conversations overheard clued her into what was happening in the Space race, and what was happening more broadly in the stalemate war they'd called the cold war.

"The Americans are making leaps in their rocket technology. Moscow needs to know why." The strangers talked quietly passing by her on the street,

"*two women have tried to infiltrate the Americans inner circle, both failing,*" the other man said in return before they turned the corner of the street and walked away.

The pressure must be on, and she was the woman who wouldn't fail.

Perhaps that's the part Anna could play.

Anna knew if she got in and earned a slightly better living, that she could get the information that the Kremlin wanted. Her mind wandered back to the day she spent with that American who had been a tourist in Leningrad a couple of years ago.

Frank? Wilson? Charlie. That was his name, she thought, Charlie. Such an American name, unlike the Charles of the English.

Didn't he say he was working in the American Government buildings here somewhere?

Perhaps she could track him down and get a job. Certainly, she could skilfully transform him into a useful asset if she chose to...

October 1962

Anna, aged twenty-five | Moscow, Moscow Oblast, Russian Soviet Federative Socialist Republic

Anna gasped as she collided with the solid chest of a man, the impact jarring her, as she walked out of the grocer without looking. A few weeks back in the city, the constant bustle and concrete jungle made her acutely aware of Moscow's comforting familiarity and beauty. How the autumnal leaves fell. How the Moskva river sounds as it took its time lazily flowing through the city. She and Vladimir lived in a quiet corner of the city, a refuge from the frenetic energy and constant movement of the urban sprawl, where the only sounds were the gentle breeze rustling through leaves and the occasional distant murmur of traffic.

"Sorry!" said the man she had run into. His Russian was accented. American perhaps? That would be surprising.. That accent was unusual in these parts…

Much like finding a gold nugget on the banks of the Moskva.

Anna looked up into familiar sage-coloured eyes, and spent a moment trying to remember that face, that voice and who it matched. She hadn't met many Americans, and those she had met she kept in a mental catalogue.

"Charlie?" She asked, disbelief colouring her voice at the idea of running into the American stranger she spent a day showing around. A warm afternoon in Leningrad, an escape. She was just thinking of him again, only months ago.

Charlie was looking more worn and aged than when she last saw him, the optimism of change or international diplomacy with Russia seeming to have taken away the shine of the new country. He had dark shadows under his eyes, and frown lines permanently marking his beautiful face.

"Oh, it's you!" He said as recognition hit. He remembered that day vividly, a brief respite from the strained silences and veiled accusations of international meetings.

"How have you been?" He asked, then remembered, that despite them spending the better part of a day together, they were pretty much strangers. He caught himself out of that and gave a rueful grin.

"I'm good, though tired from moving."

"Moving?" he asked, interest piqued.

"Yes, I've moved down from Leningrad with my husband," Anna answered curtly, nixing any chance of a man wanting to take advantage of a single woman on the streets of Moscow.

"I didn't realise you were married, please accept my congratulations," he said politely.

Anna wasn't sure what his intentions were, only what her intentions were. But she made sure the ring on her right finger was visible, before she caught herself remembering something she had learned about other cultures in her espionage education…

"Yes, I understand that Americans wear their wedding rings on their left hands, correct?" Anna asked, looking pointedly down at Charlie's empty left hand.

"Ah yes, ma'am yes, we do. I didn't realise that wasn't the same here. I thought that it was universal across all cultures." He looked down sheepishly. And here is where the American stereotyping came in. Anna bet he was surprised to find out that Russians didn't call each other comrade.

"It's okay. Have you started your new job? At the embassy, right?" Anna asked keeping her tone light, trying not to raise suspicion at all. A job at the embassy could be ideal.

More than ideal.

The American embassy was the perfect target, and somewhere the KGB had been trying to get into for a long time. Occasionally a bug gets placed, and slight intel is gathered, but to be a full time staffer in there… The chances to change everything for her country was vast. Even if she had to work behind the walls of that obnoxious golden painted building.

She could spend some time away from her husband, which may help their relationship, but she could also gather intel for the union. Work was a good idea.

She could finally use the skills she had acquired at the institute and actually feel like she was making a tangible difference. Maybe even get the union into a better position in its race with the USA into space. The thought made her long for the chance.

Did she have a chance?

“Yes, I'm an aid to the ambassador.” Charlie said in response, “I know the embassy has been around for a while, when I was in Leningrad it was just nice to get a different experience of Russia, and not just hearing all the propaganda from both sides…” He continued, but Anna just felt an opportunity on the horizon.

It seemed that he wasn't unsympathetic to Russians, and the communist plight. Perhaps he doesn't see America as the democratic and capitalist utopia it touts itself as.

He could be turned.

He could be a source.

Anna just had to weave the web to catch him.

Anna looked up at him again, giving him a once over, she hadn't noticed how tall he was. She noticed he was a tall man last time, but she didn't realise just how much she had to crane her neck to properly have a look at him.

“Why are you looking at me that way?” Charlie asked Anna, breaking her out of her staring and intense thoughts about how she could best manipulate the poor man.

"I was just wondering if the embassy ever hires local staff. Like cleaners, and admin ladies. Anything really. I lost my job when we moved from Leningrad." Anna said, figuring this was going to be the best way to angle getting a role in the embassy. A hapless woman, in need of help.

"Yeah, not usually," Charlie said, lifting his arm and scratching at the back of his neck. His biceps bulged in the action, and Anna had the realisation that perhaps this man wasn't as weak and maybe weedy as she thought.

She let her face fall at his word though, to really drive the point home.

"I'd need to check, but I'm pretty sure we're looking at hiring some cleaning staff. With the tensions between our countries, we've upped our staff count, and someone has to clean up after those messy boys." He finished with a chuckle.

Anna wasn't particularly fond of the idea of cleaning up after a bunch of what she assumed would be entitled men, but it could be a way for her to earn an income. And if she was careful, get back into spying. She would just need to come across as an American sympathiser while she applied and acted in the job. At least when she was around others. She could do that.

That might take some creative acting. Nothing that the institute didn't teach her, however.

"How would I apply?" Anna asked, hoped she wasn't coming across too eager, though maybe that was a good thing with the Americans.

"I want to earn a little bit of money to help support my family before we settle down and have babies."

Not untrue. Anna wasn't keen on having children and quickly adding further burdens to her already heavy load, but she wasn't sure how much longer she could hold off Vladimir's advances. The act of having children might just break her.

"Oh, I can ask the head of housekeeping. I'm sure it would be a straightforward process." Charlie responded.

"I can do that this afternoon if you'd like?"

Anna nodded and silently pled for it to all come together for her. God, she could use this break.

"Then maybe we could meet up for tea? Could go over what they say? Perhaps this time tomorrow over there?" He pointed at a tea shop on the corner of the street. It was sweet-looking, and Anna knew it sold good tea and food so was interested. If it also meant she could get an in with the US Embassy, then all the better.

"Da," Anna responded in the affirmative.

Charlie nodded his head, "I will bid you a good day then. I will see you tomorrow."

Anna had to contain her excitement, feeling tight in her own skin until Charlie had left her and walked away. She let out a quiet squeal and jumped twice before regaining her stoic posture and heading home.

November

1962

Anna, aged twenty-five | Moscow, Moscow Oblast, Russian Soviet Federative Socialist Republic

Anna had secured the job, but she was not so naive as to believe the Union would allow a freelance operation to run completely untethered. The taste of varenye and tea left a bitter feeling in her mouth as she considered her next steps. She didn't have an assigned handler after her time at the institute, she went dark as far as her trainers were concerned.

Anna walked down the old familiar streets towards where she studied. Her skills were coming back to her as she walked, before remembering the class on contact after being forced to be isolated away from the service.

On the sixth page of the Pravda every day an advertisement for volunteers for state frams will be run. If you need to get back in contact you will need to leave the paper, with your number written and the misspelling corrected on the bench of the biggest park of the city you're in. Someone will get in touch.

Anna needed to get a copy of today's Pravda and a pencil.

Twenty minutes later she was sitting in Gorky park, the paper in hand with the advertisement for state framers wanted. The misspelling made Anna giggle slightly, the code was strange but it worked for her situation. She wrote down her address, not wanting Vladimir to pick up a phone call and corrected the spelling to farm. She gently folded the paper, placed it down on the bench and walked away.

She was preparing supper for Vladimir who was in a foul mood, reading the days Pravda and muttering under his breath about the forgotten heroes in his own regiment, when a knock at the door startled her.

She went to the door, and found a slip of paper slipped underneath.

10am tomorrow, tea shop down the street from school. Male will be wearing a coat and a red scarf.

She was back in it.

***

Two weeks later Anna was dressed in her new 'housekeeping' uniform as she shed off her jacket she had worn to stay warm on the way to the job and put her handbag away in the provided lockers.

The woman running the cleaning team at the embassy was a West German. Sympathetic to the American plight but wanted to also keep a tight ship when it came to running a team. Also hated Russians with a passion. Anna wasn't the biggest fan of Natalie.

But it was a job and in that, it was also a way for her to get some intel on what the Americans were doing and planning. She wasn't completely in the dark, she had a little support, though because she got this job on her own she was on her own if anything went wrong.

It didn't bother her so much.

She could help her country.

"Anna!" Natalie barked. Anna struggled not to roll her eyes, or snap back at the stout woman.

"Yes Natalie?" she responded instead.

"You're on the east wing offices. Spotless you hear. I need those desks clean enough to lick."

Gross, Anna thought, turning to roll her eyes. But at least she had a reason to go into those offices.

The east wing of the building was where more of the administration staff, rather than the consular support or ambassador staff were working. These were just those who handled the costs, made sure their calendars and dairies weren't double booked and handled the mail going from the embassy back to America.

Anna had to claim she didn't understand a lick of English in order to get the job, getting to the point of seeing English in a written form and asking why there was Spanish documents around. It was important for the staff to not be insiders of the Russian Government.

But of course, she was reading most of those documents as she went through office by office, tidying, and cleaning. Vacuuming and dusting, straightening things up to make sure that the offices were incredibly clean, but also presentable if someone important was to visit. Gleaning as much information as she could, frequently jotting points down on a notebook stuffed deep in her cleaning gear and snuck out so she could debrief her handler after her shift.

There was one office, in particular, she was interested in getting into and snooping around a bit. And that was the personal assistant to the American ambassador to Russia. Surely there would be helpful information for the Government there. Anna knew she couldn't rush things though. Patience was a virtue, and in her line of work, she knew that people usually got caught by being too impatient.

Anna spent months, day in day out, cleaning those offices. Often under the ever-present and watchful eye of Natalie, she was careful only to glance at documents as she was piling them and dusting around any messes the staff had left. So far, she had found nothing of importance. Her handler was getting impatient and Anna couldn't blame him.

Not that there weren't some interesting things she had seen, but from what she had heard from her colleagues back at the institute, what she had been seeing, about visits and movements of people, were things they already knew.

Anna was getting frustrated with the process. Not that she wasn't thankful to have her job, but she knew she had to step up and get something that would be useful.

She was told by her handler to look out for things that had to do with weapons, like the nuclear bomb that America dropped on Japan at the end of the great patriotic war. Not that that's what they called it at all, World War Two, but only further proved to Anna how America perceived itself.

She needed to look for military movements, or documents pertaining to the movement of nuclear-powered weapons. Listen back to recordings from the secret bug that was put in the office of the ambassador and see if she could maybe get someone to be more sympathetic to the cause. Someone who would talk to her about what the Americans might be planning or how their system might work. Monotonous work. But it needed to be done.

January
1963

Anna, aged twenty-five | Moscow, Moscow Oblast, Russian Soviet Federative Socialist Republic

The fluorescent lights of the embassy buzzed overhead, casting long, skeletal shadows across the plush carpets.

It had been just over six months since they moved and Vladimir was getting more forceful about intimate relations and her getting ready to produce his heir. He claimed her cleaning job wasn't a career move or a worthy job. She would be better off as a house wife.

Anna, meticulously dusting the surface of the Assistant to the Ambassador's desk, felt a tremor of excitement course through her. Nestled amongst a stack of disorganised papers, she spotted a manilla envelope. It was slightly thicker than the others, and the embossed seal bore the insignia of the new CIA department from america. It wasn't sealed shut and the pile didn't look strange without it there.

Her heart hammered against her ribs. Could this be it? The kind of information she was looking for?

With practised ease, she slipped the envelope into her pocket, her fingers tracing the outline of its contents. The assistant was notorious for misplacing document and realistically she would return it first thing tomorrow. It was hard to contain her excitement.

Later that evening, back in her small home, after Vladimir had gone to bed, Anna cautiously opened the envelope. Inside, she found a series of coded messages, intricate patterns of nonsensical English words taunted her. This was no ordinary diplomatic correspondence. This was raw intelligence, the kind that could shift the balance of power between the two superpowers.

A surge of adrenaline washed over her. This was her chance. She had to get this to her handler. She started to meticulously trace the patterns on the page on to blank paper so she could hand deliver it to him in the morning.

The next few hours were a tense dance between fear and exhilaration. Anna meticulously transcribed the codes, translating the symbols into a series of numbers and letters.

She copied them exactly as well but made sure to give context where a typographer would require it. Writing, having to occasionally stop and stretch to avoid her hands cramping up.

Finally, after what felt like an eternity, it was done. She had coupled everything. She glanced up at the clock on the wall. 5.30am. She had been going for eight hours, she might only get one hour of sleep before she needed to go and deliver the message.

She had her foot in the door. Now, she just needed to keep it open.

April 1963

Anna, aged twenty-five | Moscow, Moscow Oblast, Russian Soviet Federative Socialist Republic

Anna was dusting the heavy mahogany desk when the edge of a draft memo caught her eye. It was headed: INTERNAL - CI TARGETS - DRAFT – DO NOT SHARE UNTIL FINALISED.

The paper felt suddenly heavy, alien in her latex-gloved hand. The scent of stale tobacco and the sharp, chemical tang of the cleaning polish she'd just used vanished as her internal world dissolved. She pulled the sheet from the pile. Her eyes scanned the list, dropping straight to her name, underlined and highlighted in a chilling fluorescent green ink: Anna Zaitseva.

It was over.

A wave of intense, paralyzing heat washed over her skin, instantly followed by a deep, numbing cold. Her heart slammed against her ribs—not a regular beat, but a frantic, disorganized drumbeat trying desperately to escape her chest. She couldn't feel her fingers, yet the paper crinkled sickeningly loud as she clutched it. Training snapped the panic back into a focused, icy needle. *Eliminate the proof.*

Her eyes locked onto the heavy-duty diplomatic shredder in the corner, a dark, industrial beast. She lunged, snatching the page and twisting the thick cotton blend paper into a tight, desperate ball. She forced the wad into the machine's narrow mouth. The industrial gears roared a grinding whine of protest, the noise so violent and sudden it sounded like an engine exploding in the silent, polished sanctity of the embassy. She pushed, jamming the paper hard until the machine shuddered, swallowed the evidence, and finally settled back into an unnerving silence.

The sudden silence was worse. It amplified the slight squeak of leather soles behind her.

The noise of the shredder had masked the presence behind her. Anna spun around, her face instantly drained of all color, her hands still trembling uncontrollably from the violent act. Natalie stood in the doorway, her lips pressed into a tight, exasperated line. She wasn't terrified; she was furious, her posture radiating contempt.

"Anna! What in God's name are you doing?" she snapped, her German accent clipping the words with cold precision.

Natalie's voice lowered, hard and final, her eyes narrowed in contempt. "Don't lie to me. You are in a restricted office, fiddling with government equipment, and you look like you've seen a ghost. I'm tired of your excuses. You've been wandering and snooping for months. I warned you about touching papers." She took a step closer. "Get your belongings and go. You are fired. Now. I don't want to hear about this from security. I can't believe I took that advisor's favor to hire you," she muttered under her breath, loud enough for the sting to land.

Anna played the part of the disgraced employee, nodding once, unable to meet the fury in Natalie's eyes. She clutched the sudden, agonizing knot in her stomach, the familiar sting of Natalie's disparagement barely registering. She turned and hurried out of the office, closing the door softly — the last vestige of good housekeeper.

She moved quickly, but not running. Running was conspicuous. She maintained a forced pace through the immaculate, polished hallway, the scent of the same cleaning wax she had been using for months suddenly smelling like a trap. Her uniform, usually a source of anonymity, felt like a flashing beacon on her back.

The KGB will assume I was compromised the moment I was fired. The thought was a cold, sharp injection, eclipsing every other fear. They wouldn't wait for proof. If the Americans had found her, she was a liability to Moscow. Her priority had shifted from gathering intelligence to immediate, desperate survival. She didn't know how much proof the Americans had beyond that list, only that the target list was real and the time to run was now.

As Anna reached the front doors, she lost the pretense of dignity. She didn't take her usual careful steps. She almost fell on the couple of steps outside the front door, catching herself wildly on the granite railing. Her heart hammered against her ribs, a violent, desperate sound only she could hear. This undignified scramble, this desperate flight down the public street, was only the beginning.

April 1963

Anna, aged twenty-five | Moscow, Moscow Oblast, Russian Soviet Federative Socialist Republic

Rain lashed against the windows of the small cozy cafe, blurring the reflections of the already dim streetlights into smudges of yellow on the glass. Anna huddled under her umbrella, praying the wind wouldn't pick up and watched the pedestrians scurrying past, her mind matching the speed of the rain pelting her umbrella. Natalie's suspicion hung over her like a guillotines blade, threatening to end her. Anna had too much to live for and didn't want to end up on the wrong side of Natalie's wrath. She couldn't return to the embassy, not without risking exposure. Or at least not when she was compromised. Perhaps in a few years it would be safe.

Charlie, her mark, or at the very least her entry into the embassy had been suspiciously absent from the embassy while Anna had been working recently. Though the thought of that twisted Anna's gut, the idea she was just using the man. He was more than a mark, and she'd grown dangerously reliant on his company over the last few months. He was also a friendly face in an otherwise cold environment. She couldn't call him a friend, but he was her only constant.

He was sitting in the book shop next to the café Anna was expecting him in, hair still damp from the rainfall and the commute to get there.

He might be her only hope. The thought felt like an anchor, grounding her, and allowing her a precious moment of stillness in the middle of the shit storm she had found herself in.

She crossed the street, her heart pounding. "Charlie!" she said tapping on the window and entering the café and bookstore.

He turned, a surprised smile lighting up his face. "Anna! What a coincidence. I was just about to leave."

They found a small, secluded table in the back of the cafe, the murmur of conversation and the clatter of cups providing a welcome distraction.

"I... I can't go back to the embassy," Anna confessed, her voice trembling slightly. "Natalie... she distrusts me."

Charlie's smile faded, replaced by a look of concern. "Why?"

Anna shakes her head. "Not here." She says to him.

He looks at her, eyes narrowed.

"If not here then where?" he asked.

Anna had to think. There was no ideal place as such to tell this man the truth.

"Lets walk." She says, as she grabbed her own umbrella.

And it was on that walk, Anna pulled him toward a dark, secluded corner of the park where the overgrown bushes provided a shield from the streetlights. Both heads were under umbrellas, walking more secluded areas where people are less likely to understand Anna's broken English, which was less conspicuous than Charlies heavily accented broken Russian.

Anna hesitated, then poured out the story – the coded messages, the list of names, Natalie's growing suspicion. As she spoke, she watched for micro expressions that would give away Charlie's thoughts on what she was telling him. She read him carefully, searching for any sign of alarm, any hint of betrayal. Any hint he would tell his bosses and have Anna condemned by the Russian Government.

The mood hung heavy with the unspoken, the rain had stopped but left the air feeling heavy and humid. Anna, perched on the edge of a wooden bench in a park, head lowered to avoided his gaze, one hands clasped tightly around her umbrella, the other resting on her lap.

Charlie leaned in, his voice dangerously low and intense. "Are you a KGB agent?"

The silence stretched between them, a taut, invisible thread. Tension that even the sharpest knife would struggle to cut. Anna felt the weight of his scrutiny, the rigors of her professional discipline, suddenly crumbling from under what she thought was her unbreakable resolve. She wasn't sure why, but she couldn't lie to this man.

She looked up, meeting his gaze. "I… I can neither confirm or deny that," She whispered, her voice barely audible. "The name itself is a conviction, Charlie. It puts you in danger."

Charlie leaned forward, his elbows resting on his knees. "Why not?" he pressed gently, "Don't you trust me?"

Anna hesitated, the words catching in her throat. Trust. It was a big word despite its five letters. Weighted. Could she trust him? Could she trust anyone?

"It's not about trust," she said, her voice gaining strength. "It's about… about safety. Protection. For both of us."

Charlie nodded slowly, understanding dawning in his eyes. "Of course. I understand."

He reached out, his hand hovering over hers. "But if… if you ever need help, if you ever need to talk, to someone…"

Anna looked at him, her eyes filled with a mixture of fear and gratitude. "Thank you, Charlie," she said, her voice thick with emotion. "Thank you for understanding."

As she left the park that night, Anna knew her life had taken a dangerous turn. The lines between friend and foe had blurred, and the shadows of suspicion had grown longer. But she also knew that in Charlie, she might have found an unexpected ally, a lifeline in the treacherous waters of espionage.

May 1964

Anna, aged twenty-six | Moscow, Moscow Oblast, Russian Soviet Federative Socialist Republic

The air in their small apartment crackled with palpable tension. Anna was against the kitchen bench, preparing the evening meal as Vladimir blocked the only exit, the doorway. "You're seeing someone else," Vladimir accused, his voice a low growl. "Someone at that… that fucking embassy." His rage was obvious, his face blotchy and red, the venom in his voice.

Anna recoiled, hurt and angry. "What are you talking about? This is ridiculous!"

In part because she wasn't working there anymore. She instead spent her time in the tea shop nearby, attempting to gather something, anything useful for her handler to report. She'd ruined her chances of helping the union, and its something she didn't want to tell Vladimir. She was ashamed, and still in denial about the whole situation.

"Don't play innocent with me, Anna," Vladimir sneered, slowly making his way from the door into Anna's space. "You're always gone, you come home too late, you smell… different." He gestured vaguely towards her; his eyes narrowed. "Of some other man's scent. Filthy with the scent of lies." His outburst caused his spittle to hit the bench next to Anna, who was disgusted by this roared back at him,

"If that's the case Vladimir you're carrying the stench of paranoia and dear husband, it doesn't suit you."

Can Anna play any lingering smell on her clothes off as cleaning chemicals? It was the faint smell of Charlie's pipe tobacco, lingering on her clothes after their last meeting. Guilt gnawed at her. She knew nothing had happened with Charlie. It was innocent. A shared concern, a mutual distrust of their respective governments. Regardless of that, Anna couldn't help but feel a flicker of panic shoot across her breast bone. But the line between friendship and something more had blurred, dangerously close to crossing. He was a friend. He was her mark.

She opened her mouth to deny Vladimir's accusation, to explain, but the words caught in her throat.

Vladimir knew she worked for the state, but not exactly how.

The words "American intelligence" burned on Anna's tongue, but she bit them back. How could she explain that the information clinging to her clothes, the reason for her secrecy, could shift the balance of power in the Cold War? He wouldn't understand. He couldn't.

Information she held could change the future of Russia.

The argument escalated, voices rising, accusations flying. Finally, exhausted and heartbroken, Anna stormed out of the home, slamming the door behind her. She stood on the stoop for a moment, wondering if Vladimir would follow.

She sat on the step down to the street and started counting to 300 at a steady pace.

Five minutes and he never came for her.

Where could she go?

The streets were a dangerous and cold place. A dangerous place for a woman alone at night, carrying the raw, visible distress of a crumbling marriage. She caught the train and went towards her father's apartment. She knew he was highly unlikely to be in. This time of the year he went south, as the cold was too much for him at his age, preferring the mild temperatures down by the Caspian sea.

She left the sparsely used train, and trudged down the street to her father's apartment block. She knew this time of the night the block would be quiet so made her way up to the 3rd floor, and reached above the doorframe to the place her father kept his spare key in case he locked himself out or became forgetful.

This was the only place left. Vladimir knew her family and her routine, but he only knew of this apartment; he wouldn't think to check it, simply because he wouldn't care enough to try. She had also never visited, why would she do so now?

She felt the same old, bitter resentment settle in her chest, the same one she had harbored since 1945. Papa had come home, but only his body; his spirit had been lost to the war, leaving her with a distant, broken man. He was the first man who taught her that promises of protection were always brittle.

Vladimir, with his own brand of rage and emotional abandonment, was merely the second. Her choice of husband was a brutal echo of her father's failure, a strong man who couldn't be trusted.

Anna quietly unlocked the apartment, the stale air a sign of her father's absence. She curled up on the couch of the unfamiliar home. She had only known about this place in conversations with him, but had never visited after her mother's death and his moving to Moscow. The entire apartment was cold, sparsely decorated and suited the man to a tee.

She needed the quiet, cold safety of this forgotten space to simply stop running, if only for a few hours. She was tired, feeling the drain of energy leaving her at the same rate the tears tracked down her face, she continued to weep until she fell into a restless slumber.

June 1964

Anna, aged twenty-six | Moscow, Moscow Oblast, Russian Soviet Federative Socialist Republic

The café across the road from the embassy, usually a safe haven of warmth against the cruel Russian winter and comforting aromas, felt cold and sterile to Anna. She sat hunched over her coffee, the slightly burnt, slightly bitter taste mirroring the despair that gnawed at her. The argument with Vladimir still echoed in her ears, each cruel word a fresh cut across her heart.

Suddenly, the chair opposite her scraped against the floor, startling her out of her thoughts. It was Charlie, his face etched with concern. "Anna," he said softly, his voice filled with a genuine concern that surprised her. "You don't look so good."

Anna forced a smile, a brittle, lacklustre attempt to mask the turmoil within. "Just a rough couple of nights," she mumbled, taking a large gulp of her now cold coffee.

Charlie noticed the way Anna's fingers nervously traced the rim of her cold coffee cup, her gaze fixed on some distant point. He reached across the table and gently placed his hand over hers. "You can talk to me, you know," he said quietly. "Whatever it is."

Anna wanted to scoffed at him. Of course, an American would say she can talk to him. She wasn't that naive.

Anna looked at him, her gaze drawn to his kind eyes, the lines of concern etched on his forehead. At that moment, a wave of honesty washed over her. "It's... it's Vladimir," she confessed, her voice trembling slightly. "We had a terrible fight. He... he accused me of cheating."

Charlie's hand tightened slightly around hers. "I'm so sorry, Anna. That sounds awful."

"He said I was seeing someone else," she continued, her voice dropping to a whisper. "Someone at work; you"

Charlie's eyes widened slightly, but he said nothing. Anna her gut tightening at the idea that he could be misinterpreting her in the silence, blurted out, "It's not true, of course. I wouldn't do that to him, and while you're a friend I don't think I could ever see you that way."

Charlie's hand slipped from hers, and he leaned back, his gaze fixed on his coffee cup. "Anna," he began slowly, "I... I think you should know something." He paused, seemingly searching for the right words. "I... I'm not attracted to women."

Anna stared at him, bewildered. "I... I don't understand."

Charlie took a deep breath. "I'm... well, I'm gay."

The revelation hung heavy in the air, a strange silence settling between them. Anna felt a mixture of emotions – surprise, confusion, and a strange sense of relief. Relief that her fears about Charlie's feelings were unfounded, relief that she hadn't unintentionally crossed a line.

"I... I see," she managed to say, her voice still a little shaky.

Charlie looked at her, a hint of apology in his eyes. "I'm sorry if I've confused you. I just... I wanted you to know."

A beat of silence stretched.

Gay.

The word felt cold and forbidden. In the Union, such a thing was criminal, punished by labour camps; it was officially dismissed as a symptom of Western decadence and moral failure.

A flicker of confusion crossed her face. It didn't fit the image she had of American men, or Charlie.

Anna, despite the turmoil within her, felt a surge of respect for Charlie's honesty. This was an immense secret, one that carried a life sentence if revealed. "Thank you for telling me," she said, her voice sincere. "It takes courage, especially in this country."

The awkward silence that followed was broken by the gentle clinking of spoons against cups. Anna, feeling strangely lighter, took a sip of her coffee. The bitter taste seemed to have faded, replaced by a sense of calm, a sense of unexpected understanding.

September
1967

Anna, aged thirty | Moscow, Moscow Oblast, Russian Soviet Federative Socialist Republic

The few years that followed were a whirlwind. Anna and Vladimir, their relationship tested but ultimately strengthened by shared secrets - specifically, the frank discussions about what the both of them do for a living, after almost coming to blows over it and causing a close call during a visit to Vladimir's sister. They fell into this fragile peace, neither of them particularly happy, just existing in each other's orbit.

This was not the kind of love Anna had imagined, and they weren't the people who had fallen in love not that many years ago. Vladimir apologized for his part of having her flee from their home, and they settled into a routine where it felt much less like walking on eggshells, waiting for the sharp emotional pain to penetrate.

They had even started becoming intimate again, though Anna did make Vladimir work for it after he made her feel the way she had leaving the house. For weeks she wouldn't sleep in the same bed as him, choosing the couch instead, if only to feel safer in her own company.

The fluorescent light hummed over Anna's desk in the corner of their little home, illuminating the rows of Cyrillic text she meticulously analyzed. They could be nothing, there hadn't really been opportunities since that one big one where she was almost caught. She was still trying, she wanted the rush of getting the information to her handler. Information she knew mattered and could change things. Instead she could only give scraps of information gathered from her time in the nearby café and hanging out in a nearby apartment watching and trying to lip read the English the Americans spoke.

The thrill of direct involvement was gone, replaced by the quiet tension of intellectual warfare. Still, a sense of purpose remained, a knowledge that her insights, though bloodless, were valuable.

Sometimes, while walking to the dead drop, Anna would catch the scent of strong cleaning fluid emanating from a nearby building. A ghost of her former life would flicker – the quiet satisfaction of a spotless room, the unexpected opportunities for observation. Now she just sat and drank tea with varenye. Or she pretended to live in one of the apartments next to the embassy, pushing out microwave waves the union promised would block the bugs others had apparently placed in there.

One evening, while preparing dinner (usually a comforting task), Anna felt a sudden, strange shift within her core; less a physical sensation than a moment of profound, unsettling awareness, which was swiftly followed by an intense bout of nausea that caused her to avoid food for a day or so.

Nausea wasn't normal for Anna, she was known at her boarding school and at the institute for having a steel stomach. The visit to the clinic the next morning meant that the wait to find out what was happening to her would be revealed before the end of the day.

She dutifully peed into a small container and was told to come back towards the end of the day.

The waiting was torment. She paced the room she had been put in near the embassy for the day.

Back and forth,

Back and forth.

Her co workers gave her a side eye and wanted to tell her to sit the heck down.

Hours dragged on until later she was in the doctor's office alone. The words he had just spoken echoing around the room, struggling to penetrate her mind.

"Positive."

Anna's gaze was fixed on the wall, her mind consumed by a whirlwind of emotions. Disbelief shook her, fear trembled, but beneath it, a seed of an unknown emotion began to sprout. Hope?

Tears welled as she touched her belly, and a wave of poignant tenderness washed over her, imagining the future.

A hollow emptiness quickly consumed the tenderness, leaving a desperate plea echoing in the silence.

Was she right to bring this child into the world as it was? It seemed to be teetering on the thin line between peace and complete destruction unlike anything anyone had experienced.

What dangers might her child face simply by being born in this time, to her?

But when she saw the miniature clothes at the local market on her way to work in the weeks following she smiled, a warmth spread through her chest, the unexpected tenderness coming back to settle just below her belly button.

It was almost time for Vladimir to repeat his action with her in their bedroom, as unromantic as it was, and this time, this time she could put a stop to it. The fortnightly ritual had been in place since Vladimir decided he wanted her to bear his children. Now Anna could just relax for the next however long, maybe forever and not be coerced into touching her husband out of martial obligation.

She found Vladimir in his workshop; his brow furrowed in concentration as he worked on some delicate mechanism under the cars hood. He looked up, startled when she entered.

"Vladimir," she began, her voice trembling slightly, "I have something to tell you."

He rose to his feet, concern etched on his face. "What is it, Anna? Are you okay?"

She took a deep breath, then met his gaze. "I'm pregnant."

Vladimir eventually drew back, but the relief Anna felt was instantly replaced by a sharp, cold dread. The wonder in his eyes curdled into a hard, calculating glint. His hands, still resting on her waist, tightened, a possessive, almost painful grip.

He stepped back further, his eyes tracing the contours of her body, as if trying to locate the child already. The fluorescent workshop light, which usually cast a harsh, unforgiving glare on the concrete floor and the dismantled engine block, seemed to soften, reflecting the sheer, unadulterated joy in his whiskey-coloured eyes.

"An heir," he murmured, the word was heavy in the oil tinged air.

"He will be an heir," he stated, his voice dropping from a soft whisper to a low, guttural command.

The word *he* felt heavy, predetermined.

"My father's business, my legacy... it all goes to him."

He let out a loud, booming laugh that echoed off the metal walls, a sound Anna hadn't heard in years, a sound that seemed to chase away the quiet tension of intellectual warfare she lived with. Just as she started to find a small delight in the sound, the laughter cut off, sharp and sudden, like a transmission failing.

Anna's breath hitched. The hope that had blossomed only a few moments ago shrivelled, replaced by a cold knot of dread. *An heir.* Not a child, not *their* baby, but a tool, a symbol, a continuation of the very darkness she wanted to escape. This was the volatile side she feared, the military-honed control she couldn't fight. She was suddenly keenly aware of the grease and oil on the floor, the exposed metal of the car, the danger that permeated his world.

She managed a shaky whisper. "A boy? You already know?"

He didn't answer the question, dismissing it with a careless wave of his hand.

"He is a boy. He has to be." His voice was low, resonating with an alarming certainty that brooked no argument.

He stepped close, crowding her, and placed both hands firmly on her shoulders, his thumbs pressing into the sensitive spot near her collarbone.

"No more risks. No more working." He stated. Anna was aghast. Her mind screamed a protest. She was a skilled asset, a contributor to the Union, not just an incubator for his legacy. He had just reduced her to a vessel, a piece of his property, and the heat of her anger was quickly smothered by the cold certainty of his control.

"Vladimir, I don't —" she started, but he cut her off with a warning squeeze to her still helpless arm.

"Silence. You are carrying my heir. Your duty is to him, and to me. Now, no more of this nonsense." He gestured vaguely at the blueprints and tools scattered around the workshop, as if dismissing all the years of her life that weren't devoted to him.

He pulled her in for a final, almost painful, crushing embrace that felt less like love and more like a claim of ownership.

"You are mine, and he is mine," he murmured into her hair. "We will celebrate tonight. Now, go." He turned back to his engine, and started tinkering in the hood again, dismissing Anna completely.

She stood there for a moment, absorbing the cold reality: utterly empty because of her husband, yet profoundly full of love for the little life inside her stomach.

A contradiction, would this be the main theme of her life?

December
1967

Anna, aged thirty | Moscow, Moscow Oblast, Russian Soviet Federative Socialist Republic

Early pregnancy for Anna was not easy. She didn't have her mother to talk to, she didn't have close friends to talk to, and she had all but lost touch with her school friend Darya…

Having a friend who was a nurse would have been helpful. She couldn't talk to Vladimir's mother. Her mother-in-law really didn't think she was good enough for her petit prince. Why Vladimir's very Russian father married a French woman was beyond Anna comprehension. The woman was snobby and highly intolerant to anyone who wasn't Vladimir or his father Josef.

She couldn't talk to anyone she worked with. Natalie was a vile excuse for a woman at the best of times, and trying to be friendly with anyone was a struggle without risking someone else becoming ostracised.

She was welcomed back into her role at the embassy after they caught another cleaner red handed with classified documents. Well, she had them in her hands, while one of the senior embassy staffers was pounding into her over his desk. But Anna wasn't one to judge. It got her job back. And the income from this as well as the KGB was welcome. As meagre as the income from her cover was. But no one doing the right thing by the union was really rich like the Tzars had been, so Anna counted herself lucky.

And perhaps it was a blessing in disguise that Natalie was still openly hostile towards Anna, assigning her alone to clean bathrooms, because it meant that when the nausea hit like a freight train, she had the chance to vomit in peace before tidying it up again.

She was exhausted. Anna just wanted to crawl into her bed and rest. Have a cold flannel pressed to her forehead and Vladimir petting her hair gently telling her that she was doing good, and that it would all be alright. Only a few months of this.

Instead she's out here scrubbing down yet another urinal.

Leaving the men's room in a better state than she had seen when she arrived, Anna released a breath.

Can't be too much longer of this.

Keeping her head low, she pushed her cart of cleaning materials down the hall until she heard a yelp come from in front of her.

Her head snapped up at the noise, and she mentally chastised herself for not keeping an eye on where she was going, instead trying to remain under the radar and passive.

Little luck there. Instead she ran into someone.

"Anna?" a familiar voice, the same voice that yelped only seconds ago, asked.

Anna glanced up, and into familiar whisky-coloured eyes. A jolt of awareness shot through her as she recognised who those eyes belonged to.

"Yes sir, how can I be of assistance?" She answered meekly in Russian. She knew Charlie wouldn't do anything, demand anything from her.

"I actually have a matter I need to speak with you about…" He started trailing off realising perhaps in the middle of her shift isn't the best time to bother her.

"Okay?" Anna asked in return. Trying to read the expressions on his face. If she could read minds, she thought, she would be unstoppable. And it would also mean less chance of moments like these where she might run into someone with her cart.

"Um yes. There's a mess in my office, and while I know your team isn't allowed to clean up messes after the last incident—only American personnel are allowed in private offices—I thought it would be alright if I supervise. If you would be amenable."

Anna needed to clean his office? That wasn't typical. As Charlie had said, no one was allowed to clean those offices unless they were American. Was this just a flimsy excuse?

"I can help, sir. But you need to speak to my supervisor Natalie first."

"Bring me to her," he demanded.

Charlie's voice was unusually sharp and cold as he asked.

They walked the hallways, which at this late hour were deathly quiet, Anna leading head down feigning meekness around a man she knew well.

"Natalie?" Charlie barked into the break room for the cleaners.

They could hear a chair shoot back and some stifled giggles, likely from the other cleaners. Charlie was aware of the absolute hell Natalie had been putting Anna through. So, he put on a stern American general eques act, something that would have created a visual reaction for Natalie, after seeing Americans and their reactions to the German warfare in her native Berlin.

"This not cleaning the offices thing is getting ridiculous. I need to borrow Anna's services for a short time to clean up a mess. Understood?" He asked. Him asking was an opening Anna wasn't overly keen on. It gave Natalie the chance to say no.

"Charlie, wouldn't one of the other girls be better suited to this task?" Natalie said in her thickly accented English. They always spoke English around the cleaners, assuming we remained oblivious. Natalie flourished her arms across the break room to gesture to the other women in the room. "Anna is due for a break shortly. And while these things can be skipped, she does look tired."

Charlie however looked very unimpressed and shook his head. Anna had to stop herself from rolling her eyes at the woman. She wasn't meant to understand English so couldn't know what Natalie was saying about how she looked. Also yes, she was tired, and perhaps lighter duties would have helped.

Ugh.

“No Natalie, I need Anna. She's the one I asked, and she's the one I want to clean up my messes.”

Anna gulped. There was an unexpected authority in the way he told Natalie that Anna would clean up his messes, a commanding tone she hadn't heard from him before. It was surprising, especially given his recent vulnerability with her.

She knew he would never but couldn't help but wonder if anyone else knew his secret. Surely not. It is illegal.

“Anna!” Natalie snapped at her. Anna straightened up, promptly taken out of her daydream where people could love whomever they wanted without persecution. *Oh, to imagine.*

She lifted her chin to her boss, who told her to follow Mr Rodin as he had a job for her to complete in his office. Anna did as she was told. She trailed behind, a sense of quiet urgency urging her forward, until finally she and Charlie were alone in his dimly lit office; the only sound was the faint hum of the air conditioning.

A soft click was the warning she got before Charlie asked in Russian, “Do you know if this room is bugged?”

Anna eyes widened. Bugging was something the KGB was into, and she wasn't aware that any of their major bugs had been discovered.

Charlie walked over to a small white noise machine on a shelf, flipping the switch. A low, constant, electronic hiss filled the small space, muffling their words.

“I'm going to take that as a no, do you mind if I switch back into English? It is easier for me to explain things that way.”

Anna nodded slowly at the man in front of her, trepidation in her stance.

“First I need to ask you a question,” he starts, and he points to the spare chair for Anna to sit.

He sat at his desk, the weight of what he was thinking, what he was about to do, heavy on his shoulders.

“It was a close call with Natalie, but I know exactly what you're doing Anna. I've caught you on camera sneaking documents from my boss's office.”

Anna's breath hitched. He knew?

“I promise that the intelligence in it is stable though. I kind of left that document as a bit of a honey trap.”

As he talked, he started to relax into his seat a little, though Anna stayed ramrod straight in her own, admittedly very comfortable seat.

"I wanted to know who on Natalie's crew would take the bait. The opportunity to work as a maid in this place would be too enticing for an operative to give up."

"Do you have a way out of this place?" He asked her, staring her in the eye.

She nods timidly. She had to. Her growing body would betray her cover in five months. The tiny, vulnerable life inside her had already set a timer on her entire operation.

"Okay. I am leaving for home again in about three months' time. I will need you to leave this job at the same time. It will be a coincidence. I want you to be my conduit to the KGB. I want to give over information about the USA that might help the situation over here."

Anna's eyes widened.

Fuck.

She was sitting across from someone who was willing to betray their nation and help hers.

Why?

She could feel her eyebrows shoot up to her hairline, lines undoubtedly marring her normally clear forehead.

"You're probably wondering why the hell I would do this? Simply put I am sick and tired of the way of life in the United States. I am sick of our country constantly being at war, touting the perfection of their capitalism and democratic society when the communist way actually makes more sense to me."

He chuckled lightly at that and scrubbed at the back of his neck as he spoke. A tell that he was nervous. Nervous because what he was saying was treason, in both Russia and in the United States.

"I could be shot for saying that back home. I plan on taking my partner and moving to the other side of the Pacific. Maybe to one of the islands, but I can't stay in America."

Anna's mind raced. Betrayal. Alliance. Danger. Could she trust him? The alternative was exposure, death. "Alright Charlie," she began slowly, her voice still tinged with disbelief.

"Tell me what you need to tell me."

January
1968

Anna, aged thirty | Moscow, Moscow Oblast, Russian Soviet Federative Socialist Republic

Leaving the room she was ordered to 'clean', Anna slipped out, checking the hallway for people her instincts taking over despite her heart jackhammering out of her chest.

Clear.

There was no one and Anna knew, from her many shifts cleaning just the hallway that there were no cameras or Americans bugging themselves. The action was automatic, proving that the spy was still underneath the exhaustion.

Anna got back to the cleaning supplies room, which acted as a bit of a base for all the cleaners on breaks, or when they first got in for their shifts.

Anna was mentally reciting the information she just got from Charlie, intelligence that could change everything in the proxy war between the Soviet backed North Vietnamese and the Americans.

They're making a move on the north Vietnamese at the beginning of February in the form of a major land and sky offensive. The General seems to think the troops are invincible. I'm not the only one who wants this senseless war over.

The moment Anna exhaled deeply, she was unexpectedly overcome by a wave of nausea that seemed to come from nowhere. Lately, her pregnancy symptoms had been easing up, but now, a wave of nausea washed over her, and she desperately needed to...

Her stomach lurched, and a cold sweat slicked her forehead as she emptied her stomach into the bucket, the metallic tang filling the air. The bucket next to Natalie's shoes which promptly had her sent home.

Anna was pleased to be out of that building. She was fearful of the knowledge she held. She paused for a second at the curb, checking for vehicles, before forcing herself to move, putting physical distance between herself and the American Embassy.

She never used to feel the walls close in around her, both physical walls of the embassy and those in her mind. She had knowledge, something dangerous enough to change a war's outcome and she needed to get to her handler.

It was obvious that America had no desire to look after its people, sending them off to war when a country wants to try a different type of government is only one example of this. They seem to not be able to help but flash their wealth and tell the world how they're so much better than everyone else.

Anna hurried down the street, the American arrogance she'd witnessed at the embassy still rankling, the information she held however serving to temper any hostility she could hold to those in that embassy.

She'd been taught the value of community, of shared sacrifice. She picked up her pace, the image of Londoners during the Blitz – keep calm and carry on – a stark contrast to the boisterous American exceptionalism.

Even under fire, the British had maintained a quiet resilience. The Americans, it seemed, equated worth with wealth, their “almighty dollar” overshadowing any real sense of humanity.

She reached Lubyanka Square, her breath catching in her throat, and pushed herself into a dead sprint towards the imposing yellow building.

She arrived at the base of the stairs, arms raised above her head, trying to stave off a stitch in her side. She hadn’t been as active as she had been during the service, and she regretted that. She was doubled over, this time not from nausea, but catching her breath quickly before she was to take the stairs.

She felt like she flew up four flights of stairs, the building being nine stories high from the street. There was the basement, which as most joked, made it the tallest building in Moscow, because you could see Siberia from the basement. The laughter about the basement always felt forced, a way to mask the underlying dread.

Torture.

The rumours were horrifying. Anna pushed those thoughts away, focusing on her mission. Those who ended up down there…

The only option in Anna's mind was that they must have done terrible things. She couldn't dwell on it.

She knocked on her superiors office door, and doubled over her knees trying to catch her breath after storming up the stairs in the fashion she had.

"Come in," comes a masculine bark from inside the room. "Sir! I have information from a source close to the embassy…" Anna settled into the soft, yielding leather of the chair, the musty aroma of aged paper and pipe tobacco filling her nostrils.

She begins outlining the details Charlie had told her and watched her handlers face for any kind of tell of the importance of this information.

She detailed the plan she had for Charlie as an asset and her own plans to leave the role when she was late in her pregnancy.

She promised she would scrap every little bit of American intelligence she possibly could from Charlie before he moved away from Russia and America.

Anna noted the spark in the handlers eye, and she knew she must have given them, the state, something useful.

The glow in her chest grew when he commented "Well done comrade. Now get more." Before nodding and gesturing her to leave and close the door behind her.

Anna felt useful. At long last. She felt like she had purpose for the state, she had made a tangible change.

A plan set in stone. Relief washed over Anna, quickly followed by a tremor of apprehension. This was it. There was no turning back now.

March
1968

Anna, aged thirty | Moscow, Moscow Oblast, Russian Soviet Federative Socialist Republic

This is hell, Anna thought.

It must be.

Why the heck would anyone do this?

Anna was on her hands and knees, belly almost touching the floor for her advanced state of pregnancy, cleaning the men's bathroom on her last day working at the embassy before taking time to give birth.

Everything ached.

She was told she ought to be on bed rest, but she wasn't a fan of doctor's orders.

Charlie was even starting to worry that their arrangement was taking a toll on the normally strong and stoic woman.

Obviously, expressing those concerns couldn't happen, as a hormonal Anna would probably rip his head off, no matter how useful he was to her country.

“Anna?” Charlie had just found her in the men's bathroom. His brow furrowed as he took in her pale face and the way she leaned heavily against the cool wall obviously uncomfortable.

Anna released a big sigh and clambered up to her feet.

“I cannot wait for this child to be out of my body. I love them, but goodness, I just want to not feel so exhausted all the damned time.”

Charlie could empathise, in the sense he had seen his sister go through the same thing before he came over to Russia.

“My sister had my niece just before I came here, children are a blessing and we mustn't loose sight of that Anna.” Anna shot him a look that could curdle milk.

A blessing that made you feel like you were carrying a watermelon on your front and was sapping the energy from you constantly.

“I need to get back to work Mr Rodin, its my last day, and I am not sure but I think I want this job when I come back from having this child.”

That was a dead giveaway to Charlie that they had moved into a space where they could be heard.

“Cafe Chernyy. 1400 hours on Tuesday. Do not be late.” Charlie said before he walked away from Anna.

Tuesday came around quickly, the four days since she finished work having flown by in subtle nesting in her home.

Anna took a break from cleaning, and made the excuse that she was going to stretch her legs to Vladimir who seemed to be hovering around her more and more recently. She wasn't sure if he was anxious on her part, needing an heir or what. But Anna needed space. Preferably before she snapped.

"Anna!" Charlie called, from across the cafe.

He was sitting in a seat towards the back and no one was near him. Good.

"Hello Charlie. What have you got for me?"

Tensions between their two countries was ramping up. Soviet Russia had been pretty aggressive in America's eyes, America was putting on a pearl clutching façade, but was really a ruthless beast of a country according to the Russian papers.

The Vietnam war, a war that Americans didn't even need to be a part of, Vietnam being half a world away. A war where Americans dropped literal poison, something they've called Agent Orange. claiming to clear the Viet Cong from the jungle. Persistent whispers from the Vietnamese of it causing severe gastrointestinal issues and skin problems. But it was the Tet Offensive, where the Viet Cong attacked the Americans before they could be attacked, according to the information Anna had been given. And while the attack was technically a military loss for the north Vietnamese, it decimated American moral. Anna's handler couldn't resist a rare smile when Anna reported rumours of political strife in the inner walls of the white house.

The propaganda strife between both countries, and no amount of talks in 'friendly' western countries seems to alleviate the pressure cooker that was international politics between the two countries. America stating that "KREMLIN BEHIND EVERY THREAT TO DEMOCRACY, SAYS SECRETARY OF STATE" and "MOSCOW TIGHTENS GRIP: CRACKS DOWN ON CZECHOSLOVAKIAN FREE PRESS REFORMS".

The soviet also had their own propaganda, "THE SHAME OF WASHINGTON: CAPITALIST STATE UNABLE TO GOVERN ITS OWN RACIAL CONFLICTS" and "CAPITALIST PROFIT OVER HUMAN LIFE: NUCLEAR DISASTER LOOMS AS US MILITARY CUTS SAFETY CORNERS."

"Disengagement." Charlie stated.

Anna cocked her left eyebrow.

"Disengagement?" She asked him, needing more.

"They meet yesterday and there's going to be a speech." Charlie gulped, and reached for his glass of water sitting on the table.

"Last day of the month. And there is... How do I put this..." Charlie had turned his eyes up to the ceiling, finding the words that felt impossible for his political system.

"Lets just say one elected term only."

Anna looked him.

"A single term? Hes... Giving up?" she asked, voiced hushed so quietly but needing to confirm what she heard was correct. From what she understood the president of the united states was not standing for a second term, for the first time in Anna's lifetime.

Charlie gave her a single nod. And Anna made sure to file the information away. She was due to meet her handler right after this, and this kind of information that the American government was seemly unstable was ideological gold for the union.

Charlie sighed across the table.

"I know its not everything, but it's the best I could do. In about a week, people will learn that I leaked the information, but my partner and I will escape to Cyprus. Changing my name and living out our lives in peace." He looked up at her then.

"I honestly wish you all the best Anna. I hope the risk justifies the end of this whole thing because we both know there is no way things can continue in their current state for either major power."

Charlie pushed back his chair, the legs scraping softly against the wooden floor. He stood, a fleeting, almost sad smile touching his lips as he turned towards Anna. With a slight dip of his head, the brim of his hat shadowing his whisky-colored eyes for a moment, he turned and walked towards the cafe's entrance, disappearing into the bustling street.

That was the last time Anna met, or saw a friendly American born person.

May 1968

Anna, aged thirty | Moscow, Moscow Oblast, Russian Soviet Federative Socialist Republic

The screaming of Vladimir's child after 13 hours of exhausting pain was meant to make it all worth it, but by the end of it Anna was spent.

The hospital was a sterile environment, smelling of bleach and reminding her faintly of that sensory depravation room she had once been in. Everything was pastel, like the world was muted when you were in the room.

Anna awoke, groggy and aching. The room was q uiet... Too quiet.

Weren't babies loud creatures when first born?

Her body ached, and her middle felt profoundly empty. The little life she had been growing was go ne...

A clock on the wall read 07:45. She tried to recall the time of the birth. *Approximately 40 minutes ago,* she realized. She hadn't heard a single cry since the initial, piercing wail that had confirmed it was real.

She pushed herself up slightly. The baby's crib was empty.

Anna had the strange fleeting thought that maybe she had completely lost her mind, and imagined the last 8 months. Though her body had the signs of recent birth.

The sound of rubber soles squeaking heralded the arrival of the Senior Nurse, a stern woman in a crisp white uniform, carrying a small, tightly swaddled bundle.

"Anna Zaitseva, you may feed him now," the nurse stated, her voice efficient, not gentle. She presented the bundle—a face barely visible over the white cotton edge. "This is your son. He is healthy."

With the nurse's help, Anna was sat upright. She accepted the small weight, surprised by how stiffly the child was wrapped. The nurse held the infant steady, ensuring there was no fumbling.

"His registration is required now. Name?" the nurse prompted, already preparing her clipboard.

"Ivan. His name is to be Ivan Zaitsev."

The nurse quickly wrote the details onto the state form.

"So what do I do now?" Anna asked, tired and lost. She was trained to be a spy, not a mother.

"You adhere to the schedule," the nurse corrected her, adjusting the tight swaddle. "He will be brought to you every four hours. You will attempt to offer the breast. He requires 15 minutes on each breast to stimulate production and receive his colostrum. If you feel you are not producing enough by day three, we will begin supplementary feeding with formula prescribed by the doctor."

Anna looked down at the infant's face, which seemed too perfect and too distant. *Fifteen minutes?* It sounded like a state quota.

The nurse leaned closer, pointing a clean finger at the baby's mouth. "Encourage the latch. This is his feeding time. He will not be returned to you until 11:40, so you must ensure he attempts to feed now."

"What about... what if he soils himself?" Anna asked, confused by the strict instructions.

"The nurses in the nursery are responsible for the nappies, Anna. You are responsible for feeding. Now, the state records indicate your delivery was normal. You need rest to recover your strength and to ensure adequate milk supply for your child. Feeding schedule is four hours. This is to allow your body and your breasts to rest and replenish the necessary volume for the next session. Your husband may visit this evening during the designated hour."

The nurse took the child from Anna's arms, the small weight gone instantly. She did not cuddle him; she placed him quickly back in the sterile metal bassinet she had carried in.

"He will now be returned to the main nursery. Sleep now, Anna. Rest is essential for a productive recovery."

And as if on cue, Anna closed her eyes, the soft *snick* of the door closing was the final noise she heard before she succumbed to her slumber, alone again

June 1968

Vladimir, aged thirty | Moscow, Moscow Oblast, Russian Soviet Federative Socialist Republic

Vladimir had changed with the birth of his son. A sense of vindication had settled deep in his chest. He became more attentive to Anna, his eyes constantly tracking her movements, his mind already calculating the timeline for the next one.

He needed to create a sibling for Ivan. He would not let the boy be alone.

He knew Anna was tired. He could see the exhaustion in the slump of her shoulders, the way she moved as if walking through water after nine months of growing the boy and now feeding him. But Vladimir felt the urgency like a physical hunger. His own brother had been lost to the silence of the Great Patriotic War. One son was not enough. One son was vulnerable.

He wanted the same security for Ivan, regardless of the cost.

So in stolen moments, Vladimir cornered her. He caught her in his arms, his kisses not asking for permission but claiming territory. He felt her stiffen, felt the familiar resistance in her frame, but he ignored it just as he had before. Her hesitation meant nothing against the necessity of his legacy. She had fought him on Ivan, too, and look at the perfect result.

He pulled her into him, his touch insistent, ignoring the bone-deep weariness that clung to her. He whispered pleas that sounded more like commands against her skin. *Another,* he thought. *We must have another.*

Only the baby's cry stopped him.

Vladimir released her with a sigh of frustration. Ivan was a peaceful baby, usually, but his timing was poor. Anna pulled away, relief flashing across her face before she masked it with motherly duty. Vladimir watched her go. He helped where he could, but he adhered to the natural order: the woman reared the infant, and the man built the dynasty.

Later, in the dark, Anna groaned as the soft murmuring of Ivan's crying drifted through the walls.

Vladimir's hand shot out, gripping her arm as she shifted to rise. "Honey," he said, his voice low in the darkness. "Leave him for a moment. Stay here."

"He's hungry," she whispered, pulling against his grlp.

"And so am I," Vladimir countered, tightening his hold.

But she twisted away, the maternal instinct overpowering his command, and padded down the hallway. Vladimir lay back, frustration simmering. He felt like his head had only just hit the pillow, but his mind was already working. She was healed now. The waiting period was over.

He got up and followed her to the nursery. He opened the door quietly.

Anna was in the rocking chair, head tipped back, eyes closed in exhaustion. Ivan was at her breast. Vladimir watched the two of them, his gaze heavy and possessive. His son was precious, and he would protect him with his life.

But as he watched Anna drift into sleep, his resolve hardened. She was tired, yes. But she was his wife. She had given him one son, and she would give him another. He would ensure it.

May 1970

Anna aged thirty-two | Moscow, Moscow Oblast, Russian Soviet Federative Socialist Republic

It was the nausea that gave it away, a familiar lurch in her stomach that was accompanied by a hollow, dropping feeling, like an elevator suddenly plunging a few floors. Ivan was now two years old, still a toddler and very much in his chubby cute stage. He was walking confidently now, stringing two and three words together, demanding his mother's attention with clear intent.

Vladimir's friends' wives doted over his little fingers and toes, and loved his chubby wee cheeks and gurgling babbles as he tried to communicate with them. They were women Anna saw mostly at the compulsory factory social functions, wives of men in Vladimir's expanding professional circle. Their praise for Ivan often felt like a necessary performance, part of the social contract of being Mrs. Vladimir Sokolov.

Thinking of it, she couldn't remember when she last had her period. Time had become a blur of feedings and naps, housework, and the endless demands of both Vladimir and Ivan. Two years had passed since Ivan's birth, and the last two attempts she'd made to reclaim her body had ended violently, both times under sterile, unforgiving lamps. Her own body's cycles a distant afterthought.

She dragged herself up from the rocking chair where she had rested these past few hours, feeling she had occupied it more than her own bed since the nausea began two weeks ago.

And now she will need to see her doctor and see about confirming her suspicion. The very thought of the clinic made a dull, persistent ache bloom low in her abdomen, a familiar reminder of the scarring left by the last hurried procedure. That pain, more than the nausea, fueled her fear of the diagnosis.

She gently moved Ivan from her arms and placed a sleeping Ivan into his small wooden cot.

He was sleeping a bit better. During the last month he was sleeping through the night from 11 pm to five am. And Anna was more than thankful for the six hour sleeps she was able to have now. She would never take sleep for granted again.

A roiling sensation started in her stomach, and she padded quickly out of Ivan's room, trying not to slam the door, then sprinted down the hallway to her bathroom. Just making it before she vomited up any food she had consumed in the past few hours.

"Great," Anna thought, wiping her mouth with the back of her hand, "I didn't want nutrients anyway."

Waiting until she was sure there wasn't going to be a second bout of nausea, Anna lifted herself off the floor, taking stock of how weak she felt as she walked over to the bathroom sink and splashed cold water on her face and drank some of the tap water to feel human again.

Anna wasn't overly excited about the prospect of another eight months of being uncomfortable, especially while there was a small human who ruled her sleeping patterns. She was not the young woman who had once navigated the cold streets of Moscow, carrying secrets, not babies. That life felt like a character in a book she had been forced to close.

Another small human to feed, clothe, and care for. A wave of weariness washed over Anna, quickly followed by a flicker of warmth at the thought of Ivan having a sibling, a companion in a world where she often felt alone. But the greatest relief came from the chilling calculation: nine months of pregnancy, plus six months of recovery—fifteen months of sanctuary. She would be safe. A world where the demands of the husband, the state, and the home threatened to consume her whole.

December 1970

Anna, aged thirty-three | Moscow, Moscow Oblast, Russian Soviet Federative Socialist Republic

The next eight months were arduous. Ivan's will had become an intense, almost palpable force, resulting in daily defiance, tantrums that echoed through the house, while Anna was in the throes of morning sickness. As far as she could tell, the child within her was healthy, a constant weight that made each step difficult. The child was kicking her bladder constantly with a dull, rhythmic thumping, not sharp strikes like she remembered with Ivan.

It was mid-December, snow was blanketing the ground outside, muting sound and creating peace when Anna felt like there wasn't much in her home. The windows crying with condensation that Anna wiped away every morning, she was glad she wasn't in the same state, it was only a couple of weeks until her due date. The reprieve Anna had so carefully calculated was only a few months until it expired, a thought that sat like a stone in the pit of her stomach. She couldn't handle the idea that she only has a few more months before...

Vladimir had taken over the majority of duties regarding Ivan recently. It was perhaps a little early for her husband to take over in the child-rearing duties, but she was thankful as it gave her the chance to get some rest while she carried their next child. Her body had scarcely recovered from the last childbirth before the next one started growing slowly sapping away her strength.

Anna rolled out of her bed, her joints stiff, and padded down the hallway to the kitchen. She paused at the nursery doorway to ensure Vladimir was still distracted, the floorboards cold beneath her feet. She saw him in her rocking chair, snoring with the small toddler nestled against his chest snoozing quietly, a blanket draped over the toddlers small body to keep him warm. Vladimir's face looked softer in sleep, almost like the man she'd met at those dance halls so many years ago, but she didn't linger on the thought. As she reached the kitchen doorway, she felt a distinct, undeniable popping sensation low in her belly, as if a balloon had burst deep inside her. It was followed by a warm gush of liquid that made its way down her legs, soaking her nightdress and pooling on the linoleum.

"Blyat!" Anna gasped. Her waters had broken.

She heard a sharp crying from the nursery; her sudden yell had likely woken up poor little Ivan, and it would definitely wake Vladimir. In spite of the fear prickling at her skin, she knew she couldn't do this alone. A contraction ripped through her core, like a band tightening across her middle until she couldn't breathe. It was a blinding, white-hot pain that winded her and caused her to double over.

"Vladimir!" she cried out, the sound echoing off the walls. She dropped onto the floor, her knees hitting the cold hard ground as she sank onto the puddle of her own fluids, and simply cried.

Through the fog of agony, she heard Vladimir stirring, followed by Ivan's distressed wail from the nursery. The sounds were a chaotic assurance: he was awake, he was coming. He appeared in the hallway a moment later, a dark silhouette against the dim light, the sound of his heavy footsteps magnified by the pounding in her ears. He had Ivan clutched tightly to his chest, the boy's face red with crying.

"What's wrong?" His voice was rough with sleep and a jagged edge of shock.

"Vladimir... help..." Anna gasped out, her voice strained as another wave of pressure rolled over her.

Anna lay groaning as Vladimir rushed over to the phone attached to the wall and dialed 03. She listened to his panicked, barking voice on the phone, his words a blur of "emergency" and "floor" and "blood." She felt a strange, detached gratitude for the force of his authority even as she resented the way he took charge of her body.

Within a couple of minutes, she heard the phone clatter back onto the hook and felt his presence next to her. His breathing was heavy, smelling of stale sleep. Her own groans and screams had weakened as she tried to save her breath for the next surge of pain. She tried to focus on his rough hand petting her hair—the touch was awkward, lacking true tenderness, but she knew it was likely the only soothing she would receive. He was quietly murmuring that help was coming, that her boys were here.

A loud knock rattled the front door, making Vladimir jump up from his sitting position on the floor.

"Ambulance!" a voice called through the door.

Vladimir scooped up Ivan, who had gone eerily quiet now, possibly worried about his mother, and ran to open the door.

"Help her!" Anna heard him bark. The hallway suddenly swarmed with heavy coats and the smell of cold winter air. The medical staff maneuvered the stretcher with practiced, brusque movements, lifting her into the back of the ambulance. The transition was a shock—the freezing December air hit her damp skin like a physical blow, turning her sweat to ice. She squinted against the streetlights, her vision blurring as another contraction seized her.

"Help her god damn it!" Vladimir roared from behind the medical staff.

"Sir, we're going to Botkin Hospital, meet us there."

As they began to pull the heavy doors shut, Anna's eyes locked onto Vladimir standing on the threshold of their home. He looked small and rigid in the cold, but it was Ivan who broke her heart. The boy was squirming violently in his father's iron grip, his small hands reaching out into the dark, kicking his legs in a desperate, wordless struggle to get free and follow her. He was a small, frantic blur of red-faced terror against the grey Soviet backdrop.

The doors slammed shut with a heavy, metallic thud, severing the connection. The sound echoed like a cell closing, cutting off Ivan's screams and leaving only the hum of the engine. And with that, the world outside the ambulance's thin walls vanished. She was alone with the pain, the smell of antiseptic, and the growing dread of what the blood on the floor mixed with her waters really meant.

December 1970

Anna, aged thirty-three | Moscow, Moscow Oblast, Russian Soviet Federative Socialist Republic

The rush to the hospital through the slush and biting December wind was a blur of sirens and her own screams. She could feel her life draining from the strain of what was happening to her. The child had turned and become stuck, tearing her open from the inside. She couldn't get out, couldn't fit turned the way she was.

The ambulance had called ahead, and Anna was rushed into a sterile, white-tiled operating theatre for an emergency caesarean.

The surgery wasn't exactly what Anna wanted to happen preferring the more natural route she took last time, and she knew the uncertainty would terrify Vladimir, who was forced to wait behind the heavy ambulance doors in the freezing cold with their two year old. She wasn't overly keen on dying either, though; she had a son she needed to live for.

A few hours later Anna woke to a silent room, the sedative still making her head swim. The air smelled strongly of bleach. She expected the sounds of a busy maternity ward, or the distant crying of newborns from the nursery down the hall, but there was nothing.

The room was cold and emotionless, and she was entirely alone. There was no cot; only the metal frame of her bed and a worn bedside table.

The only sound was the heavy ticking of a clock on the wall and her own raspy breathing.

Anna tried to sit up, though she felt a sharp pulling at her centre. She knew the baby had left her body, her abdomen felt empty without the presence of the babe, who had been nestled and safe inside her.

Where was the child?

Some time later, a nurse in a stiffly starched white cap came around. Seeing Anna was staring listlessly at the ceiling, she left to fetch the head doctor. When the door opened again, it was the doctor. He stood at the foot of her bed, his expression unreadable and clinical. The nurse bustled into the room behind him and with a cold hand grabbed Anna's wrist, counting under her breath as she observed her watch.

"Do you know what day it is?" the doctor asked as he shone a light in her eyes.

"It's... mid-December? The 17th?"

The doctor took note of her answer and checked the wound on her stomach – where they had cut into her to rescue her child.

"86 doctor," she stated as she released Anna's wrist, and the doctor nodded at her, dismissing her from the room.

"Doctor?" Anna asked, her voice a thin whisper. He raised his head. "Where is my baby?"

The doctor straightened his back, his eyes finally meeting hers with a flicker of sombre pity.

"There were complications. The reason you went into labour early was because your body knew something was wrong. The baby had turned, and in doing that, had caught the umbilical cord around her neck. She died as you were prepped for surgery, and we were unable to revive her." He looked down, unable to meet Anna's eyes when he told her,

"It was a stillbirth."

The room felt as though the oxygen had been sucked out of it. Anna released an animalistic howl of pain that echoed off the cold tiles. The doctor remained still, watching her for a moment before nodding and stepping out. No one came to hold her hand. No one was there to comfort her in the most agonising moment in her life.

Her heart was being torn apart. The baby she had carried for eight months, a little girl, had managed to strangle herself before she was born.

Not ready for this world.

The grief hit Anna like a train, and she felt like the hospital was crumbling around her.

Night fell early, as it always did in Moscow's December, and the hospital, the room Anna lay in became decorated in long shadows before lights automatically turned on.

Anna could feel her face was puffy, her nose burned from the tears she had shed, and hadn't seen anyone in a couple of hours. The door cracked open and through it came a familiar face.

Vladmir.

He later told her that he managed to slip past the nurses station, and was let in by a nurse who took pity on their plight.

He looked tired, his heavy wool coat still dusted with melting snow.

He didn't come to her bed side at first. He stood by the door, his body silhouetted in the dim light from the hallway.

"Anna," he said, his voice cold and brittle.

"Vladimir," she whispered, reaching a hand out toward him.

He didn't take it. He looked at her, his eyes dark and hollow. "The nurse told me what happened," he said. His voice was flat, but the words were razor-sharp. "They told me that you couldn't keep her alive."

The statement cut deeper than the surgical knife ever could. Anna gasped, the air catching in her lungs, and tears rushing to her eyes.

He stood at the door for a moment, looking at Anna. She could only imagine the state she was in, rumpled in a crisp bed. Bedraggled hair, flushed and swollen face, belly much flatter than it had been when he last saw her.

Anna was sure he saw her as a failure. And perhaps that could be her salvation.

Or a curse.

He turned and disappeared back into the hallway, leaving her alone with the crushing weight of his blame.

The following days, recovering from the caesarean during the darkest part of the year, weren't any easier. Vladimir wasn't back after that first visit; he could only send up small parcels of fruit and notes on scraps of paper, though Anna could hardly bear to read them.

She was scared they would be laced with the blame he felt towards her for their loss.

Anna woke up most days, and if the nurse was in the room, she always asked where her baby was. The trauma had made her mind foggy, and she would momentarily forget, only to have the memory of Vladimir's words rush back to haunt her.

Vladimir's parents had taken Ivan away to their dacha for the next few months so Vladimir and Anna could both recover. Anna had simply drifted through the decision after Vladimir bribed a nurse to tell her. The house would be even emptier without him.

Recovery felt impossible. Their daughter was dead before she even got to live.

Two days after Christmas, ten days after the surgery, they were told she could go home.

Anna didn't want to leave the hospital. Home felt like a foreign concept, and she wasn't sure how she was going to face the house where her son played while she had been trying to grow another.

She was heartbroken.

When she finally walked out of the hospital gates into the freezing December air, Vladimir was waiting. He looked completely lost. He didn't hug her – it wasn't something they did - but his hand shook as he took her bag. He wouldn't look her in the eye, the silence between them heavy with the accusation he had hurled at her in the dark.

January
1972

Anna aged thirty-four | Moscow, Moscow Oblast, Russian Soviet Federative Socialist Republic

Ivan was growing into a bubbly boy, a burst of color against the gray backdrop of their apartment. He was the only thing that moved Vladimir to emotion. When Vladimir looked at his son, his face softened, but the moment he turned to Anna, the mask returned — a heavy, glacial "coldness" that felt like the moment a cold Moscow winter gust hits ones face.

Slowly, tentatively, Anna and Vladimir had found their way back to each other. Not the version of them from their youth, where love was much more abundant, but a fragile truce where Anna accepted her marital duties with a quiet, hollow resignation. They were two actors on a stage, performing the role of "parents" for Ivan, while the space between them in their bed felt like the distance between the east and west of the Soviet Union.

"He needs siblings." Vladimir declared to Anna five months after they left the hospital feeling more hollow than any parents should.

"Don't we owe it to our daughter, our son, to give them siblings? To honour our loss with a new life?"

It was the first time Anna saw even a spark of emotion regarding the loss of his daughter.

Not long after they left the hospital, they made the trip to bury their little girl in Kazan, next to Anna's mama. Her little girl was with her babushka now. Anna only hoped that the two of them were having the time of their lives in the heaven the priest at the Zaitsev family's Sunday church spoke of. A place far warmer than the frozen earth of Russia. Even as the little coffin was lowered into the melting earth, still recovering after a particularly rough winter, Vladimir didn't have much emotion other than disappointment in his eyes. No tears welled, even as they spilled down Anna's own face. As the rope was loosened and her baby girl was lowered into the earth Vladimir's eyes flicked to her.

Anna imagined that the depths of a Siberian winter would be warmer than the look her husband gave her. Her eyes welled further as she looked away from the whole moment. Anna couldn't handle his disappointment, his blame only added to her own.

Like clockwork, nausea hit Anna eight months later. She was scared of it. She felt like a marked woman. She knew if she could fail again, she would. She didn't tell Vladimir. She couldn't bear to see the flicker of hope in his eyes, knowing how quickly he would turn to stone if it vanished. That was probably going to be the nail in her and Vladimir's coffin.

She knew that going through that grief again would hurt more than she might be able to bear, so she lived in a state of quiet, terrified thievery, stealing four months of motherhood that belonged only to her. She hid the pregnancy until she physically couldn't anymore.

Four months in, she decided she had to tell him. Her morning sickness had quickly dissipated, and she felt the first, faint flutters—a delicate tapping against her ribs that felt like a secret language. It made her feel better about the whole process, until the afternoon the silence was broken by her own scream.

It wasn't a "gush of liquid." It was a sudden, violent heat—a dark, heavy rush of blood that pooled on the linoleum, smelling metallic. Surely her waters couldn't have broken. She had months left. She was only just through the first trimester.

Then another cramp ripped through her, a white-hot blade that stole her vision and left her clawing at the kitchen table until her fingernails bled. The pain was a ten, a blinding roar that brought her to her knees.

Once the pain subsided enough for her to gasp, she grabbed her son and rushed to the neighbor's apartment. She couldn't look at Ivan; she was terrified he would see the blood on her legs and be scared something was happening to his mama again. Something that could kill her.

The recovery ward was a hall of iron beds and the sharp, burnt-hair scent of quartz lamps. There were no beeping monitors, no soft digital pulses to tell her she was alive. There was only the rhythmic, hollow *clink* of the glass IV bottle and the heavy silence of a Soviet hospital.

It turned out the cramps and the blood were a miscarriage. The hard kick had been the final straw before her placenta dislodged itself, killing her child. She was rushed in for an emergency hysterectomy. The doctor hadn't used a soft voice; he had simply told her she was "cleared out." There was no chance she could ever have children again.

Anna watched as Vladimir walked into the room. He didn't rush to her side. He stood at the foot of her bed, with his coat still buttoned, his hands shoved deep into his pockets. He didn't look at her face; he looked at the empty space where her womb used to be.

"The doctor says you are empty now," Vladimir said. His voice wasn't sad; it was flat, clinical, and utterly devoid of mercy. "He also told me how long the child had been there. Four months, Anna."

His words were an accusation.

He stepped closer, his shadow falling over her like a shroud. "You carried my child like a thief. You hid them in the dark as if I were the enemy. And because you were too weak, too afraid to let me see, you let them die in silence."

"I was scared, Vladimir," she whispered, her voice breaking against the sterile, oppressive silence of the recovery ward.

"You were selfish," he snapped. The words didn't come with the red-hot passion of a man in a rage; they came with the searing, clinical precision of a blue flame, the kind of cold that doesn't just freeze, but cauterizes the soul. He didn't move an inch toward her. He remained rooted at the foot of the iron bed, his hands like stones in his pockets.

"You have left the Zaitsev name to wither on a single, lonely branch because you wanted a secret," he continued, his eyes as flat as the concrete outside. "You think Ivan is enough? In this world, a single son is a target for fate. He needed siblings, brothers. He needed a wall of men behind him to survive what is coming, and you have left him alone."

He finally looked at her, but there was no recognition of the woman he had once loved. There was only the cold appraisal of a man looking at a broken tool.

"You are not a mother to the sons we needed, Anna. You are a graveyard of secrets and dead things. You turned your womb into a tomb and kept the door locked until it was too late. And now, after the doctor's knife, you are a useless woman."

He turned on his heel without a single touch, the sound of his boots on the tile echoing like a gavel striking a final judgment. Anna realized then that the grief hadn't broken him—it had simply confirmed his suspicion that she was the one thing in his life he could no longer use.

January 1972

Vladimir, aged thirty-four | Moscow, Moscow Oblast, Russian Soviet Federative Socialist Republic

The loss of a second child in a row, the second in two years, and the medical certainty that Anna could never conceive again, broke Vladimir. It was bad enough that he suffered flashbacks to the day Anna gave birth to their first daughter, a little girl who never was given the chance to draw a breath.

The sterile smell of the hospital and the drawn look on Anna's face after she woke from the operation that rendered her infertile triggered the old, cold military discipline he thought he had buried deep in his bones. A cold knot tightened in his chest, the memory of lowering a empty box signifying his daughter into the dirt in Kazan causing a ripple of coldness to flow through his blood stream.

It was empty, get a grip.

Ivan's bright laughter was the only small spark in the darkness that had settled over him and the household. He could still perform the role of the doting father but when he looked at Anna, a familiar bitterness rose. It was the same resentment he'd felt toward those in war. The weak links were the entire units weakness. They were only as strong as their weakest in the field, and it was the same in his family...

She couldn't even do this right, a cruel voice whispered in his head. He found himself short with her, his responses clipped, his touch absent.

Their son adored her, a fact that Vladimir found increasingly difficult to tolerate. His mother's death, so soon after the miscarriage, felt like a tactical blow aimed directly at him. She had been his anchor, silently making sure he never drifted too far. Now, only the echoing silence of loss remained. A void where his children should have been, and where his mother's presence used to be.

God, their children. There were more of them in heaven than there were on this mortal plane.

Vladimir found himself retreating into silence, the weight of his grief a physical barrier between him and the world. Small tasks felt monumental. Only Ivan's cheerful chatter offered a balm to soothe the emptiness in his soul.

"Vladimir?" Anna asked one evening in their cramped kitchen, a few months after her emergency surgery.

He looked towards her. His eyes were drained of colour, an eerie kind of amber that looked dead, a dull wasteland compared to the man she had married.

He waited to hear what she wanted to say to him, feeling as though there wasn't much left to discuss. Ivan was tucked up in bed, having started school recently, leaving Anna home alone with her thoughts for most of the day.

“Do you…” Her voice trailed off, hesitant. He watched her, a weariness etched on her face. The silence between them weighed like lead, stretching taut with unspoken accusations.

What now? he wondered, the familiar distance already widening.

The thought flickered in his mind, unbidden and unwelcome. His own control felt fragile these days. He saw her not as a grieving wife, but as a failing asset. The years ahead felt less like a shared future and more like a tightrope walk over an abyss.

“Those are the first words you've spoken to me in week, wife. What do you want?” he asked, his eyebrow raised in a challenge.

Anna sighed deeply, looking away for a split second before coming back to meet his eyes. She looked reluctant, forcing each word out as if it were a physical effort.

“I want my husband back. The man I fell in love with. The one who doted on me, the one who was filled with life. I want that.”

A sigh escaped Vladimir's lips, heavy with resignation. He saw the set of Anna's jaw and her defensive stance.

Here we go, he thought, the familiar bitterness rising. He knew the words forming in his mind were cruel, but he felt powerless to stop them. Cruelty was the only weapon he had left to defend his own ego.

A part of him recognized the cruel words forming on his tongue, a dark echo of his own pain. He knew what he was saying would probably break his wife. But the grief he felt had no bounds.

"Yes little wife and I want a wife, a true woman who can produce children. We don't always get what we want now, do we?"

It wasn't logical, and on some level, he knew that. But the emptiness inside of him screamed, and she was the one who couldn't fill it. A bitter resentment coiled in his gut that screamed at him to hurt. To have others hurt just as much as he did.

Vladimir watched as his words hit Anna. Her slight, still-recovering body flinched as if under a physical blow. Twenty-five words in his rant. Twenty-five blows to her heart. Her shoulders slumped. The light in her eyes flickered out, confirming the raw wound he had deliberately ripped opened.

Anna recoiled under the weight of his harsh words. Then, a look of hurt and resentment flickered across her face. He saw her jaw tighten, the argument continuing in the hard, unforgiving set of her mouth.

"Only a spoilt boy would regard a woman in such a manner," she spat back at him.

The insult snapped the last thread of his restraint. Before he could think, he raised a hand. Her defiance felt like a strike against his authority. His hands clenched into fists, the blood pounding in his ears. A red haze threatened to cloud his vision. He lunged forward and slapped her across her cheek.

The impact sent her head whipping back, causing her to fall heavily to the floor. Normally, a strike like this wouldn't have downed her, but she hadn't been in peak physical shape since Ivan's birth. Her body was weak from surgery, her reflexes dulled by useless grief.

Vladimir stepped back. The sound echoed in the sudden silence. A cold dread washed over him.

What had he done? His hand felt alien, heavy. A knot of revulsion tightened in his stomach.

What have I done? The thought screamed in his head, but his face remained impassive. A mask he desperately clung to.

Anna clutched at her cheek and glared up at him as she stood up. There was no fear in her eyes, only a challenge he recognized. It was the look of a predator evaluating a threat. He swallowed hard. He knew what she was capable of, and he realized with a jolt of adrenaline that hitting her again would be suicide.

Vladimir didn't rise to the challenge. He chose the coward's retreat because he could see she was ready to unleash hell on him for touching her in the way he had. Instead, he turned on his toe and strode out of the room.

He didn't look back to see the wreckage he'd left behind. He only knew that the boy who had once danced with her and exchanged letters at school was finally, irrevocably dead. He had done his duty to his own pride, and as he walked away, the distance felt like an iron curtain falling between them.

May 1975

Anna, aged thirty-seven | Moscow, Moscow Oblast, Russian Soviet Federative Socialist Republic

"Are you Anna Sokolova?" the man asked curtly as Anna opened the door to her home.

It had been an age since she had heard her maiden name. It was almost strange hearing the two words strung together, like a ghost from a previous life suddenly appearing on her doorstep.

"I am she," Anna responded, her voice steady despite the sudden prickle of apprehension. The man shoved a heavy, wax-sealed envelope into her hands.

It had been a couple of years since Anna's incident with Vladimir - the night he had raised his hand to her. In the wake of that violence, they had come to an arrangement born of necessity and mutual loathing: she worked during the day and he the nights. They shared dinner in a suffocating silence, and independently parented Ivan, but they occupied separate rooms and were hardly on talking terms. Anna wished divorce was more common in Russia, but she knew the cost. To leave a man like Vladimir would be to sign her own death warrant, sealed with a kiss of fear.

"Thank you?" Anna said, but the man didn't meet her gaze. He offered an abrupt nod before turning sharply and walking down the path. A shadow of something. Sadness? Pity? flickered across his face before he composed himself and vanished into the grey Moscow afternoon.

Anna was a little confused. Post wasn't uncommon, but official documents weren't typically hand-delivered by men who looked like they were more comfortable in the shadows of society. Shaking her head, she walked back into the home and fetched a small knife to open the seal of the envelope. Inside was a stack of papers, mostly in the stark, typed legalese of the Soviet bureaucracy — a language designed to obscure as much as it revealed. Her stomach dropped, the weight of the paper feeling like a leaden weight pulling her toward an uncertain future.

She flicked through them, a knot tightening in her stomach as she registered phrases like "In the event of his death..." and "His only daughter is to..."

Wait.

Her eyes scanned back to the formal address on the first page, a familiar block lettering suddenly leaping out at her amidst the unfamiliar text.

Papa?

A cold wave washed over Anna. She hadn't heard from him in a few months, but after her mama's death so many years ago, that wasn't unusual. Since the incident with Vladimir, she wasn't especially inclined to get in touch with her papa, fearing his volatile temper might ignite against her husband and catch little Ivan in the crossfire.

Her papa. Her strong, stoic papa. The one who always stood tall, who went to war for the country. The man she looked up to as the single example of strength in her world.

He was gone.

Anna felt a part of her break. He was her last parent. Her last link to her childhood. Her high school friends had long since become too busy to respond to letters, and her tertiary years were filled up with the slow erosion of Vladimir. She had friends, sure, but at this stage in her life, she felt utterly isolated.

She was an orphan.

She sank into the kitchen chair and started reading through the documents more thoroughly, this time not skipping over the handwritten letter at the front.

Anna,

If you are reading this, then I have departed Russia and have gone to join your mama in the afterlife. As you will see, my organization's lawyer, Igor, has made sure to keep a few items under the radar, and out of government view. I know how you feel about the current political situation, but there is no reason my daughter or her family should ever go without when I have worked hard to provide a cushion against the world.

I will admit, I lost part of my humanity and soul in that war, especially in Berlin. Please do not be surprised if you are to ever meet a German person who looks like me, and doesn't have a father. I know not of what happened to the women I found comfort in while I was there. The hunger of those days drove us all to do things that cannot be washed away.

I hope, in admitting my darkest sins, that you, my dear daughter, can find it in your heart to forgive and absolve me. I love you, though in my own way, which I realized too late was very different from the soft, easy love of your dearly departed mama's. And for that, I am sorry. More so than I think I would ever be able to explain in a letter. Please read the details Igor has included. The property and the funds are all yours now, and in your maiden name, as I know Vladimir and you are no longer what a husband and wife should be.

Perhaps that, too, is my fault. I shouldn't have paid him and his family to woo you to secure a future deal among the families. Maybe it was my own war-forged pragmatism that led me down that path. I saw a strong, ambitious young man from a well-connected family—a secure future for you, or so I rationalized at the time. Business and family became dangerously intertwined in my thinking. I bought you a protector, Anna, but I see now I only bought you a cage.

It was a selfish act, projecting my own needs onto your life and manipulating your choices. The weight of that realization is heavy, my dear daughter. I again hope you can forgive me for my many misdeeds. Live well, Anna. I will make sure to give your mama a hug when I see her, but also please know that we are both watching down to watch little Ivan grow, and you come into your own as a woman.

Sincerely, your papa,

Grigori Sokolov

Anna felt the papers drop from her hands.

Shock. That must be it. A numb, ringing silence in her ears. Her papa cheated on her Mama while he was at war? Her papa, who was her picture of the perfect man, and who until she read that letter had been completely infallible? *And found comfort?* The casualness of the word belied the potential darkness beneath. Had it been a mutual seeking of solace in a brutal world, or something more... predatory? The thought sent a fresh wave of nausea through her. Anna had heard the whispers of the horrors of the war, but she had chosen to keep her blinders on so as not to taint her own memories.

And the business deal? The one that shaped her into a Zaitseva? Her marriage, the cornerstone of her adult life and the life of her son, rested on a lie—a cold, calculated transaction engineered by her father. She wasn't a wife; she was a purchased asset. Little more than livestock for barter in the grand scheme of things. The weight of this knowledge pressed down on her, heavy and suffocating.

Anna felt her face fall into her hands, and she wiped her brow, trying hard to get rid of the stress induced lines in the middle that she knew must be deepening by the second.

A deep sense of betrayal hit her like a sledgehammer. She wanted to yell, scream, punch something. She wanted to cry deeply and allow herself to drown in her tears.

But there was no one to scream at, and her tears felt as dry as the Moscow dust.

Hopelessness.

Fuck. What was she to do with this information? What was she to do with herself? Anna wasn't sure who she was anymore. The foundation of her entire adult identity had just dissolved into ink and old paper.

She picked up the rest of the papers, which contained the deed to a little cottage on the shores of the Caspian Sea, and some instructions on where some of the family heirlooms were kept—including where some black-market Rubles were stashed away from the government's prying eyes. Perhaps a trip to the sea would be a good idea. It was obvious she had missed her father's passing and however he was laid to rest. Igor's own letter advised where a headstone for him was, but that he had been cremated and scattered to the winds in the far north.

The headstone was near the cottage, and while Anna and her Papa hadn't been on the best of terms, she felt a desperate need to stand before his name and demand an answer the wind couldn't give. Ivan was the only part of her that cared for her anymore. She didn't have any other blood relatives.

June 1975

Anna, aged thirty-seven | Moscow, Moscow Oblast, Russian Soviet Federative Socialist Republic

The sun warmed Anna's bare skin as she sat on her towel, legs stretched out and brushing against the soft sand of the beach. Ivan was out towards the water; with many other mothers around, she knew he was safe. She knew they would visit this cottage more frequently, so she had made sure that Ivan was enrolled in a state school that taught children to swim and survive in the water.

Anna lay back down, stretching out in the sunshine like a cat that had just woken from a long nap. She felt safe here. No Vladimir, who she was quietly scared of, and no risks to Ivan from him either. Vladimir had chosen to stay behind, citing he had a lot of work to catch up on. It was a flimsy excuse, but it meant she and her son were safe, and that to her was all that mattered.

Anna suspected it was a lie, and that perhaps he was just sick of his wife and was instead courting another. Anna didn't care. As long as he never laid a hand on her or her son, she was content enough to maneuver around him the best she could.

She allowed the sun's rays to warm her alabaster skin, still pale from the long Moscow winter, and released a sigh while she closed her eyes. She hadn't realized she had fallen asleep in the heat until her son came running up, dripping wet, and shook himself like a dog before her.

Anna released a shriek at the abrupt wakeup; getting splattered by water droplets wasn't her ideal way of waking from a nap.

"Mama!" he yelled down at her. She did wonder some days if she was still Anna, or if a legal name change had occurred without her knowledge and she was now simply *Mama*.

"Yes, my darling?" she asked, sitting up to spy the lean eight-year-old at the end of her towel. The boy was all arms and legs, sprouting so rapidly that it was hard to keep up with his growth. The thought of her child becoming a man, no longer needing her, caused a deep ache in Anna's heart, a future she found difficult to accept.

"Mama! You must come for a swim, the water feels incredible!" Ivan said as he tugged at her arm.

"Okay, darling, but please allow me time to get up. I'm not sure if you noticed, but I was enjoying my time in the sun just now." Ivan looked sheepish. Which was good; it meant he knew he had done wrong—an attribute his father didn't possess.

Anna groaned as she dragged her body from the towel and followed her child down to the shoreline. Anna wasn't overly confident in the water, preferring to paddle. Since the trauma of the hospital years ago, she felt a strange disconnection from her own body; she felt fragile, like a piece of mended porcelain that might crack if the waves were too rough. More often than not, she covered up more skin than the younger beachgoers.

Crossing her arms across her belly, she waded into the water behind her son. Ivan was running through the water with reckless abandon, chasing after young girls and kicking water up at them if they got too close, resulting in raucous laughter.

Anna smiled to herself and walked over to one of the other mothers who was also keeping a watchful eye on the children.

"Which one is yours?" Anna asked the woman.

"The girl in the white swimsuit," the woman answered. The young girl must have been about seven. She was a delicate thing, her long auburn hair meticulously braided, a mother's careful work against the salt and sun, Anna noted with a pang of familiarity. The girl turned on her heel and ran away from Ivan again, rushing through the surface water towards her mother.

"Mama!" the girl shouted, a small whirlwind of energy heading their way. The woman raised a silent eyebrow, and Anna saw the girl's exuberant approach falter, replaced by a slightly more demure dip of her head towards Anna in greeting.

"Mama, forgive the interruption," Valeriya said, smoothing her swimsuit as she stood straight. "I wished to ask what time we are departing. I would like to play further with Ivan, but I understand we must not be late for dinner." The girl looked up to her mother.

"Okay, Valeriya, you can go and play. But only for another half an hour."

The girl looked up with big brown eyes, before glancing towards Ivan, who was kicking up water in the shallows, then back at her mother and Anna.

"Mama, might it be possible for Ivan and his mother to join us for dinner? Please?" she asked, her voice softening with hope.

The woman looked over to Anna, who offered a small, hopeful smile. Anna gave a subtle nod, and the little girl screamed in excitement and ran back towards Ivan.

Anna softly let a chuckle loose. "Is she your only daughter?"

The other woman looked at Anna and nodded solemnly.

"Yes, and she's growing up much too fast. Is Ivan your only child?"

Anna nodded, the phantom weight of the daughters she never held brushing against her heart. Both women looked towards the ocean where the two children played in the surf, two small figures chased by a tide that never stopped coming.

July 1978

Anna, aged forty | Moscow, Moscow Oblast, Russian Soviet Federative Socialist Republic

"I'm sorry, Ivan, but you will need to go." Anna's tone brooked no argument. His protests bounced off her resolute exterior, achieving nothing as she put an end to the quarrel she was having with her eleven-year-old son with her signature *Don't argue and do as you're told* look that all soviet mothers have mastered.

Ivan stood in front of her, arms crossed over his scrawny chest, jaw locked in place, malice in his eyes, horrified at the idea of being sent away. The red scarf of his Young Pioneer uniform was knotted crookedly at his neck, a symbol of the state's discipline that he seemed currently intent on mocking.

Boarding school.

Anna had gone to one herself, and while her memories were a mixture of friendship and a lack of privacy, she knew it had its upsides. One, it meant that Ivan would be away from Vladimir. His father's moods were getting more unpredictable, his late-night returns more frequent, and the smell of expensive foreign cigarettes and nervous sweat clung to his clothes like a second skin.

Two, it meant Ivan would have a superior education. The school in Leningrad was a prestigious bastion of discipline; it was a world away from the gritty Moscow streets where Vladimir's influence loomed like a shadow. It gave him a chance to see parts of the world he might not have seen before.

The child was being petulant, and had already threatened to move himself down into the Dagestan region where the dacha was, so he could go to the same school as Valeriya, the girl he had met a few summers before and had become pen pals with. Ivan had poured his heart into scrawled letters that Anna had sent for him. She probably shouldn't have read them, but in a house where secrets were the primary currency, it was a valuable insight into her son's mind. He wrote to Valeriya about the sea as if it were a Promised Land, a stark contrast to the stifling silence of their Moscow apartment.

Anna gave him a stern, "don't mess with me" look. It was the look of a woman who had been trained by the KGB to stare down diplomats. Ivan promptly picked up his feet and headed towards his suitcase placed on his bed to pack.

“I'll go, but note I am NOT HAPPY ABOUT IT!!” he yelled down the hallway before his door slammed with a force that rattled the framed photographs on the wall.

She had braced herself for teenage rebellion, but the sheer force of Ivan's opposition felt like a constant drain. It exhausted her every day, and it wasn't helped by Vladimir's constant absence. Even when he was home, he was a ghost, a presence that offered no authority, only a cold, judging silence, unless his son was in front of him.

Anna sighed and began to prepare dinner for a family that she felt was falling apart at the seams. She sliced the dark rye bread with practiced, sharp movements.

Anna loved her son dearly, but she was keenly aware that in the world as she knew it, he would be eaten alive if he remained soft and pining. Hopefully, the structure and routine of school would help him forget about the Valeriya. She secretly wished that, in Leningrad, far from their shared memories, Ivan could build his own life, unhindered by the Zaitsev name and the shadow of criminality bought on by his father.

Anna had looked into the girl, knowing that Ivan would probably run away to her if he ever found out. After Anna got in touch with some old contacts, she didn't find anything of interest, but seeing parallels between the girl her son was smitten with and her own life unsettled her.

The mother went to the same school as Anna in Gorky, and their fathers had served together closely before hers passed away in the Battle of Berlin. The

Soviet world was vast, yet the circles of the elite and the military were dangerously small.

A knot of unease tightened in Anna's stomach. Gorky, their fathers... the threads of their past felt too tangled for comfort, a potential complication she desperately wanted to avoid for Ivan.

Ivan's heavy stomping around his room brought her out of her thoughts. She listened to the sounds of drawers opening and closing, the angry energy of a boy trying to pack his life into a single trunk. She knew she was going to be travelling with the surly teenager on the Red Arrow train up to Leningrad. The overnight journey would be long, filled with the rhythmic clatter of the tracks and the unspoken words that had piled up between mother and son like winter snow.

She looked at the three plates she had set on the table. One for her, one for Ivan, and one for a husband who likely wouldn't show. She realized then that sending Ivan away wasn't just about his education; it was about ensuring that he had a way of escaping the shadows before they caught up to the family as she knew it.

January 1982

Anna, aged forty-four | Moscow, Moscow Oblast, Russian Soviet Federative Socialist Republic

"What do you mean by that?" Vladimir retorted, his voice rising with the raspy edge of a man who had spent twenty years smoking despite his wife's complaints about the nasty habit.

Money, children, their dead marriage… the arguments blurred into a monotonous hum. Anna felt a detached weariness, a strange sense of not being able to muster the energy to truly care about the specifics anymore. At forty-five, she felt the weight of every secret she had ever kept, a leaden pressure behind her eyes. It was a dangerous level of apathy, the kind she been taught never to fall into, that of people who had finally given up, but she simply had no emotional bandwidth left to be mentally whipped by the man who was meant to be her comrade in arms until the end.

Releasing a heavy sigh, Anna looked him in the eye. “Vladimir, I cannot have more children. I cannot have a career because in this system, I am a grandmother-in-waiting before I am a working woman. As for this marriage, let’s just say I’m regretting this more than I can express in words.”

Vladimir turned a shade of deep, bruised crimson. Anna didn't flinch; she simply waited for the sharp sting of an open-handed slap against her cheek. She had already braced her neck muscles, a reflex from the combat training at the Institute that her body remembered better than her own wedding vows.

Instead of hitting her, he turned and lashed out at the thin, plywood door of the pantry. His fist punched through the cheap veneer with a splintering crack, leaving a jagged hole they couldn't afford to fix and certainly couldn't explain to the block’s housing committee.

Anna was glad she had secreted away the rubles her parents had left her to send Ivan to boarding school. She didn't need him to see his father’s anger. This slow, inevitable descent into a different kind of violence that seemed to be rotting the men of their generation. Vladimir's face was contorted in rage, a raw, unfettered emotion that consumed him. He looked at her with a clinical kind of hatred, his eyes devoid of the tears that might have offered some human release. He had been raised on the same Soviet lie as all men born in the shadow of the war. Tears were a Western decadence, a sign of unforgivable weakness.

Anna noted with a grim, internal irony that she had been trained to resist torture at the hands of foreign agents, yet here she was at forty-five, using those same breathing techniques to survive her own kitchen. It wasn't okay—she knew that—but compared to Ivan, she could take it. She was a seasoned shield; her son was still only glass.

"Clean that mess up!" Vladimir yelled, gesturing vaguely at the splinters on the linoleum before stalking down the hallway.

Anna sighed. She wasn't one for divorce; in their circle, especially as they approached their senior years, a failed marriage was a black mark on a dossier, a sign of 'unstable character' that would strip away their access to the better grocery stores and the dacha. But as she looked at the shattered wood of the door, she wondered how much more of Vladimir's demeaning anger she could absorb before she, too, finally broke.

February
1984

Vladimir, aged forty-six | Moscow, Moscow Oblast, Russian Soviet Federative Socialist Republic

Vladimir pulled into his parking spot at the garage. The familiar scent of oil and gasoline filled his nostrils, a scent that usually grounded him. To the neighborhood, he was just a mechanic who worked long hours on the heavy Volgas and Ladas of the local elite. In reality, the grease under his fingernails was a convenient mask. The garage served as the perfect front for the "family business"—a place to swap plates, stash merchandise, and hold meetings that the KGB wouldn't overhear.

He knew he wasn't the smartest man, but he was reliable. However, the quiet of the morning was a stark contrast to the turmoil brewing inside him. Since Ivan started boarding school, Vladimir had all but stopped drinking, turning instead to pills when he could afford them. He had envisioned strong sons carrying on his name; instead, he had Ivan—sensitive and thoughtful. A dreamer.

One of his clients, Natalia, pulled her car into the drop-off zone. She was married to one of the "business's" biggest associates, a man named Kolya. Vladimir felt a familiar heat as she sauntered out of the vehicle.

“Morning, Vova!” she said, her voice chirpy.

“And how can I help you today, Natalia? Why isn't Kolya here?”

She let out a lyrical peel of laughter. “My husband is much too busy for mundane tasks like driving. You're stuck with me.”

The two had been having a sporadic affair for six months. It had started during a winter storm when the power cut out, leaving the garage in total darkness. They had found warmth in each other's bodies amidst the cold of the workshop.

Nat strode into the back office. “Vova, honey, can I speak to you? It's about a charge I don't understand.”

He followed her, the door clicking shut. She kissed him with a desperation he hadn't felt in months. His back slammed against the door and his hands started to roam as she deepened the kiss, causing an uncomfortable sensation in his pants. Too tight.

She pulled back, putting a foot of space between them.

“I'm pregnant,” she said, as he made to take a step towards her.

Vladimir's world tilted. He froze and cocked an eyebrow, waiting for the punchline.

"Kolya is infertile," she whispered. "We've tried for years. But six weeks ago... with you... it happened."

Vladimir did the math. Six weeks ago, he had stormed out of the house after a violent row with Anna. Breaking a door and putting his fist though another wall. The woman infuriated him to no end. He had come here, and Natalia had been waiting. They had been reckless. Irresponsible.

"I'm going to tell Kolya it's a miracle," she said, placing a hand on her stomach. She wasn't showing a "bump" yet, but she looked slightly bloated from the early hormones.

"I need you to never mention this. I want this child to have a normal life. I won't come looking for you, but I will put your name in my testament so they know their biological father one day."

Vladimir scrubbed a hand through his hair. He had told himself the affair was a contained transaction. He was able to find release and she was able to get release and her husbands cars fixed at a discount, using the money to fund her own extracurriculars. Now, it was a runaway train. His child—born to a criminal associate's wife.

The guilt stirred. Not just for the affair, but for the few times he had seen red and struck Anna over the last year. He never left a mark, but the way she recoiled from him now was a reminder of the man he had become.

"Vova, I can see you're losing your head. Please, stop. I need you to just do the oil change, and then I'll leave. You won't see me again."

Vladimir felt like he was suffering a short circuit. He had thought he was in control, satisfying a simple urge. Now, Natalia's pregnancy felt like a runaway train.

"I'll keep a letter for them," she added quietly, her voice barely a whisper over the sound of a distant pneumatic drill in the garage. "Something tucked away where Kolya won't find it. If I don't survive, they will know who you are. I'll make sure the truth is left in my papers."

March 1984

Anna, aged forty-six | Moscow, Moscow Oblast, Russian Soviet Federative Socialist Republic

"Hello Anna, and welcome. We're excited to finally have you on board."

Anna was starting her new job as a secretary to a minister in the House of Soviets. It was a simple prospect, but it got her away from Vladimir. The office gave her an 'excuse' for things at home to be less than perfect.

She set herself up in the booth next to her new boss's office. The pay was decent, which was vital now that Ivan was at that expensive boarding school. She knew her son hated it, but she couldn't let him stay home to see his father act the way he did with Anna lately. It was better for him to be away than to be a victim of Vladimir's wrath.

As she read through the pile of notes handed to her, a knot of curiosity tightened in her stomach. She hadn't realized she would be handling such sensitive information—internal memos regarding regional dissent. She took it as a sign of trust, but it made her pulse quicken.

Later that afternoon, the phone rang. She knew, based on the time, it would be Ivan.

"Hi Mama!"

"Can I come home for the holidays?" Ivan asked, his voice trembling. "No one is staying behind."

"No, Ivan. Your Papa is still... not well."

It was the excuse she had used for a while. She couldn't tell the boy that his father was violent, even if he didn't hit her, or that he came home reeking of cloying, sickly-sweet perfume that didn't belong to her. She refused to make Vladimir the boy's villain.

"But Mama! I miss you."

Tears pricked her eyes. She missed him too. "How about we go to the Dacha?" she offered. It was a small house away from the city. The sea breeze and the Dagestani locals would help them both.

"Really? We can go?"

"Yes," Anna said. A daunting task lay before her, and she knew it wouldn't be easy. Lately, Vladimir's paranoia had grown, leading him to hide the Dacha keys. If she wanted to get them back, she'd have to be sneaky, almost as if she were a burglar in her own home.

"Let me know the dates, Ivan. We will find a way."

August
1986

Ivan, aged eighteen | Stalingrad, Russian Soviet Federative Socialist Republic

Ivan released a sigh of relief when he spotted the familiar look of a city upon the horizon. Stalingrad was a welcome sight after he had spent the better part of the last twelve hours driving from Moscow. The barren landscape driving down had given him plenty of chances to think. He was eighteen, just finished secondary school in Leningrad and his mother had set him up in the family Dacha for the summer so he had some time to relax before he had to figure out his next step. As he drove closer to the city, he knew in his heart that the reason he was spending the summer away was the situation at home in Moscow.

He hummed a tune, tapping in time on the steering wheel and allowed his mind to drift back to what he had left behind him.

He had watched his mothers face trying to hide her discomfort every time his father walked into the room. His father, Vladimir had changed a lot in the last year or so since Ivan had last seen him. There were uncharacteristic bouts of forgetfulness, and seemingly unprovoked angry outbursts. Vladimir was a dark storm cloud in that home, and it was only a matter of time before the storm broke, potentially breaking everything in its path.

His mother had made a point to "Enjoy the freedom and sea air", when handing him the keys and closing his fist around them. There was a note of sadness in her voice. Could it have been a wistful wish to escape the fate she had found herself in?

Ivan shook his head as he pulled into the car park of a slightly rundown hotel. The modest place, chosen for its halfway point between Moscow and the coast where Valeriya's train would soon arrive, had peeling wallpaper and a lingering, faint scent of old cigarettes. He grabbed his overnight bag, the click of the car lock echoing in the quiet air after he'd secured it, walking towards the front counter.

He entered the lobby, and there she was. Valeriya wasn't the spindly "little girl" he had played with in the Caspian waves ten years ago. She was a woman now, her auburn braid thick and lustrous, her shoulders draped in a light cardigan as she pored over a book of Russian literature. She was beautiful and Ivan couldn't wait to spend more time with her.

With any luck perhaps she will accept the ring that felt like it was a lead weight in his bag. Something he had saved up for months for.

"Valeriya!" he called out.

She looked up, her glasses sliding slightly down her nose, and a radiant smile transformed her face. She dropped her book and flung herself at him, her impact nearly knocking him back.

"Ivan! You're actually here," she laughed into his neck.

"I wouldn't be anywhere else," he murmured, pulling back to look at her. "I missed you every single day I was in Leningrad. The letters weren't enough."

"I thought you might forget me once you got to the city," she teased, though her eyes held a trace of genuine vulnerability. "With all those city girls and your studies."

Ivan took her hands in his, his expression turning serious. "You've been my anchor since we were children, Valeriya. There isn't a girl in Leningrad who could compete with ten years of us."

"Ten years," she whispered, reaching up to brush a stray hair from his forehead. "We've grown up together, haven't we?"

"We have," Ivan agreed. "And I think the best years are just beginning. But first, I need to get the key to our room so we can actually sit down and talk without the concierge watching us."

Reluctantly, he released her curves to check in. They walked up the hallway hand in hand, a familiar comfort settling over them. They weren't the "good chaste children" their parents might have hoped for; they had found comfort in each other's bodies a few summers ago, seeking a private world of their own while the political crisis between the United States and the Soviet Union escalated outside.

Later, lying next to a sated Valeriya, Ivan listened to her soft, rhythmic snoring. He felt a profound sense of luck. The girl he had met by chance a decade ago was now the woman he intended to keep forever.

The next day, the drive south felt shorter with Valeriya in the passenger seat. When the wooden gates of the dacha finally swung open, the contrast to the previous night's hotel was stark. This wasn't a grand estate; it was the little stone cottage Anna's parents had held onto for decades. The salt air of the Caspian Sea whipped across the shore and the modest porch, where they had spent so many childhood evenings, looked out over a private stretch of sand. To their left, the sea was a vast, darkening expanse of blue, while to their right, the sun was flirting with the tip of the jagged peaks of the Caucasus Mountains.

"I forgot how peaceful it feels," Valeriya said, stepping out of the car and looking at the familiar architecture of the small home. "Compared to the stifling coldness of Moscow, this feels like a dream".

"It's home," Ivan said, dropping their bags in the foyer. "Or as close to it as we can get right now. No more cramped lobbies or leaking faucets. Just the sea and us."

They spent the next few days settling into the rhythm of the coast, but the beauty of the dacha only intensified Ivan's nerves. Every time they sat on the porch or walked the grounds, the ring in his pocket felt heavier.

The sky turned a deep violet over the water, reflecting the last of the golden light hitting the land. Valeriya was in the sea, swimming and frolicking in the waves.

Ivan walked to where their towels lay on the sand. He reached into his shoe, his fingers closing around the small velvet box. He kept his back to her for a second, checking the ring to ensure the stone was still there, it was an irrational fear to have the stone fall out into the sea. He couldn't imagine a future without her.

The salty air filled his lungs as he turned. Forever. The word resonated with the vastness of the ocean.

Sucking in a fortifying breath, Ivan walked toward the shoreline. "My love?" he called over the water.

Valeriya stopped, turning slowly to look at him. Ivan dropped to one knee in the shallow surf, the cold water soaking into his trouser leg.

"Darling," Ivan started as she drifted closer, her eyes widening in realization. "I've known for years that you're the one. I know it sounds cliché, but I couldn't imagine myself with anyone else. Valeriya

Lepyokhina, would you do me the immense honour of becoming my wife?"

Tears threatened to escape Valeriya's eyes. She looked down at him, the man who had been her constant for over ten years. His eyes looked up at her, hope painting the irises a glacial, brilliant blue.

"Valeriya? Don't leave me hanging down here," Ivan said with a nervous grin.

She nodded quickly, unable to find her voice, and extended her right hand. Ivan gingerly took her hand and slipped the ring onto her finger, ensuring it was secure so it wouldn't be lost to the tide. Valeriya held her hand up, letting the last of the day's rays catch the gem.

Ivan stood and pulled her into a fierce embrace, her damp skin pressing against him.

"Darling, let's go back to the dacha and dry off," he whispered. "We have so much to celebrate."

September 1986

Anna, aged forty-nine | Moscow, Moscow Oblast, Russian Soviet Federative Socialist Republic

Anna lingered in the doorway after Ivan and Valeriya left, the scent of the spring air they carried in with them still faintly present. A soft smile touched her lips as she pictured the hopeful light in her son's eyes, the shy pride with which Valeriya had displayed her ring. A good day. A rare bloom of warmth in the often-frozen landscape of her life. But even as the memory lingered, a familiar tightening began in her chest, a cold dread that Vladimir's fragile civility wouldn't last.

Thankfully, Vladimir had been cordial to the both of them while they were here, but a knot of anxiety twisted in Anna's stomach about his inevitable reaction now that they were gone. His moods were a shifting landscape, and she was always braced for the storm. This simmering tension felt familiar, a precursor to the psychological games he preferred since the last time his hand had connected with her face. The isolation, the insidious whispers that twisted blame until she wore it like a shroud – those were his usual weapons.

On a theoretical level, Anna understood the patterns and manipulations, but the barbs still hit home, causing a sharp, stinging pain that she couldn't seem to shield herself from.

A few days prior, Anna had contacted Sef, her friend from boarding school. The years had stretched between them, but the thought of a shared history, a potential understanding of their respective battles, offered a fragile lifeline.

"Anna!" Vladimir's voice, sharp and laced with impatience, sliced through the quiet of the apartment.

Anna winced, the sudden noise a physical blow. Loud sounds still clawed at her, echoes of childhood dashes to the bomb shelters.

"Has the boy left?" he demanded, his voice tight with barely suppressed anger.

Anna arrived at the door to his cramped office and offered him a curt nod.

"Good." He said, his chair scraping harshly against the floor as he made to stand up. He didn't just stand; he loomed, filling the small doorway and forcing her to take a half-step back.

Anna was still in the doorway, eyebrow crooked.

"I hate that he's marrying that filthy peasant girl. You know this is your fault, right?" He punctuated his words with a jab of his finger that stopped inches from her eyes.

Confusion flickered across her face. How could she dictate who their adult son chose to love? And those two were clearly, deeply in love.

“We could have built a legacy if the boy hadn't inherited your stubbornness and your appetite for trouble. We could have been positioned for the coming changes, Anna. Perhaps we would have been if you had managed to carry a child to term without breaking,” he spat at her.

The accusation landed like a physical blow, stealing her breath. It had been a long time since he had wielded that particular cruelty.

A cold dread settled in Anna's stomach. She suspected this outburst had been brewing for days, the undercurrent of his resentment finally breaking the surface. It still stung, the old wound tearing open anew.

The doctors' reassurances , “freak accidents,” they had called the miscarriage and still born , offered no solace against Vladimir's poisonous words. They cut her deeper than the incisions they had to make to remove her reproductive system. A constant reminder of her failure.

Anna closed her eyes against the pain, the tears she could feel welling.

Vladimir bridged the gap between them in a single, predatory stride. He grabbed her chin, his thumb digging into the soft tissue under her jaw, forcing her to face him. Her eyes flew open, wild and scared.

He smirked, the expression looking cruel on his once handsome face. “Don't you dare hide from me. You look at me when I talk to you, Dryan.[1] ” Anna swallowed hard, the movement restricted by his grip. His mood was a volatile thing, a storm brewing without warning. Usually, his words were enough to inflict damage, each syllable a carefully aimed shard of ice. This physical touch, the bruising grip on her chin, felt like a dangerous escalation, a disturbing shift in his control. He was upping the ante, and a cold tendril of fear snaked down Anna's spine. He wasn't just angry anymore; he was enjoying the terror in her eyes.

1. Vile thing

January 1987

Anna, aged forty-nine | Moscow, Moscow Oblast, Russian Soviet Federative Socialist Republic

Anna brushed her hair carefully and twisted it into an intricate knot that allowed her hair to flow down one side of her neck and over her shoulder and collarbone, strategically masking the faint, yellowing bruise near her jaw. She swept a brush with some rouge over her pale cheeks—pale because she hadn't slept properly for weeks since Vladimir last lay a hand on her. She was worried that one morning she wouldn't wake up, so she had taken up residence in Ivan's old bedroom and installed a lock on the inside of the room so Vladimir couldn't break in while she was sleeping. But the sanctuary of Ivan's room was a lie. Though the locked door offered a sliver of security, every creak of the floorboards, every sigh of the wind against the windowpane, sent a jolt of adrenaline through her, a constant reminder of the potential danger lurking just outside.

He hadn't struck her again, not yet. But the glint in his eyes, the dismissive curl of his lip, those were the harbingers of a different kind of pain. The fear of his raised hand was potent, but the slow erosion of her self-worth, the constant blame – that was the poison she truly feared.

She shook off the dark thoughts and shrugged on her dress for the day. Her son's wedding day. She was excited for him just probably not in the way she 'ought' to be. She was excited that he was getting out of his father's sphere of influence. She was excited for her boy to find love. She was excited to see Valeriya's family embrace him. For him to have his own family and finally spread his wings.

She was deeply unimpressed with Vladimir. During the ceremony, he was sullen. He didn't smile or wave over to Valeriya's family, instead choosing to mutter derogatory remarks about her family's heritage—calling them "dirt-under-the-fingernail peasants" just loud enough for her family to capture some of the worst of it.

The precise angles for a fatal strike, the mental exercises to endure agony, her old training flickered through her mind, a stark contrast to the simmering rage threatening to boil over. Every muttered insult Vladimir directed at Valeriya's family was a fresh spark, igniting a fury that even years of discipline struggled to contain. Her own pain was a familiar burden, but the thought of Valeriya's family hearing his venomous words and judging the man who had raised the son she loved was a different kind of torment.

Anna's jaw throbbed, her knuckles white, her gaze fixed trying to hide the rage she was harbouring towards her husband during the ceremony. She was fine... until the speeches.

A fork clinks against a champagne glass. Vladimir and Anna stand up to give their speeches. Vladimir had already told Anna he "had it covered" so she could remain "pretty on his arm" rather than speak, to which he received an eye roll behind his back.

“Most people would have met their new daughter-in-law more than once,” Vladimir started, and Anna could feel the hairs on the back of her neck rise. She could see Ivan starting to tense, knowing that his father's words were like javelins. Straight to the point and rarely missing their intended target. “But this wasn't the case with Valeriya and my son, who chose to hide their little union from me until the very last moment.”

It had actually been months, and Vladimir had met Valeriya several times when she was a child.

“A father always hopes that his son is going to carry on his empire, and I had hoped that for Ivan, that would mean marrying someone... with a pedigree that matched his own. Someone whose blood wasn't diluted by the mud of the provinces.”

Anna choked on her drink and glared across at her husband. The room went deathly silent. Poor Valeriya and her entire family looked shocked; Ivan had turned a vermillion color.

How dare he suggest that Ivan needs to marry rich or powerful in order to keep Vladimir's name 'good' for future generations. Did he not understand that the boy was his only child? His only chance at the redemption he so badly needs?

Ivan looked moments away from clocking his father at his own wedding, and Anna wouldn't have blamed him. She noticed Valeriya's hand slide from her open mouth to Ivan’s knee — a subtle command to back down.

Vladimir finished his speech with a cold, perfunctory toast, which wasn't met with the enthusiasm he was looking for.

A cold resolve settled beneath Anna's simmering fury. There would be a reckoning. She knew the cost – the potential sting on her cheek, the icy silence that would follow. But the thought of Vladimir poisoning Ivan's happiness was a price she refused to pay, even if it meant facing the monster in her own home.

Anna was sure Ivan was already vowing that his father would never lay eyes on his future grandchildren.

As they sat, Anna gripped Vladimir's knee under the tablecloth with a vice-like pressure, her nails digging through the fabric of his suit. She felt him stiffen, his breath hitching in a way that wasn't out of pain, but out of a dark, surprised challenge.

"Not another word," she hissed under her breath, her eyes fixed forward with a terrifying calm. Vladimir didn't pull away; instead, he covered her hand with his own, squeezing back until she could feel the bones in her hand rubbing together, causing her to stifle the need to snatch it away or cry. The war had officially moved back behind closed doors.

The front door had barely groaned shut with the soft snick of the lock slotting into place before Anna was launched upon. Vladimir swung around, his body a wall of iron, and caged her against the door.

"IN FRONT OF PEOPLE?" he bellowed. Standing over her, his face was a mask of purple-veined rage, spittle flying. Anna had long ago given up on the idea of a happily ever after; love was a currency she would never receive from her husband.

"How fucking dare you!" He pulled back and swung his fist. Anna flinched, the air of the punch whistling past her ear as he lodged his knuckles into the wood of the door next to her head. Anna's face remained impassive, a tactical mask that she knew maddened him further.

"Yes," she replied calmly. "Because you, dearest husband, did something unforgivable. You caused a scene. And in the worst possible place. Your son's wedding. Your only child, I might add."

This only fueled the fire. Her calm demeanor, laced with a cool, cutting anger, was a direct challenge to his dominance. He lifted his hands from the doorframe for a split second, and in that heartbeat, Anna ducked under his arm, refusing to be cornered any longer.

"YOU FUCKING WHORE!" Vladimir bellowed, turning to stalk her like a predator.

The first blow landed hard in Anna's shoulder. He had been aiming for her face, but her ingrained instincts took over, shifting her weight just in time. She ducked away again, her voice steady even as her heart hammered. "You humiliated a family because they don't come from the same part of Russia as us."

She managed to avoid another swinging fist, but she couldn't miss the heavy boot that clipped her ankle, tripping her. She hit the floor hard. Before she could roll, Vladimir was on her, straddling her chest and pinning her to the rug. "You think a few old tricks make you my equal?" he spat, his grip tightening on her throat until her breath hitched. "You are a failure. A hollow woman who couldn't even give me a second son. You are lucky I haven't turned you into the authorities for your 'clandestine' letters to your school friends."

As he loomed over her, Anna felt a sickening shift in his weight. She could feel his body thickening below her—the disgusting, unmistakable pressure of his arousal blooming from the violence. The realization that his rage had turned into a dark intent to take her by force snapped the final thread of her restraint.

Anna didn't scream; she calculated. She hooked her legs behind his, using his own forward momentum against him. With a sharp, practiced twist of her hips, she flipped them. In an instant, the power dynamic inverted: he was on his back, and she was the one straddling him, her knees pinned firmly into his biceps.

"Dearest husband," she whispered, her face inches from his. "Your time has run out. The days of being your warm body, the punching bag, the woman you are intent on torturing—they are over. I am overflowing with the hate and anger you've shoved down my throat for the last eighteen years, and I am full, Vladimir. There is no more room."

Anna looked him directly in the eye, her expression terrifyingly vacant. "Do it. Turn me in. We will go down together. I know where the rubles are hidden, Vladimir. I know whose pockets you've been lining to keep your 'empire' afloat. If I go to the Gulag, I'm taking your status, the dacha, and your name with me."

Vladimir's body went rigid, but the predatory glint in his eyes was replaced by a flicker of genuine uncertainty. He saw not his wife, but the operative she had once been. He realized she wasn't bluffing; she was willing to burn the world down just to stop him from touching her.

He released a jagged breath and gave a violent shove to get her off him, though it lacked his usual conviction. “Get out of my sight,” he snarled, scrambling to his feet and smoothing his suit with trembling hands. “Go to your cage in the boy's room.”

Anna stood up, smoothing her own dress with a terrifying calm. She didn't run. She walked slowly, her footsteps echoing in the hallway, leaving him alone in the dark with his vodka and his fear.

September 1991

Anna, aged fifty-four | Moscow, Moscow Oblast, Russian Soviet Federative Socialist Republic

It was late, and the silence of the apartment Anna shared with Vladimir was broken by a knock on the door.

It is well past ten pm and not an appropriate time for visitors Anna thought as she tied an old robe around her waist and padded to the front door.

There was only one working light, the apartment a dismal excuse for a home after they had to sell their old home on the outskirts of the city because of the hyperinflation that was ripping through the entire union. This was all they could afford after the ruble's values started tumbling. It wasn't comfortable, but no one was, it would do.

Anna went to the door, checking the peephole. Her heart jumped seeing her son, Ivan, with his daughter, Mikhaila, wrapped around his left leg. It felt like an age since she had last seen them, she had only met

Mikhaila once. Mikhaila was still young, having just had her second birthday. Her hair was tied into pigtails at either side of her head.

Anna opened the door to them both and got down to the floor. “Mikhaila, look at you,” she whispered, reaching out. The toddler shyly hid behind Ivan’s calf before stepping forward to give Anna a tentative, sticky hug.

Anna pulled her close, breathing in her scent and holding her tight, terrified the moment would end. Ivan hadn’t been the biggest fan of visiting, especially not while Vladimir was still living under this roof, but he obviously had pretty big news to share if he was breaking his own rules and coming here so late.

“How are you both?” Anna asked, stroking Mikhaila’s cheek as the toddler yawned and Anna picked her up to prop her on her hip so the little girl could fall asleep against her Babushkas shoulder if she needed to.

Ivan shifted slightly as he entered, his eyes flicking around the apartment with a barely perceptible unease. “Is he asleep?” he asked, nodding toward the closed bedroom door where Vladimir lay, snoring as Anna had padded past the room to get the door. “He’s out cold, Ivan. It’s safe,” Anna reassured him.

“Actually, Mama,” he began, reaching out for his daughter and putting her on his hip as Anna handed the little girl over. His jaw was set tight, creating a mask of calm he had perfected over years of dealing with his father's outbursts. "We've been better. That's why I'm here."

Anna's brow creased.

"We're moving," Ivan said, his voice flat and controlled, though his grip on Mikhaila's coat tightened. Anna knew her son was hiding something. She watched the way he carefully avoided her eyes, his face a practiced blank slate. He had always been too smart for his own good, learning early that showing emotion in this house only invited conflict. He wasn't aware of his mothers past life, but it was those instincts that came to the forefront as Ivan spoke.

"Spare me, Ivan. Where? And why so suddenly?" Anna said, crossing her arms.

Ivan let loose a deep breath, and Mikhaila drooped in his arms, resting her head against his shoulder and falling into a light sleep. "There is a fishing position open in Vladivostok. It pays in hard currency, Mama. We can't afford to stay in Moscow anymore."

"Vladivostok."

That was one of the few cities whose name hadn't changed in Anna's lifetime. She had never visited; it was on the other side of the country.

"Okay, and you'll be taking Valeriya, Konstantin, and this little one I suppose?" Anna asked. "Valeriya is okay with leaving her family behind? It's quite the trip from there down to the Caspian."

"She's home packing as we speak," Ivan nodded, and Anna could feel her heart break a little. The thought of her six-year-old grandson, Konstantin, being thousands of miles away was a physical pain.

She was looking forward to watching her grandchildren grow up, find themselves, and fall in love. She wanted to be their Babushka, an active part in their us and lives. She couldn't do that if they were on the other side of this vast country.

Konstantin was due to start school soon, and perhaps that was one of the reasons Ivan was so keen to get out of the city, away from the memories here.

"And will I see my grandchildren grow up?" Anna knew it was a nasty question to ask. She wasn't there to guilt her son, but heck, it was his own fault for wanting to take the children to the Pacific Ocean with only two days' notice.

"Yes, Mama. I'm not stopping you from visiting. And we can consider putting the children on a flight over to Moscow when they're old enough."

Anna let loose a sigh. She thought of the thousands of miles of track on the Trans-Siberian Railway. She didn't want to have to travel for days to visit her family. Though perhaps it was her own fault. She had spent a solid amount of Ivan's childhood shielding him from his father's mental health struggles, but that came at the cost of Ivan's trust. He saw her protection as a lie, and now he was putting an entire continent between them.

"Is that all then?" Anna asked, nodding at the sleeping toddler in his arms.

"Yes. We will be moving in a couple of days. I would appreciate it if you didn't tell Papa until we are gone. I don't want a scene, and I don't want him upsetting the children. I must go home to put this little one to bed," he said.

She snuggled into his neck, and Anna couldn't help but feel a pang of grief. She wished Ivan and Vladimir could have had a relationship like that.

Perhaps in a different lifetime.

"Okay, Ivan. Please look after yourself. If you need help, please reach out. I know I don't show it all the time, but I do love you, and I am proud of you you have built despite everything."

Ivan smiled back at his mother, a real, fleeting smile that reached his eyes. He nodded and exited the apartment, closing the door behind him with a soft snick.

A soft snick that signified the end of Anna's hopes for a reunited family.

December
1991

Anna, aged fifty-four | Moscow, Moscow Oblast, Russian Federation

GORBACHEV RESIGNS. A NEW ERA OF RUSSIA BEGINS.

The stark headline in the morning paper swam before Anna's eyes.

Gorbachev resigns.

It felt surreal; the grainy image of the weary leader was a confirmation that the late-night broadcast hadn't been a trick of her tired mind. Last night at 7:35 p.m. Moscow time, former president Mikhail Gorbachev signed Declaration No. 142-H, formalizing the dissolution of the Soviet Union and its control over the other nation-states still under the power of Moscow.

The lukewarm tea did little to soothe the unease that had clung to Anna since the late-night broadcast. Gorbachev's weary voice, his final address, replayed in the silence of her sleepless night: "I am leaving my post with a feeling of anxiety. But also with hope and with faith in you, in your wisdom and strength of spirit."

A long sigh escaped Anna's lips. The leader spoke of hope, but all she felt was a gnawing anxiety. She scrubbed the countertop with unnecessary force. The mundane act was a desperate attempt to ground herself in a world that suddenly felt precarious. She looked toward the living room. With a final glance at Vladimir sprawled on the couch, lost in his drunken slumber, Anna prepared to leave. His oblivion was a separate world from the urgency gripping her. He had become entirely withdrawn since the wedding years ago, especially after the bitter words he had hurled at Ivan. Now, as she had discussed with Ivan just months before, their son only allowed supervised visits with the grandchildren. It was the tangible consequence of Vladimir's toxicity: a chasm widening within their already fractured family.

Oh, the grandchildren, Anna thought.

They were celebrating Christmas together in only a couple of weeks. The thought of Mikhaila's bright eyes and Konstantin's eager questions spurred her into motion. She had to protect their future and their innocence. She heard what happened to the Germans when their government fell as a child, and she feared the same hunger and chaos would now find her family. She tied her hair back with a scarf and stepped out into the uncertain morning.

The residential streets of Moscow weren't as busy as Anna expected. A strange, heavy silence hung over the neighborhood as if everyone was holding their breath behind closed doors. However, as she bustled her way onto one of the trains, the atmosphere shifted to one of quiet desperation. The train grumbled its protest at having to move again and started to make its way through the Moscow cityscape.

The rhythmic clatter of the train was a backdrop to Anna's desperate calculations. If she could just get their money into dollars or marks, surely those currencies would remain strong. They would be a lifeline in the turbulent waters ahead. She needed to get supplies as well: flour, oil, and butter. She could also do with some oats and buckwheat but would do the best with whatever the stores had. She assumed the shelves would probably be pretty picked over, or even raided overnight.

When she reached the commercial district, the eerie quiet of the morning vanished. The bank line was a testament to the fear gripping the city, stretching down the block in a jagged row of shivering bodies. Seeing the crowd, she made her way to the grocery store first. She discovered she was right: things were very much picked over. Because she knew the owner, she was allowed to get some stock that hadn't made it to the shelves yet. She loaded up on wheat flour, oats, and oils. She made sure to pick up her favorite spices, juniper and black pepper. She knew that she would need to source some bay leaves at some point for her stews, but that wasn't at the top of her list at present.

Inflation was already a bitter taste in her mouth as she paid for the meager supplies. She felt a pang of guilt spending the dwindling rubles, but then she saw a brightly painted train and a small doll. Christmas might be the last time they were all together before Ivan moved the family to the coast. She bought them as a small act of defiance against the unknown darkness.

She thanked the cashier and bustled back to the bank. She cursed the line, which hadn't gotten any shorter. She knew that if she waited too much longer, she wouldn't have much left as life savings. Every minute she stood there, she felt the value of her hard-earned money evaporating.

Finally at the counter, Anna felt a chill despite the crowded room. The knot of her scarf had loosened in her haste. A red thread was unwinding and catching on the icy December air outside. The teller's disapproving glance didn't deter Anna. She requested the full amount in American dollars, the crisp notes feeling alien in her hand. Let them scoff; stability was worth more than ideology now.

Uncertainty swirled around her like the Moscow snow. Political speeches and crumbling empires were abstract concepts. To Anna, the collapse of the Union meant only one thing: the potential for her grandchildren to go hungry. She would not let that happen.

Clutching the precious dollars, Anna stepped back onto the street. The December wind tugged at her scarf until it finally slipped free, a vibrant red streak against the grey. It danced away towards the frozen river. It was a poignant farewell to the familiar world she had known, a visual echo of the uncertain journey ahead for Russia and for her family.

May 1993

Anna, aged fifty-five | Moscow, Moscow Oblast, Russian Federation

The rhythmic clinking of the wooden spoon against the pot accompanied Anna's thoughts as she prepared dinner. The television murmured in the background, a news report mentioning something vague about inter-Russian travel. A sharp pang of longing pierced through her. Ivan's last call, his voice filled with the excitement of Misha's first school play, felt like a world away, a joy she wouldn't experience

Her thoughts had more recently been her only company. The familiar rumble of Vladimir's complaints about the news or the neighbours had been absent for days. The silence in the apartment felt heavy and unnatural. He moved with a sluggishness Anna hadn't seen before, his eyes holding a distant, unfocused quality. He had been losing his grip on the present, often forgetting what year it was or where their son had gone. A cold dread seeped into Anna's bones; this unsettling calm always preceded a storm of his unpredictable moods.

Vladimir's arms encircling her waist made Anna stiffen, a jolt of surprise shooting through her. The last time he had touched her with anything resembling affection, she couldn't even recall. The distance between them had become a physical thing. They chose to sleep apart because the empty bed felt warmer to Anna than the frosty reception she got from her husband daily.

“Honey, we need to talk,” Vladimir’s deep rumble murmured in her ear.

A shudder rolled down Anna’s spine.

Was he lucid? Or did he think they were twenty again? It was terrifying how fast he could slip between the man he used to be and the shadow he was slowly becoming.

A familiar prickle of unease crawled up Anna's neck. This sudden shift in Vladimir's demeanour felt like a trap. She forced a sweet smile, her mind racing. She had learned long ago that with Vladimir, appearances could be deceiving. Caution was her only weapon, especially when his lucidity was a flickering flame.

“What about?” she asked sweetly as she turned in his arms to face him.

His hands moved from her waist to her hips and held her in place, gripping her hard against the benchtop and his own body. He seemed present, his eyes sharp, but the question he asked proved his mind was still drifting. “Why is Ivan moving away? Really?”

Anna’s heart sank. Ivan had been gone for two years, yet to Vladimir, the wound was fresh and new today. A multitude of reasons for Ivan's move sprang to Anna's mind, each one a silent indictment of their life in Moscow. The constant strain of Vladimir's temper, the subtle ways it had chipped away at Ivan's spirit over the years. She thought of the hopeful tone in Ivan's voice when he had first spoken of Vladivostok, a chance for a fresh start for his family. The atmosphere in Moscow felt increasingly oppressive, a weight she knew Ivan felt keenly.

"Anna," he said, a dark undertone tainting his deep voice. "Answer me."

Anna gulped. A demanding and non-lucid Vladimir was not a nice man to be around.

"He wants a better life for his children and wife, Vova," Anna replied meekly. This was a weak response, but maybe it would placate him for a time.

He sighed.

"This would be easier if you told the truth. No wonder Ivan can't stand you."

Vladimir's words struck Anna like a physical blow, a cold fist clenching her battered heart deep in her chest. The truth of his accusation was less devastating than the casual cruelty with which he delivered it. A familiar fear, the constant whisper of inadequacy as a mother, resurfaced. She had made mistakes, every parent does, but did that mean her son could hate her?

A pained look flashed quickly across Anna's face while she considered the venom that Vladimir just spewed.

Not quick enough.

He released her hips.

“Don't be such a damned drama queen. It is not that big a deal. Christ Anna, it is like I told you that he died or something. Though moving as far east as he has, perhaps they would be better off dead.”

A cold wave of disbelief washed over Anna. Better off dead? The words echoed in the stunned silence of the kitchen, monstrous and incomprehensible. How could a father, a grandfather, utter such a thing about his own flesh and blood, simply because they chose to live far away? Her mind recoiled from the sheer callousness of the statement.

Anna tried to reason with him. “Vova, he's our only son. Misha and Kostya are our only grandchildren. Surely you can't believe they would be better off dead than safe and thriving away from us out east?”

Vladimir scoffed. As he started to turn back, he whipped around and grabbed Anna by the chin.

“Listen here Anna. They wouldn't be our only grandchildren, he wouldn't be our only son if you had managed to keep a single other child alive or perhaps had been able to produce more. One child is a disappointment to this nation. You're a disappointment.”

On that note, he released her chin and strode out of the room. Anna sank to the floor, sliding against the cabinets , her mind reeling at the cruelty he had unearthed from the past. The venom in Vladimir's voice resonated with the long-held fears that gnawed at Anna's self-worth. His words were a cruel confirmation of her deepest insecurities. The chill of the floor was seeping through her clothes, a physical manifestation of the cold emptiness that her husband had just thrown her way.

A door clicked open, and Vladimir called out, “I'm going out with my brothers in arms. I won't be here for dinner, and don't wait up for me.” The front door slammed. It was nice of him to at least let Anna know what was happening, even if she had put considerable effort into making them both a nice dinner.

Anna was alone.

Cold.

Numb.

Isolated.

September
1997

Anna, aged sixty | Moscow, Moscow Oblast, Russian Federation

The anticipation thrummed in Anna's chest, a counterpoint to the airport's general hum. Soon, the doors would open, and she would see them. Mikhaila, her five-year-old whirlwind, whose every giggle was a tiny explosion of joy. And Konstantin, now a thoughtful ten, a hint of a smile always playing around his lips. Though he was only ten, he often carried the gravity of someone much older.

The silence in the apartment had become a constant companion, punctuated only by Vladimir's distant muttering. She craved the uncomplicated joy her grandchildren carried.

5 minutes to go.

The airport was bustling, people checking in for the next international flight, Moscow to Istanbul. She imagined the people were going to enjoy the warmth the city would provide. Revel in the history. Soak in the atmosphere. Perhaps attend important international business meetings, to be an important business person attending said important international business meetings.

Her gaze lingered on the stream of passengers heading towards the Moscow-Istanbul gate, a wistful sigh escaping her lips. The thought of sun-drenched streets and the scent of spices offered a fleeting moment of escape. But the image of her passport, tucked away in the locked box in Vladimir's study, a petty act of control, quickly grounded her. Even if the desire was strong, the means were simply out of reach, their finances as constrained as her freedom. She had managed to squirrel away just enough from her meagre salary at the Soviet House to afford some treats and activities for the children, but a flight across the country was an impossible dream.

Two minutes until they landed.

Anna could see the plane now. It was a dot in the sky, but getting closer and closer as it approached.

Her heart ached with a fierce desire to fill these precious days with joy for Mikhaila and Konstantin. She envisioned them tracing the ancient stones of the Kremlin walls, their young voices echoing in the vast cathedrals. The simple pleasure of ice cream after a visit to the zoo. These were the memories she wanted them to take back to Vladivostok, bright spots against any shadows they might sense at home. Whether they could venture beyond the city limits, perhaps to the sprawling estates outside Moscow, remained a question mark hanging over their visit, dictated by Vladimir's unpredictable nature.

The weight of Vladimir's changing behaviour was a constant presence in their small apartment. When the fog in his mind briefly lifted, a sharp anger often surfaced, a volatile echo of the man he used to be. Sometimes the past bled into the present, and he would call for their daughter, his voice thick with a grief that never truly faded, a grief that had fractured something within him decades ago when they lost the babies.

To the children, Anna offered gentle explanations for their grandfather's forgetfulness, careful to steer him away from the painful memories, even inventing stories about Ivan's childhood to bridge the gaps in Vladimir's fractured timeline. The constant vigilance was exhausting, a tightrope walk with an invisible precipice.

Early onset Alzheimer's, the doctors had told them. No cure, and it was only going to get progressively worse.

It was taking its toll on Anna, and she was not sure what the future was going to hold for them all. His mental breakdown after the death of his daughter, the stillborn baby, may have been thirty odd years ago, but it was one of the triggers for his decline.

As Anna released a breath, she heard the announcement of the children's flight arriving over the intercom.

"Flight 238 from Vladivostok has just touched down. Customers from this flight are expected to depart through gate 116. Anyone waiting for these passengers is advised to wait in the domestic waiting area near the gates exit. Thank you".

Only a few more minutes, the time it takes people to disembark, then she would hold her precious grandbabies in her arms again.

A high-pitched squeal of delight pierced the airport hum as Mikhaila spotted Anna. Mikhaila, her pigtails bouncing, collided with Anna in a burst of giggles and a tight hug that squeezed the air from her lungs. Ten-year-old Konstantin followed at a more measured pace, a serious, guarded look on his face, waiting patiently until his younger sister had her fill of Babushka's embrace before offering a more reserved, but equally heartfelt, hug.

It made Anna's heart happy hugging her grandchildren. She had missed their joy filled presence. She was grateful Ivan had agreed to this visit, knowing she would keep the children shielded from Vladimir's worst days.

She bustled them into the train to head back to the apartment that she shared with Vladimir. He was out today, going to spend some time with his brothers in arms, the men he had served with in the Red Army before Anna and him had even wed.

The small apartment, usually quiet and still, vibrated with a newfound energy. Mikhaila's infectious giggles punctuated the clatter of toys, a whirlwind of youthful exuberance. Konstantin, ever the responsible older brother, kept a watchful eye on her, even intervening with surprising speed when a baking experiment threatened to engulf a tea towel.

Later, he took charge of dinner, his quiet competence in the kitchen hinting at a passion for cooking. He boldly declared he wanted to be a chef later in life. Anna observed him, a thoughtful frown creasing her brow. While many of the greatest culinary masters were men, it felt like a humble path compared to the military legacy Vladimir cherished. A chef? The thought was unexpected. Perhaps a cook in one of the military canteens? Vladimir would want more for his only grandson.

Mikhaila, still exploring the world with wide, curious eyes, trailed after Anna, asking endless questions. Anna made a mental note to take her to the planetarium later in the week, maybe the natural history museum, to open her eyes to possibilities.

She wanted to keep the children busy so they did not need to spend time with her husband. Vladimir had been increasingly withdrawn since his night out with his former comrades.

When she was not at her administration job at the Soviet House, Anna was walking on eggshells. She was not sure how to deal with Vladimir anymore.

The days flew by in a flurry of activity: the roar of lions at the zoo, the hushed reverence of the art museums, even a glimpse into Anna's surprisingly mundane office at the Soviet House. The train journey to St. Petersburg was filled with Konstantin's quiet observations about the city's grandeur and Mikhaila's excited chatter. But as they boarded the return train to Moscow, a knot of unease tightened in Anna's stomach.

Their visit was drawing to a close, with only a couple of nights left before their flight back to Vladivostok. Anna's mind drifted back to the start of the trip. Ivan's casual mention of his and Valeriya's week-long trip to Australia, which they had taken while the children were safely in her care, replayed in her mind.

There was a nonchalance in his tone that did not sit right. A familiar instinct, honed by years of knowing her son, whispered a warning she could not ignore.

June 2001

Anna, aged sixty three | Moscow, Moscow Oblast, Russian Federation

The bright morning light seemed to cruelly highlight the unhealthy pallor of Vladimir's face. Anna watched him, all the while a familiar ache settled in her chest. The ache wasn't unusual. It came from the feeling of watching a man she had once loved. Even when she shouldn't have. The man she once knew was getting swallowed up slowly by the fog of his illness. The vibrant spark had left him so long ago, each year chipping away at his spirit. But this… this felt different. Anna had known for some time that his strength was failing, but she became truly worried when he started snoring for the first time consistently a few nights ago.

He was spending more time sleeping. In the last day or so, he started the weird snoring and was gurgling during the day.

Anna had called Darya, her old friend from high school who became a nurse.

"It sounds like a death rattle, Anna," Darya's voice was calm and professional as she described the gurgling sound. "His body is shutting down. There is little a hospital can do except annoy him in his final hours. Just keep him comfortable."

Anna sank onto the edge of the bed, the finality of the words a physical weight pressing down on her. After so many years, Vladimir was dying. The passage of time had changed the vivacious and lively young man into a dying old man alone in his bed. Life was cruel. But in the end, Vladimir had been cruel too.

Within forty-eight hours of Anna's call to Darya, she needed to make another call.

To her son.

She was not upset or crying, which surprised her. She had anticipated a wave of grief, a crushing weight of loss. Instead, there was a quiet numbness. It had been a long time coming, she realized, a faint ache behind her eyes. The Vladimir she had loved had slipped away years ago, stolen piece by piece by the relentless illness. This felt final, but not entirely unexpected.

Ivan was on a flight from Sydney now, coming to help her sort things out. After his move to Vladivostok, he had eventually sought a life even further away, in Australia.

A funeral? Medical professionals? Morgues? It all felt overwhelming, so Anna hoped that Ivan would help her navigate through everything.

Vladimir's death made her brain feel washed out. Simple tasks felt monumental, and each thought was a struggle to grasp. She glanced down at her hands resting on the table, surprised by their lack of clarity, as if they belonged to someone else. The world around her felt muted and distant, like trying to see through a dense fog rolling in from the sea.

The need to pack soon surfaced, unbidden, in the swirling mist of her thoughts.

The practical reality of her situation settled in over the following days. Ivan would need a space while he stayed with her. She stood before Vladimir's side of the wardrobe, a sense of trespass washing over her. The faint, lingering scent of him, pipe smoke and something like sandalwood, felt like a tangible presence. To disturb it felt like a violation. Yet, Darya's quiet reminders of the arrangements pressed upon her.

Her movements were heavy, each action requiring a conscious effort. A worn jacket, a faded photograph of their youthful faces, full of a joy that now felt impossibly distant; each item was a weight, a tangible piece of a life that had reached its final chapter. Her movements felt slow and disconnected. Each item she touched, a worn sweater of Vladimir's or a photograph of them young and laughing on the beach, seemed to carry a faint echo of a life that was now definitively over.

A strange sense of quiet washed over Anna, a feeling of a long journey finally reaching its end. The years of uncertainty, the constant vigilance, and the faint, persistent hope that Vladimir might somehow return to her had all dissipated with his last breath.

The arrangements after he was gone were a blur of hushed voices and official forms. Ivan, his face etched with a weariness that mirrored her own, navigated most of it. The quiet dignity of the small ceremony and the weight of the earth falling onto the simple wooden casket were moments that passed as if viewed through a shroud.

The vastness of her loss felt like an open chasm. To avoid falling into it, Anna clung to the immediate. The delicate curve of a chair back became a point of intense focus. The way the sunlight fractured into jewel-toned hues as it passed through the chapel window held her captive. These small observations were lifelines, tethering her to the present moment and preventing her from being swept away by the overwhelming void.

Once the funeral was over, the decision to move Anna out of that small apartment felt less like a choice and more like a current gently pulling her along. Ivan had found the complex, a community specifically for widows. It was a place where others understood, without needing explanations, the quiet absence that now permeated her days. It felt sensible enough. It was a place to navigate this new landscape, surrounded by others who were also learning to live in the aftermath.

The taxi ride to the complex was silent. The late afternoon sun cast long shadows across the unfamiliar buildings. Each identical window seemed to hold a story of loss, a silent testament to lives intertwined and then severed. As the taxi pulled to a stop, a woman with kind eyes and a gentle smile approached, offering a hand.

"Welcome, Anna. We've been expecting you."

Stepping out of the taxi felt like stepping onto a new, uncertain shore. The fog of grief still clung to her, but in the woman's warm hand, there was a faint spark of something else: a possibility of friendship and a shared understanding in the quiet landscape of widowhood. The relief that Vladimir's long suffering was over was a quiet undercurrent, a truth she would not voice aloud just yet. But it was there, a small, fragile seed of peace in the vast emptiness.

July 2001

Anna, aged sixty-four | Moscow, Moscow Oblast, Russian Federation

The apartment, stripped bare by the packing, felt haunted by Vladimir's absence. The silence permeated every lingering thought, every quiet moment. Ivan's solution loomed before her: a complex exclusively for widows.

So I will not be a sad old lady, Anna thought with a touch of bitterness.

Yet, a sliver of acknowledgment pricked at her. A complex housing mostly widows who were too young for retirement homes, yet needing the support of a community, was likely the best place for her.

She had not been overly pleased about leaving the small apartment she had shared with Vladimir in Moscow. It was where all their recent memories were stored, even if those memories were stained by his illness. But Anna guessed that all things had to come to an end and perhaps this would be a good thing for her too. It was still hard to believe she was a widow, a role she had not quite learned to settle into.

A week had passed in a haze since the funeral. Ivan moved with a purposeful energy, handling arrangements, his voice low and steady. Anna just saw things happening around her and to her. She was not actively participating in them; she was a silent, uncomprehending audience member to this part of her own life.

To her, it felt like she went to sleep one night having to call Ivan and tell him that his father had died, and the next day he was here. Now, Vladimir was six feet underground and her home was being dismantled.

As they drove toward the new complex, they passed the home Ivan grew up in. The home Anna lost two baby girls in. The home Vladimir and her bought and eventually could not hold onto because of the rising costs and the change in the nation. It was empty still as they drove past it.

"Ivan!" Anna called as they pulled up outside the front door of the new apartment. She just wanted the world to stop spinning. She needed to pause for a minute so that maybe, just maybe, she could process what was happening around her.

"Yes, Mama?" Hearing him still call her that made Anna's heart warm. Despite being a fully fledged adult himself, and with his own children, he still called her Mama. It was a sense of being needed. Wanted.

"Come in for a cup of tea, won't you?" she asked him. "You are working too hard."

Anna was actively using delay tactics. She was shameless about it; she just wanted a moment to take stock. A lot had happened in the past few weeks.

"I can't, Mama. We are due at the old apartment in an hour to hand over the keys." He looked down at his watch and let loose a string of English curses, thinking his old Mama did not understand the language and therefore did not know what the profanities meant. She remembered learning those words a lifetime ago, and she recalled the memory with glee.

"We need to get going. You know what Muscovite traffic is like."

Anna let a sigh loose and ambled down the car Ivan had hired for the move.

"I do not want to go," she stated as she reached into the backseat, grabbed a box and handed it over to him.

"Mama," he sighed. Ivan was not the biggest fan of fighting with his mother. "I live on the literal other side of the world from you. Mostly." He thought about it for a second before shaking his head. "It is at least fourteen hours before I can get here. I cannot afford to have you not looked after. I want you to have a community. It is this, Australia, or a literal retirement home."

Ivan punctuated the last point with his hands on his hips. Anna was actively screwing up her face at the idea of being in a home with other geriatrics or having to move in with her son across the other side of the world. It was probably more of a threat in Ivan's mind. At least Anna could speak and understand passable English, even if it had been a long while since she had needed to use it.

Ivan placed the box he was carrying into the truck, already half emptied. Anna had not realized that she and Vladimir had so many possessions. Ivan had apparently done a clean out while Anna was napping yesterday.

"See Mama, there are no good choices. At least in this two bedroom modern apartment, there is room if the kids are over here for an Overseas Experience, or to visit or something. Mikhaila is ten now and Konstantin is fifteen; they will be traveling before you know it. People can visit."

It was the best of the many wicked choices. She was resigned to her fate.

There was help on the other end of the move, and Ivan had to run off to speak to a real estate person about selling the apartment. Surrounded by boxes, Anna felt the weight of everything settle on her shoulders and she slumped onto a chair that had been moved in already.

Anna had only been sitting for a matter of seconds, allowing no time to start stewing on everything that had happened, before a timid knock hit the door frame. Letting out a sigh, Anna got up. The chair groaned at the loss of her weight as she turned to see two ladies in their sixties at her door.

Strangers.

Anna glanced around, making sure no one else was around, before shaking her head for being silly.

"Can I help you?" Anna asked the women. They were interrupting her wallowing time.

"You are Mrs. Zaitseva, right?" asked the first woman, putting her hand out to shake Anna's.

Accepting that handshake was letting her into the house. Anna did not know these women, so she stepped forward to shake hands.

"Yes, and your name?"

"Chiara Isava, and behind me is Ameliya Nicolaye-va," she said, gesturing at the woman at her side.

They both were small women, and Ivan had said this complex was only for widows. Anna assumed they must both be missing their husbands. Though Anna could not relate to missing Vladimir, it was strange not to have his moody presence hanging around. It was a loneliness she had only truly felt during the day it took for Ivan to arrive from Australia.

Anna had the feeling that she would never be lonely again with these two women around. Chiara breezed past Anna with Ameliya trailing close behind, their voices a low hum as they surveyed the half packed rooms.

"We brought tea and varenye," Chiara announced, walking into the kitchen space and immediately searching around for a kettle and some cups. She held up a jar of the sweet fruit preserves as if it were a trophy.

"Ameliya heard you moving in, and I ran into your lovely son Ivan as he was leaving this morning," she continued the hunt before pulling the kettle out of a box and releasing a joyous sound at the discovery.

Anna smiled. She could not help it. She watched the two women bustling around her half unpacked space, getting things set up for a tea time. Chiara seemed to be the more dominant personality of the two, though Anna thought Ameliya might have been a force to be reckoned with as well. The quiet ones, like Anna, always were.

"And he said it would be alright to come by and welcome you to the floor. Ameliya is your next door neighbour and I am only a few doors down on the other side of the hallway."

Anna looked over to Ameliya and quietly whispered, "Does she ever just stop?" so Chiara would not overhear and be offended.

Ameliya looked over to her friend before looking back at Anna with a small smile and shaking her head. The movement meant a few of her grey hairs were coming loose from her tied back braid. Ameliya was the taller of the two ladies; Anna estimated her to be perhaps 5'7". Chiara was short, shorter than Anna, but had personality in spades.

Chiara had short hair, very obviously styled into a slick bob, and unless her hands were busy, she was waving them around very animatedly as she talked. Ameliya was obviously much quieter, with long hair braided back from her face. She had a rounded face to Chiara's more square shape and had a spattering of freckles across her nose and cheeks.

"Anna?" Chiara called out from the kitchen, holding a kettle that was now warm and three mismatched mugs. "Have you unpacked chairs and a table?"

Blushing, Anna looked around and found both the table and all the chairs covered in boxes. She shot a worried look at Ameliya, who read it perfectly and started moving the boxes carefully to the floor.

"Anna, we know you are a widow, but other than that and the fact that you have a handsome son—oof, Ameliya!" Chiara complained as Ameliya stamped on her toes. Obviously, there was something going on there regarding Chiara eyeing up men when she perhaps ought not to.

"Anyway, as I was saying, before I was rudely interrupted," she said, shooting daggers Ameliya's way. "We do not know a lot about you. So Anna, who are you?"

Who was she? What an intriguing question.

April
2004

Anna, aged sixty-six| Moscow, Moscow Oblast, Russian Federation

Anna was not expecting the letter. It was found in her mailbox earlier in the day. There was no stamp, no return address, and an eerily familiar handwriting that could not possibly belong to who she thought it must belong to. In her hands she held an envelope, not unlike the ones she used to receive her love letters in during her youth. She was confused; her brows furrowed as she stared down at Vladimir's handwriting. It was bold and unwavering on the envelope. Confusion was a knot deep in her chest.

How could that possibly be?

Her husband had been dead for three years.

For three years, she had been free from his lucid moments that often resulted in her tears. For three years, she was not walking on eggshells. For three years, she had not wanted to just give up. The letter must have been held by one of his former associates, one of the "brothers" he spent his final years with, and delivered now as a final strike from beyond the grave.

She realized he must have written this long ago, perhaps in those early days when the doctors first mentioned Alzheimer's and the fog was only just beginning to drift into his mind. He had enough clarity then to be cruel, to plan a way to haunt her even after he was gone.

The paper was crisply folded in the envelope. The ink of her name was sharp and black; the letters were formed with a decisive hand. Anna's breath hitched. Her name in his handwriting. Her hands shook as she held the envelope. She was just getting back her freedom. A sense of spaciousness had begun to open up in Anna's life; the heavy weight of Vladimir's constant scrutiny was finally lifting. She remembered the arguments over a simple outing with friends; his disapproval was a suffocating blanket. This letter felt like a new chain.

Taking a deep breath that seemed to get lost in her lungs, she slowly pulled the sealed tab of the envelope open, careful not to tear the paper. A cold dread seeped into her. Even then, as the first subtle shifts in his memory began, he had been planning this.

My Beloved,

You are receiving this because I have passed away. And with my passing I was going to keep secrets to my grave, but the only way to heal things sometimes is to allow them to see the light. Sunlight is the best kind of disinfectant according to my mother.

I am still mad at you. And I do not know if I ever will not be, Anna. Your body. It failed the both of us. I know that to begin with, this was the thing that drove us apart. I know I changed after that. I know you did too.

I always thought you had betrayed us by sleeping with that American at your workplace, until one of my 'friends' found out that he sleeps next to another man at night, and not in a platonic way, and dealt to him. I would not allow your straying to ever tarnish my name. And while I knew that he was a homosexual, it was about the perception, Anna.

I was so mad at the time. Mad because you seemed to be courting another man, mad because you were incapable of producing me more children. Well, I went elsewhere. I know you probably assumed as much. But my mistress, a woman from my own childhood, has a child by me. They know of you. They know if they want to know more to come and find you.

The child's name is Matrona Puntina. She may try to find you or Ivan. Though with him leaving us for the West, I do not think she will be able to find him or any of the legitimate Zaitsev's easily. She is also getting this kind of letter upon my death.

Do not deny her family if she does reach out. I have tried to set up her mother, but my father's work falling apart like it did, and the fact that your work did not bring in much money despite the dangerous nature of it, made supporting both families difficult.

Perhaps your inability to have a second or third child was a blessing. Those babies would not have had to starve. I hope I am remembered as I was, a strong man who stood for the values of family and Russia. Who loved loyalty and held those who were not to account.

Yours,

Your now departed husband,

Vladimir

Anna could have dropped the god damned piece of paper; she was shaking so much. The casual admission that he had "dealt to" the American, the man she knew as Charlie, chilled her to the bone. Vladimir had ordered a man's death over a mere perception of an affair, a perception that was not even true because Charlie had been gay. He had carried that blood on his hands for decades while shaming her for the loss of their daughters.

How dare he come back from the grave and dare to make her feel less than. Less than a woman. Shaming her for two incredibly rare and unfortunate incidents involving their children while he had been off fathering a secret family.

How.

Dare.

He.

A raw, animalistic scream ripped itself from Anna's throat. She knew her scream would likely be a war cry to her fellow widows, and they would all come running to support her. And a few minutes later, with tears streaming down her aged face, she was proved right.

A gentle rapping on the door was followed by hushed tones of concern. The neighbours in the complex knew the sound of a woman breaking; they did not assume she had fallen or hurt her body, they knew she had been struck by a memory or a ghost. Then, a wave of reassurance came in Chiara's louder call.

"Anna? It is us."

"We heard the scream, and we can hear your crying. We have wine and chocolate. It is Chiara and Ameliya."

Ameliya had likely called for Chiara when Anna let loose that scream because she knew Anna needed more than just a neighbour; she needed a force of nature. Recovering her composure, she put down the letter, dabbed her cheeks, and rose to open the door for the visitor. Her friends, who despite all the crap that her dead husband just put her through, were still standing there.

Comfort food in hand.

September 2005

Anna, aged sixty-eight | Moscow, Moscow Oblast, Russian Federation

The air in the apartment hung heavy with the fragrant steam of black tea and the cloying sweetness of berry preserves. A low hum of conversation filled the room. It was a comforting murmur woven from the shared address and the quiet understanding that came with an empty space beside them in bed. Beyond that, each woman held her stories close, revealing them at her own pace. Everything else was totally up to the individual as to what they divulged.

Anna found herself mostly listening, content to absorb the energy of the room. Chiara, in contrast, was a whirlwind of sound and motion. “What can I say?” she had exclaimed with a shrug. “Italian by birth, married to a Russian who spoke in whispers! A woman has to adapt!” Her voice, even in casual conversation, carried across the room. The loudest people, Anna had noticed, used their volume to cover up things; however, at her age, she felt it was not her place to judge.

Ameliya, another quiet soul, sat beside Anna, the two of them sharing a comfortable silence. A clatter of a spoon against a tea cup garnered everyone's attention.

"Listen up, everyone!" Chiara said to the room of women. There were mixed ages. Anna felt like she was in the middle of the crowd. There were some ninety year old women who were as sharp, if not sharper, than some of her tutors at the Red Banner Institute. Then there were a couple of ladies in their forties who had lost their husbands in the second Chechen war.

"I would like to formally welcome Anna Zaitseva to the widows' club! I know you have lived here for four years, Anna, but since you finally decided to join our afternoon tea, we must make it official," Chiara announced. "Anna, please stand up and introduce yourself."

The prospect of being the centre of attention nearly killed Anna; she loathed public speaking with a passion that bordered on a physical phobia. She had not even wanted to speak at her husband's funeral because of it, and the thought of all these eyes on her felt like an interrogation.

The silence stretched, heavy and uncomfortable. It was broken only when one of the older women cleared her throat, a nervous sound, and Ameliya's elbow connected sharply with Anna's side. So Anna got up. Reluctantly.

“Uh, hi. I am Anna Zaitseva. I have a son and two grandchildren and grew up in Moscow. I used to work as an administrative assistant in the Soviet House.” And with that, Anna sat down.

Again, she hates public speaking. There was a polite smattering of clapping before Chiara swooped in and worked the room of women back into chattering.

“You hated that, did you not?” asked Ameliya in her typical hushed tone.

Anna chuckled. “Was it that obvious?”

Ameliya grinned. “Well, here is to never having to do that again. Za zdorov'ye, to our health.” They clinked their tea cups together.

All the while, Anna was wishing there was something stronger than tea in her cup. A shot of something strong, something that would burn the edges off her nerves, would have been far more welcome. She watched the other women and realized that this group was her new reality. The ghosts of Vladimir and the secrets of his letter were still there, but in this room, she was just Anna.

May 2010

Anna, aged seventy-three | Moscow, Moscow Oblast, Russian Federation

The four women had settled into their usual places around Chiara's worn wooden table: Anna beside the quiet Ameliya, facing the animated duo of Chiara and Roza. Chiara's laughter filled the space, with Roza's typically quippy remarks as cards were played in a theatrical manner. Ameliya and Anna across the table were quiet in contrast. The smell of black tea and sweet jam permeated the air as Anna refocused on the game of Durak.

The familiar weight of the cards in her hand brought a quiet sense of mastery. Twenty years ago, in the boisterous atmosphere of Vladimir's garage, she had learned the subtle art of Durak. It was a skill she now wielded with a deliberate restraint, the quiet power palpable in her every gesture.

"Heard Mrs. Petrova has moved to that new care facility," Chiara said, laying down a card with a sigh.

Roza nodded. "Well, at least someone else can get the flat."

Anna pictured the frail woman she had sometimes seen in the hallway; her slow steps had become increasingly labored. A small pang of sympathy touched her.

"So, I heard someone was moving in today," Chiara said to the women as Anna tuned back into the conversation.

"Yeah, and I heard they are from Moscow and have been here their whole life. That is pretty cool, right?"

Impressive, as Moscow had been the center of the Russian world since the war and during the Great Patriotic War while it was sieged upon.

"I heard the man downstairs call her Nika. Anafonika Smirnova, I think he said her name was?" Roza said.

Anna's head whipped around. She had not heard that first name in years. About forty years. She suddenly found herself in a panic as she remembered how Nika and her shared the same space during their time at the Red Banner Institute. Nika had taken a different track than Anna; she had ended up in the counterintelligence space, where she was tasked with ensuring the Americans fell for specific levels of misinformation. She was brilliant, sharp, and knew exactly how to spot a lie.

While Chiara and Roza continued their lively banter, Anna retreated inward, a cold knot of anxiety tightening in her stomach. Nika. She had to find a way to speak to her before… before what? The thought of revealing her KGB past to these unsuspecting women filled her with dread.

"When was she moving in?" Anna asked, not remembering much before Nika's name was mentioned. Perhaps a lack of foresight on her part, but it had very much caught her off guard.

"Today! I would not be surprised if her family helps her with boxes in the next couple of hours," Chiara exclaimed. "Ah ha!" she shouted as she pulled another card.

Anna could hear some noise coming from the hallway, quiet under the chatter of the ladies in the room.

"I am just going to see if Nika is here yet," Anna said as she excused herself from the room.

With a slow, deliberate exhale, Anna tightened her grip on the door handle, preparing herself to look into the face of her past. A woman about Anna's age, not unlike the girl she once knew, was striding into the apartment four doors down from Anna's own. There was a familiar set to her shoulders, a hint of the same purposeful energy Anna remembered from their youth. She disappeared inside, and a younger man came out, grabbed another box, and followed the woman.

Anna let loose a sigh and then walked over to the apartment. She was not one for approaching people typically, preferring to sit back and assess a situation before making a move, but now was not the time to be timid. No time to be timid. She wanted her past to stay there, in the past. She had spent so long escaping her shadows, and now they finally felt like they had let her free. Anna was not about to let her past drag her back.

"Anafonika?" Anna asked into the apartment as she poked her head around the corner.

A familiar face peered out of one of the rooms. Behind her, a younger man emerged, his stance radiating a protective suspicion, hands planted firmly on his hips.

"And who are you?" he asked, before Nika asked, "Anna?"

A grin spread across Anna's face. She was remembered.

A warmth spread through Anna, surprising and unexpected. To be remembered as a peer, as a colleague, was a small balm to the years of Vladimir's insidious whispers and his constant reminders of her supposed insignificance. A fragile sense of self worth flickered to life. But the past was still a place where there was too much pain. Anna could not risk being pulled back into that.

Anna nodded at the woman, who pushed the man aside and ran over to give her former housemate a hug.

"Anna! It has been what, like forty years? Forty-five? I thought we would have kept in touch."

Anna pulled out of the hug with a bit of a grimace at the reminder of the promises the girls all kept. There was no way Anna would have been able keep to any of her promises; Vladimir made sure that she was not going to have any good thing from her past, friends or not. She only got in touch with Darya when she had medical related questions; she still had an aversion to hospitals and doctors after her hysterectomy.

"Nika, we need to catch up, but quickly before the others come around to welcome you, can you pretend we met at a regular university? The other women here do not know my past, and I would like to keep it that way."

Nika took a step back from Anna. "You are not proud of your work for the Union?"

A sharp shake of her head. No. It was not just about pride. A web of loyalties, secrets, and the long shadow of Vladimir's influence made it impossible to simply embrace that past.

"Not that. Vladimir is not here anymore, hence my living here. I will explain things later, but we met at the city's university, not the Institute."

Nika nodded slowly, and just as the acceptance crossed her face, the women came down the hall looking for Anna.

"Looks like the full welcome party has come. Welcome to the widows' club, Nika," Anna said, before mouthing a quick sorry at Nika, whose apartment was suddenly filled with women.

June 2011

Anna, aged seventy-two | Moscow, Moscow Oblast, Russian Federation

The excitement coming off the two girls standing in front of Anna was palpable. Misha was there with a wide grin on her face; her best friend stood beside her with a small smile. Despite the ten years that had passed since Anna had last seen her granddaughter in person, Misha launched herself at her grandmother, not unlike when she was much littler and had arrived off the plane all those years ago.

Misha and her best friend Alexandra Komarov, whom she called Sasha, were in Russia for an overseas experience between their undergraduate years before they dived into postgraduate studies. At twenty-one, Misha was a woman now, but to Anna, she still had the same spark in her eyes.

Komarov. The name sparked a flicker of something in Anna's memory; it was a vague association with power and a certain ruthlessness that had once permeated the business circles of St. Petersburg. The Komarov name carried the weight of new money and fortunes built on the privatization of the gas industry after the Soviet collapse. A knot of unease tightened in her chest; each breath hitched as the feeling grew. Hopefully not noticeable to the excited girls in front of her.

There was a quickness in Sasha's eyes, a subtle intelligence that belied her casual pronouncements about her privileged upbringing. Anna had seen that kind of carefully constructed nonchalance before; it was a shield often used to deflect closer scrutiny. Misha, however, seemed completely charmed by the act.

"Your tour is called a conspiracy?" Anna asked the girls as they entered her apartment in the widows' complex.

"A Contiki," Sasha clarified, a slight roll of her eyes that did not quite hide a smile.

Misha was nodding along before she explained, "They are doing some sightseeing in Russia, but I wanted to see you, and Sasha has not seen her family up in St. Petersburg in ages, so we will join up with the crew when they are ready to leave Russia."

St. Petersburg with a Komarov, Anna mused. A mental image formed of elegant restaurants, hushed conversations in dimly lit corners, and the subtle dance of social manoeuvring.

"Ah, St. Petersburg," Anna commented, a small smile touching her lips. "A beautiful city. Misha tells me that is where you are from, Alexandra?"

Sasha spoke of St. Petersburg with a casual air, mentioning exclusive clubs and family connections. Anna watched her, a knowing flicker in her eyes, recognizing the not-so-subtle cues of a life lived in privileged circles.

Hugging her little Zaychik, she held on tightly. She knew the chance to visit family in Australia, with its stunning landscapes and unique culture, was slipping away, causing a deep sense of longing. Anna would only make that flight one way, and she wasn't willing to leave her mother country. To maintain her cover, she pretended not to understand English and acted like a homebody. This was a role that had become surprisingly comfortable for her. She kept the secret of her fluent English close to her chest; it was a habit born of decades of survival. If people thought she was just a simple, monolingual old woman, they spoke more freely around her, and she had always preferred to be the one who listened.

Although a bit shaky, her English was still quite fluent. Anna stayed informed about global events by listening to the BBC, absorbing the measured tones of the newsreaders and the crisp visuals of world events. The channel was considered illicit but Anna wasn't sure if the Russia she knew was the Russia she was living in now. The miles between them and Australia felt vast and unyielding. Let them live their lives there. Here, in this small space, with the lively chatter of the girls and the comforting presence of her friends just down the hall, Anna found a quiet happiness.

Anna only had the girls for one night. She felt a flicker of her old life, wondering if she could still pull strings for a night at the opera through some of the connections Chiara or the other widows maintained. But what she truly longed for was the intimacy of her small table, the sharing of stories over tea, and the familiar click of playing cards. It might not provide their usual excitement, but it was her way of holding them close and ensuring their well-being. In a city that felt increasingly predatory, Anna felt that for at least one night, the girls were safe, well, and fed.

"What would you like for dinner?" Anna asked the girls in Russian, pretending to be oblivious to the English conversation about clubbing and meeting boys going on behind her.

"Pelmeni?" Misha asked. A knowing smile graced Anna's face at the suggestion.

"Okay, but you girls have to help me make them; these old hands do not work quite like they used to." The girls nodded, and Anna smiled. Pelmeni was something her mama taught her to make when they were living in Sverdlovsk; it had been a good way to distract her from the goings-on of war. Anna was pleased to pass the tradition down to her own granddaughter.

The rhythmic thud of rolling dough filled the small kitchen. The smell of raw flour and seasoned meat was a comforting contrast to the girls' excited chatter. Sasha, surprisingly adept with her hands, expertly pleated the delicate parcels of meat and pastry, while Misha, less graceful but equally enthusiastic, giggled at her own clumsy attempts.

Anna watched them, a warm feeling spreading through her chest. The scent of simmering broth mingled with the earthy aroma of the filling; it was a fragrant tapestry woven from generations of family memories. Later, huddled around the small table that was used more for tea time gatherings than eating, illuminated by the soft glow of a single lamp, they ate. The simple meal was punctuated by laughter and the clinking of spoons.

Anna nodded at appropriate intervals, a polite smile fixed on her face. Her ears worked diligently beneath the surface, catching a familiar word here or a hesitant Russian phrase there, piecing together the whirlwind of their European travels.

February 2015

Anna, aged seventy-seven | Moscow, Moscow Oblast, Russian Federation

Chiara had quietly warned Anna of what was coming this week. The warning came through whispers from one of their many tea times where Chiara had pulled her aside while the others were distracted. This week was the anniversary of Ameliya's husband's sudden death.

Anna saw Ameliya's grief for Nikolai in her fleeting smiles and the pangs of pain when the conversation of their dead husbands came up. She had told the group that they had a love that spanned decades until one day she woke up next to a corpse instead of her husband's warm touch.

The idea of waking up next to someone who was cold in the morning was unimaginable for Anna. She was not capable of the same kind of grief. Vladimir had spent the last part of his life in separate rooms while he was in and out of a lucid state. A profound sadness often clouded Ameliya's quiet demeanor, a longing that transcended the simple grief of loss.

Anna had heard whispers from Chiara about a dark period before her arrival, a desperate yearning to be with Nikolai again that had led to a quiet, unspoken attempt to follow him. The fragility of Ameliya's recovery was a constant undercurrent in their group.

Anna was quietly envious of the depth of emotion Ameliya held for her husband. Imagine being loved like that: a love so deep and profound she would want to have followed him into the afterlife. Anna would not get that kind of love. Self pity aside, she knew the entire group of women needed to band together and make sure their friend was supported and loved.

Before the others woke, Anna slipped out of the complex, cleaning gear in hand, to visit the grave site near the Moskva River. She may not have loved Vladimir like this, but she wanted to make sure her friend's husband's grave site was looked after when she came to visit. She knew where it was from the ladies speaking about it privately. They took turns each year to make sure it was in good condition for Ameliya's visit. This year was Anna's turn.

The sun was quietly peeking over the horizon, setting everything in a golden glow as dawn hit the city. Anna could see her breath as she bustled down the streets and crossed the river bridge. The river reflected the sun and sights. It was still: a chance to reflect, a chance to take stock. Anna admired the reflections of the buildings over the water with the faint light of dawn colorizing the entire image.

As a brisk breeze followed the river, carrying with it a chill and some of the autumn leaves that had been steadily falling from the trees, it caused Anna to snap out of the temporary moment of serenity and continue her mission to Nikolai's grave site. Sighing, she knew that those trees would lose their leaves soon. The golden leaves and oranges and reds would line the streets, and the trees would soon be encumbered with snow instead. Anna knew it was going to be a cold winter; the Hydrometeorological Research Centre of the Russian Federation had advised as much.

She arrived at the graveyard and moved down to the row where she knew her friend's beloved was buried.

Here lies Nikolai Nicolayev. A beloved husband, father, and Dedushka. Survived by his greatest love, Ameliya, his two sons, Artemi and Gleb, and his three vnuki. May his soul rest forever in love and peace.

Kneeling on the damp earth, Anna's gaze traced the inscription on the smooth granite. Nikolai Nicolayev. A life summarized in a few lines. She wiped away where wild birds had desecrated the headstone and placed a small bunch of flowers down at the site.

"Thank you for loving her," Anna whispered at the stone.

Anna got up slowly from that, overcome with a mix of emotions: jealousy to have been loved like that, and sorrow because she could imagine the pain one of her closest friends was going through.

Ameliya's eyes were red-rimmed and swollen. She had been crying, something Anna loathed. Earlier in the morning Anna had gone out to get coffee and tea at one of the local cafes for everyone. Coming back, though, Anna could see the distraction perhaps had not worked quite as well as it could have.

On a plate in the center of the table sat a small mountain of persiki, the delicate peach-shaped cookies. Their caramel filling hinted at a forgotten sweetness, and their blush was a soft, natural pink. Anna had baked them with Ameliya in mind, a small offering of comfort for a friend with a fondness for sweet things.

The apartment had become a sanctuary for the day: a space for Ameliya to feel her grief safely, and a place for other women to comfort her and make sure they were able to feel anything that came up for them as well. They drank tea, ate the sweet peach treats, and allowed the grief of their own losses to wash over them.

Ameliya's shoulders trembled with each choked sob, her breath hitching in ragged gasps. The redness around her eyes spread, mirroring the faint flush creeping up her neck. Her hands, clasped tightly in her lap, were visibly shaking, the knuckles bone-white. Anna noticed the slight tremor in Ameliya's voice, a physical manifestation of the emotional turmoil she was experiencing. Even the small sips of tea seemed to cause a shudder to run through her slender frame.

The sweetness of the persiki cookies did little to alleviate the tension etched deeply into her brow, the muscles there tight and rigid. As the memories flowed, the grief seemed to physically weigh her down, her posture slumping further into the worn armchair. The women all gathered around their friend, like a shield, to make sure she knew she was not alone and she was loved and that they wanted her to stay. Even if the woman's beloved had departed, the feeling of loss was as fresh today as it was the day she woke up to his cold, dead corpse.

September 2015

Anna, aged sixty-eight | Moscow, Moscow Oblast, Russian Federation

The tea from earlier in the day was gone. In its place stood a bottle of good Vodka, clear and cold from the freezer, and a small plate of cheese and crackers the women had hardly touched. The lamp in the corner threw long, amber shadows across the room, catching the glint of tears that had finally stopped falling but had left a salt-trail on Ameliya's cheeks. The air was thick, not with steam this time, but with the heavy, electric honesty that only arrives after midnight.

Anna looked at her friends. She saw Ameliya, whose grief was a holy shrine; Chiara, who used volume like a shield; and Nika, who sat in the corner with the watchful stillness of a hawk.

"We spend so much time mourning them," Anna began, her voice cracking the silence. "But we never talk about the parts of them that we do not miss."

She reached into the pocket of her cardigan and pulled out the letter from 2004. The paper was soft now, like cloth, from years of being folded and unfolded in the dark.

"Vladimir died in 2001," Anna said, her eyes fixed on the bottle. "You know this, I moved here not long after. But he made sure to strike me one last time three years later. He left a letter with one of his associates. In it, he confessed to fathering a daughter with a mistress. He told me her name, told me she might come looking for my son, and then he blamed my failing body for his straying. He blamed me for the daughters we lost decades ago."

A sharp intake of breath came from Chiara. Nika simply narrowed her eyes, leaning forward. Perhaps she remembered Anna talking to her about Vladimir back at the institute.

"He also admitted to having a man killed," Anna whispered, the weight of the secret finally sliding off her shoulders. "An American I worked with. He had him dealt to because of a perception of an affair that never happened. He carried that blood for forty years and never blinked."

"Bastard," Chiara spat, her Italian accent thick and jagged. She poured herself another shot, her hands trembling. "You think you knew a man? I moved here for love in the sixties. An Italian girl in Moscow. My mother thought I was moving to the moon. In Italy, in the south where I was born, love is a thunderstorm. It is loud. It is plates breaking against the wall. It is singing from the balcony. You know exactly where you stand because the air is always vibrating with it."

She let out a dry, rattling laugh. "Then I came here. To the grey buildings. I married my Mikhail, and I waited for the thunderstorm. It never came. I thought for ten years that he did not love me. I thought he was made of stone. And all that time, he spent half our marriage reporting on me to the local committee. He loved me, yes, but he loved the State's approval more. Every time I acted too Italian, he would go to his little meetings to ensure they knew he was still a loyal comrade."

"Russians do not give their hearts away to the breeze," Nika interjected quietly. "The wind here is too cold. It would freeze the blood."

"I learned that," Chiara nodded, her face softening. "I remember a winter, thirty years ago. I was so sick, the fever was like a fire. Mikhail did not cry. He did not tell me I was his love. He just went out into a blizzard. He walked four kilometres to find blood oranges for juice like my mother used to give me in Naples. He came back covered in frost, his eyelashes frozen, and he sat by the stove and squeezed the oranges for juice without saying a single word. That is the Russian love. It is not a song; it is a sacrifice. My Mikhail was a snitch, yes, but he was also the man who brought me oranges in a blizzard. Both things were true."

Ameliya reached for a piece of cheese, sans cracker, her movements slow and deliberate. "It is why the loss is so heavy," she said, her voice a ghost of a sound. "When a Russian man dies, the silence he leaves behind is not just empty. It is the loss of the quiet protector. Nikolai never told me he loved me every day. He just made sure the boots I wore were thick enough for the mud. But the reason I loved Nikolai so much was because of the shattered thing he found when we met. I am from the East. Vladivostok. When I was twenty, I was beautiful, and I was foolish. A man promised me a job in a grand hotel in the West. He talked of silk sheets and big tips. Instead, the moment we crossed the border of the Oblast, he took my papers. He broke my nose so I would stop screaming, and then he sold me."

The room went deathly still.

"I spent two years being moved from city to city like a crate of cabbage," Ameliya continued, her voice devoid of emotion, which made it all the more chilling. "Trafficked across the union. I was used by men who did not want to know my name, men who stank of cheap tobacco and sweat. I was beaten when I was too tired, drugged when I was too rebellious, and discarded in a basement in Gorky when my body finally started to give out from the infections. I was waiting to die. I wanted to die."

She took a shaky breath. "Nikolai was the medic who found that basement during a raid. He didn't see a prostitute or a ruin. He saw a person. He sat with me in the hospital for months. He held the basin while I vomited from the drug withdrawals. He spent five years just teaching me how to hold a hand again without flinching. He picked up the pieces of a woman who had been ground into the dirt and he glued them back together with patience. I did not just love him, Anna. I owed him my soul. And now that he is gone, I feel like the pieces are falling apart again because the man who held them together is not here."

Nika reached out and placed a hand on Ameliya's arm. It was a firm, grounding touch.

"We are all survivors of men," Nika said quietly. "Some were cruel like Vladimir. Some were weak like Chiara's husband. And some were rescuers like Nikolai. But they all defined us. They were the sun we orbited. Perhaps that is why we are here now. We are the only ones who can translate the silence. We know the difference between a man who is quiet because he is protecting you and a man who is quiet because he is erasing you."

Nika looked directly at Anna, a silent acknowledgement of their shared past passing between them.

"But the sun has set," Nika concluded. "And look at us. We are still here. We are drinking vodka, we are eating cookies, and the walls have not fallen down."

Anna felt a strange, bubbling sensation in her chest. It was not the vodka. It was the realization that the widows' club was not just a place to wait for death. It was a fortress.

Anna looked at the letter in her hand, the ink that had once felt like a brand on her skin. With a deliberate movement, she leaned forward and held the corner of the paper over the small candle. The paper curled and blossomed into a hungry flame. She dropped it into the empty tea saucer and watched until Vladimir's handwriting was nothing but grey ash.

"To escaping our shadows," Anna said, raising her glass.

"To escaping the shadows," they echoed.

"Next time," Chiara said, trying to regain her usual spark, "I will marry a Frenchman. They are supposed to be a good middle ground."

"You are seventy-eight, Chiara," Roza quipped from across the table. "At this age, the only man you should worry about is the one who delivers the pension."

The room erupted in a small, much-needed burst of laughter. The weight of the evening had not vanished, but it had shifted. It was no longer a burden they carried alone.

March

2024

Anna, aged eighty-six | Moscow, Moscow Oblast, Russian Federation

Anna had spent a week cleaning the little apartment, making sure there wasn't a speck of dust or photo out of place. She knew that Misha was arriving soon. She was pretty sure the plane had already landed, and that she was bringing her fiancé.

She fixed the old red scarf around her head. An old faithful kind of scarf that had almost been lost during the fall of the Union. In those days, everyone was in a rush to get food and banking, but Anna had retraced her steps through the mud to find the fabric discarded on the street a day later. It was a survivor, just like her.

A timid knock came on the door. Misha wasn't sure about this. *Interesting,* Anna thought. Perhaps it was the new location, perhaps it was the man she was bringing.

Anna opened the door, noting that she was moving a little slower than usual. She had aches and pains, the lingering tax of winters where coal was scarcer than bread, but noticing the pain was what bothered her more than the ache itself.

On the other side of the door was Misha. Anna couldn't believe – well she knew it in her mind that Misha was an adult - but when she pictured her, she pictured a gangly teenager, not this full-grown woman in front of her. She was a woman, filled out in her body, chocolate eyes still sparkling with the same mischief she had when she was a child.

The man she was with, her fiancé Anna surmised, was much taller and surrounded Anna's grandchild protectively. He had striking green eyes, not unlike the deep forests in the northern part of Russia that Anna remembered, from her youth spent hiding from war. He was bulky; Anna thought he was either one of those men who was obsessed with how he looked or had some form of military or police training. He stood with his weight balanced and ready to move. Anna had seen that look on men before, usually the ones carrying sidearms.

"Come in, please," Anna said to the pair in Russian, testing the man. Can he speak in her granddaughter's mother tongue?

Misha quietly translated Anna's words to him, which gave Anna all the answer she needed.

"Babushka's English isn't great, and she will probably speak to me in Russian. I can ask her to try English, but I can also translate for you?" Misha asked the man, and Anna wanted to correct the girl. She could speak English perfectly. But it was a part of her past, the biggest secret she held from a time when knowing the language of the West was a dangerous currency, and not one she could share yet.

The man, Matt, Anna finally remembered his name, instead showed Misha his phone and told her that the device could interpret the conversation. Perhaps even respond to it, but Anna knew it wouldn't sound right. A machine has no soul because it cannot understand the rhythm of a person's heart.

Anna stopped listening to the pair and instead continued with prepping dinner and making sure the desserts she had made earlier in the day were still as delectable as she intended them to be for the evening meal.

Clearing away the plates, Matthew attempted to thank Anna in Russian. She appreciated the effort, though couldn't help but hear the thick Australian accent underpinning his words. Anna nodded at his thanks and continued her work.

Plates cleaned and tidied away; Anna offered to show the couple to their room. "I show you room now?" she asked, making sure her English was broken despite knowing full well she wasn't using correct grammar. It pained her tongue to butcher the verbs so badly. Her old teacher at the Institute would have rapped her knuckles with a ruler, but information was a vault and she was the only one with the key. The room was modelled off the one she had back in her old home she had shared with Vladimir. The only difference is now there was just one bed rather than the set of twins the grandchildren had known her to have. Anna figured everyone was an adult now, and if Konstantin and Misha visited at the same time, there was nothing stopping one of them from taking the couch.

Matt yawned and Anna wished them both a good night, noting the quick flash of... was that fear? In Matt's eyes before she closed the door. She saw the way he looked at the small bed and then at Misha, like a man staring at a beautiful fire he wasn't allowed to touch. Perhaps there was more to this relationship than she thought.

It had been amusing watching the two trying to deny their feelings for each other while also pretending they were In love for Anna's sake. More amusing when Misha, scurried her grandmother out of her own apartment and then came back an hour later to ask for ideas on what they would be best to do in Russia. Thankfully, in Russian this time so Anna didn't have to fake not understanding.

Matt's accent was thick, but Misha hadn't lost hers. She could understand them both to a point. When Anna returned from her card game later that morning, she found the apartment quiet, but her eyes immediately went to the small details. A lampshade was tilted at an odd angle. The cushions on the sofa were half an inch from where she always kept them. She hid a smile as she boiled the kettle. Matthew had been searching for bugs, microphones. It was a familiar ritual from her youth and it told her more about the boy's profession than Misha ever could.

Anna had picked up that they were going out this afternoon and perhaps, perhaps this was the best time to meddle a little bit. Finally the two had chosen to go to Moscow Zoo, a good choice in Anna's mind, though caged animals did make her a bit sad. She empathized with them, because she had spent forty years in a marriage that felt like a very clean and small cage. She considered her finances. Perhaps it wasn't much, but Anna went down to the bank and withdrew a handful of Rubles to send the couple to dinner. An intimate dinner and a walk by the Moskva River usually forced the truth out of even the most stubborn hearts.

Anna wrote a note in her tight and elegant cursive for the both of them: *I went to a game night. Please, here's some money so you two can enjoy a romantic dinner.*

And went off to challenge the other widows to a card game, wondering if the boy would check the restaurant over before he finally dared to kiss her granddaughter.

March 2024

Anna, aged eighty-six | Moscow, Moscow Oblast, Russian Federation

Anna was preparing lunch when the landline on her wall rang. Only Misha, her son in Australia, and a handful of others scattered across the globe possessed that number. Misha was currently traveling within Russia, and that thought made Anna hurry to the phone with a sense of anticipation.

"Da?" she answered.

"Babushka!" Misha's voice cracked with relief as Anna answered. "Thank goodness you picked up!"

"What is wrong, Zaychik?" Anna asked.

"We were kidnapped and are now in Kaliningrad. We have no cash and no belongings as they are still with you," Misha said quickly.

"Are you safe?"

A cold calm settled over Anna. The tremor in her hands disappeared. Her questions became concise and her tone was devoid of emotion. Decades of training, buried beneath layers of domesticity, resurfaced with chilling efficiency. The frantic grandmother vanished. She was replaced by the operative who had navigated far more dangerous situations than this.

“Okay, Zaychik. You still have that old bank account within Russia?”

“Da,” she replied.

“I need you to visit the branch and withdraw money. Get a cell phone and call me on it once you are in a safe and private space. Then I can help you properly.”

“Are you sure, Babushka?” Misha’s voice trembled slightly. “This will not get you into trouble, will it?”

“Da, it is fine. Give me thirty minutes and then find a bank.”

Misha hung up then. Anna got herself ready to head down to the local bank to transfer money into Misha's old account. The urgency of the situation cleared the fog of her quiet life. A sharp focus returned. It was a sense of purpose she had not felt in years. The intricate planning and the need for secrecy felt like slipping into an old, comfortable coat. It was a shadow of the past and a reminder of a life lived on the edge. A small, almost forgotten smile touched her lips.

While Anna walked down to the bank, she tried to remember where all her old classmates might be in Kaliningrad these days. It was a little out of the way. She hadn’t been glad of many things from her past, but for the first time she was glad Nika had moved down the hall. Rather than her deep sense of dread that perhaps the woman would relinquish their shared past to the other widows in the block. After moving a few thousand Rubles across to Misha's account, knowing Misha would return anything she did not use, Anna made her way back to knock on Nika's door.

"Anafonika?" Anna asked as she banged on the wood.

The woman opened the door with bleary eyes and an eyebrow cocked at Anna's urgency. "Anna, what is the meaning of this?"

"Do we have contacts over in Kaliningrad these days?" Anna asked abruptly. She closed the door behind her in a rush and bustled into the apartment like a typhoon.

The question took Nika back for a second. Kaliningrad was a port city of Germanic origin that was cut off from the motherland by Lithuania and Poland. It remained important to the nation as an opening into the Baltic Sea.

"I have an old contact there named Timofei. Though," Nika added with a slight grimace, "it has been a long time. I hope he is still amenable. I can give him a call and try, but I cannot promise anything, Anna."

Anna started making tea as if on command while Nika called an old number in Kaliningrad she had not called in a long while. Anna could not hear the conversation clearly. There were murmurings of apologies and promises to pay before Nika handed the phone to Anna and instructed her to give Timofei the details.

"Timofei speaking," a deep timbre came through the line.

"Timofei, it is Anna here. I am one of Nika's school friends. I need a large favour to help my family and we are willing to pay for discretion."

"Nonsense, Anna," the deep voice rumbled. "Nika has already pledged a debt. What do you need?"

Anna explained that her granddaughter needed to be smuggled out of Russia to a Western friendly country. Germany perhaps, or Poland at a pinch.

"Da, I can do that. Make sure she is ready to go and give me a call when she is so we can act quickly. I am driving tour buses between Kaliningrad and Gdansk daily. I can smuggle them in the luggage compartment. It will not be comfortable, but it will get them out of the country without tipping off the authorities."

"That would be good thanks. We shall talk soon." Anna hung up the phone and looked at an expectant Nika.

"So, who is Timofei?" Anna asked a nervous looking Nika.

Sunlight streamed through Anna's window later that day as the landline rang. The sound of Misha's voice brought a mix of relief and renewed anxiety. Anna listened intently and relayed Timofei's instructions in a low, urgent voice. She added a heartfelt, "Be careful, Zaychik," before the conversation ended.

April *2024*

Anna, aged eighty-six | Moscow, Moscow Oblast, Russian Federation

It started as a strong sense that something was fundamentally wrong. Aches throbbed where there had been none the day before. A slight sense of confusion danced at the corners of her typically sharp mind. Anna's thoughts were a little foggy, and she felt truly tired, despite sleeping like a log every night for the past week.

She was exhausted, and she suspected it was a delayed effect of the adrenaline surge she felt while helping Misha last week. The rush had been more potent than she remembered. That must be it, she told herself. I am just reacting poorly to the adrenaline comedown. Her training told her it was unlikely but Anna held onto that hope. Because the alterative was unthinkable.

She was glad she had managed to get Misha out of trouble, and that knowledge contributed to her sleeping well. Misha was in Germany now with her partner, Matt. Knowing she was safe was a relief, though Anna knew she needed to go and visit them while they were close by.

Anna had been feeling a little weaker before they came to visit, which slowed her down, but it had not been anything major. She hadn't had a fall or had to move out to a rest home. Still, a persistent unease clung to Anna like an invisible weight pressing down on her. It wasn't a localized pain, but a general feeling of unwellness. It was a quiet hum of disquiet that resonated through her body like a discordant chord. It felt like the final note at the end of a song, one that was long and haunting.

Perhaps a doctor visit was in order after all. The trip to see Misha and Matt suddenly felt less like a leisurely visit and more like a necessary escape. It was a chance to recharge before confronting whatever this insidious feeling truly was. A wave of melancholy washed over Anna as she contemplated her age and the finite nature of her time. A quiet realization settled within her: she needed to be pragmatic about the time she had left.

The thought sparked action. Pen and paper were retrieved, and the scratching of her nib against the paper filled the silence as she wrote letters. This was a forgotten pastime that had been left neglected since Ivan's childhood.

The first was to Misha, a light-hearted missive filled with hope for her future, to be opened on her wedding day. The second, to Ivan, was more serious. It was a carefully worded message containing her final words to her son. The third was to her grandson, Konstantin, giving him the best advice she could as a grandmother, to be opened when he falls in love. The final letter, addressed to a lawyer, was terse and businesslike. It outlined her wishes for her estate. She knew this wasn't the typical way of doing things. It had been a long time since she had updated legal documents with her lawyer, she just hoped this would be respected.

As the ink dried, quickly, a strange calm settled over her. The letters, like tangible anchors, grounded her in the present. They reminded her that even amidst uncertainty, there were still things she could control. Even with this persistent unease, she had taken action and laid down her wishes. It was a small measure of control in an uncertain world.

The trip to Germany suddenly felt not just like an escape, but a purposeful journey. It was a necessary step in confronting the shadows of her past and whatever lay ahead.

April 2024

Anna, aged eighty-six | Berlin, Berlin, Federal Republic of Germany

The rhythmic clatter of the train wheels against the tracks was a relentless soundtrack to Anna's journey to Berlin. Each lurch and sway vibrated through her weary bones, and a dull ache settled in her chest that no amount of stale train air could dispel. Flying had always felt like an unnatural defiance of gravity and a vulnerability she preferred to avoid. This ground-bound pilgrimage held its own kind of penance, despite the days blurring into a landscape of fleeting towns and anonymous faces. Every kilometre that brought her closer to her Zaychik chipped away at the anxiety that had been a constant companion since the news. To see Misha's bright smile again, to know her delicate little hare was safe, that was the only destination that mattered. It was worth every ache and every lost hour of sleep.

Stepping onto the bustling platform of the Berlin Hauptbahnhof felt like exhaling a breath she hadn't realized she had been holding. The sharp, unfamiliar sounds of German voices and the rush of people created a world away from her quiet home, but the urgency propelling her forward drowned out the strangeness. The aroma of strong coffee and sweet pastries hung heavy in the air of the small Berlin café. Anna's gaze swept across the tables until a knot of anxiety tightened, then released, when she spotted the familiar, slender figure tucked away in a corner booth.

It was Misha. Relief washed over her in a dizzying wave. Their initial greeting was a tight embrace, a silent acknowledgment of the terror they had both endured, albeit from afar. As they settled, the clinking of cups and hushed conversations faded. Misha's voice, still trembling slightly, began to recount the horrifying ordeal. The kidnapping happened all because of a case of mistaken identity involving her friend Sasha.

Anna scoffed, releasing a harsh, dismissive sound. "Misha," she said, her voice firm and laced with genuine affection, "Please take this as the absolute truth. That Sasha cannot even begin to possess the light you carry."

Anna knew that Misha, a naturally slim girl, struggled with her own body issues. She hoped that was something the girl would work through with Matt. A faint pink dusted Misha's cheeks at Anna's unexpected compliment, providing a brief softening of the fear etched on her face. Misha took a shaky breath and began to recount the events, her voice gaining a hesitant momentum.

“It was just a normal date,” she started, her fingers tracing patterns on her coffee cup. “We went to the zoo. The monkeys were being particularly playful that day, and I remember Matthew laughing.” A shadow crossed her features. “Then dinner, at a quiet little place near the river. Everything felt ordinary.” Her voice dropped. “It was afterwards, while walking back to the apartment.”

The recounting of their capture brought a fresh wave of tears to Misha's eyes, leaving silent tracks tracing paths down her pale cheeks. Her breath hitched, and a small, broken sound escaped her lips. Anna's hand instinctively reached across the table, covering Misha's trembling one. Nearby, the sudden scrape of a chair against the wooden floor punctuated the heavy silence.

Anna's gaze snapped towards the sound, finding Matt hovering anxiously near their booth. Anna shot a withering look across the small space, one honed over years of dealing with wayward men. It was a look that could freeze blood and empty rooms. Matt's jaw tightened, his eyes locking with hers in a silent, defiant glare before he visibly forced himself to remain seated, a statue of concern. Misha, lost in the reliving of her terror, remained oblivious to the tense exchange. She remained unfocused as she whispered about the cold, the fear, and the violation that had irrevocably altered the landscape of her and Matthew's shared world.

Misha was seemingly deep in remembering what happened to her and the effect it had on her and Matthew. The raw vulnerability in Misha's voice stirred a fierce protectiveness and a familiar ache in Anna's heart. She wanted to shield this young woman from all future pain. That desire felt particularly strong given her own recent fragility. As Misha finally fell silent, exhaustion etched on her face, Anna squeezed her hand.

"Rest now, Zaychik. You are safe." Anna watched her with a lingering concern in her eyes and a silent wish for Misha's continued healing.

The long train ride back to Moscow stretched before Anna. Each click of the tracks served as a reminder of the miles separating her from Misha once more. The relief of their reunion was tempered by the lingering worry for the young woman's recovery, though she knew they would be okay. New passports were coming from Australia so they could catch the next flight back to their home.

Anna had done her job.

Anna pictured Misha and Matthew, their faces etched with the recent trauma, yet bound together by an love. It was a precious thing, that connection. A sigh escaped Anna's lips, as the journey and the emotional weight of Misha's story took their toll. The day was fading outside the window, mirroring the subtle fading of her own energy.

May 2024

Ivan, aged fifty-six | Moscow, Moscow Oblast, Russian Federation

She was dead.

Ivan wasn't sure how to hold his grief, or the knowledge that his mother was no longer there. He loved her, and however strained their relationship had been, he could not hate her for the choices she had made. He understood now that he would have done the same if his children had been in that kind of danger. It was a realization that had taken a lifetime to reach, arriving only now, as a grown man with two adult children of his own.

His hands shook as he held the letter. It was his mother's parting words, found on the kitchen table in an envelope.

Anna had collapsed in her apartment only a month or so after his own daughter made it back to Australia. One of her friends had called an ambulance service, but she was pronounced dead on their arrival. They then called Ivan, who took the next available flights to get himself to Russia and to his mother's side.

Synok moy, Ivan, my dearest.

You are a grown man now, halfway across the world, but you will always be my little boy who grabbed my finger so tight the day you came into the world. As your Mama, there is one thing I need you to keep tucked away deep in that stubborn heart of yours. Never take your beautiful lot in life, including Valeriya and those noisy but wonderful grandchildren, for granted. This life is a mere blink. Mine has been, well, let's just say it has been painted with more shades than a Moscow autumn. It ranged from the screech of bombs overhead, which you cannot forget even if you try, to the sneaky thrill of playing my part in that ridiculous Cold War right under the noses of those Americans. You probably still disapprove, my serious son, but your Mama had her moments. It was not quite like Kostya's flashy James Bond movies, mind you. My work was more subtle and more useful. And then, of course, there was the pure, unadulterated joy of holding you, a tiny, perfect weight in my arms. That was followed by the kind of darkness you would not wish on your worst enemy. I mean the silence after your sisters... You were to have two sisters, and a still birth and miscarriage were one of the hardest things I ever had to overcome. Well, you know. A life in full colour, that is what it has been.

Speaking of messes, I still carry a knot in my gut about those years when you were small. Your father was not himself after losing the girls. That one time his temper flared at me, it lit a fire in me and a fierce need to shield you. Boarding school felt like the only way. It was a clumsy, heavy-handed way, I know now. Hearing you say you hated me cut deeper than any surgeon's blade, my darling. Forgive your old Mama for that clumsy love and for making you feel so abandoned.

But you blossomed, didn't you? You went from that scrawny lad to the man who fell head over heels for Valeriya, even back when you were still practically children yourselves. Seeing you two all moon-eyed over those summers warmed this old woman's heart, it truly did. And now you have built your own bright little rainbow in Sydney with a whole spectrum of friendships. Cherish that, Ivan. Those connections are the sturdy threads that hold us together when the storms roll in.

I have tried to leave things as neat as one can manage. These bones have not been feeling quite right lately. They have been a bit creaky and a bit off. Darya, bless her practical heart, just waved it off as age. But if you are reading this, well, she was wrong. You know my feelings about doctors ever since the girls. I was a stubborn old fool.

You will find a couple more notes tucked away. There is one for my bright-eyed Misha for the day she walks down the aisle. It is a day your old Baba wishes she could see. There is also one for Kostya for when he finally tumbles headfirst into love, as I suspect he will, dramatically and with much fanfare. My heart will be with you all, always echoing across the oceans.

Ivan folded the letter carefully. The sound of the paper and even the scent of it felt like a whispered goodbye. The scent of her perfume, faint but familiar, clung to the room. He stood there in the quiet kitchen. The silence was a stark contrast to the chaotic whirlwind of the past few days. Outside, the Russian autumn was making its mark known. Winds whipped past the apartment complex and rain came down in an almost horizontal fashion. It was a fitting backdrop to the storm within him.

Almost in a way, it was Anna's way of reminding him, even in his grief, of the colours of life. The wind picked up the wet, fallen foliage and moved it around as he left her apartment building for the final time. He began preparing to go back to Sydney.

Epilogue – February 2025

Misha, aged thirty-four | Sydney, New South Wales, Commonwealth of Australia

My dearest Zaychik, my Mikhaila.

I have passed away, but you already know this. You are reading this on your wedding day. I just wanted to leave you a short note and a final letter.

I am so proud of you, Zaychik. I am at rest knowing that you and your brother are both safe away from Russia and that your Papa and Mama are happy and thriving in their home. There was a time I was worried my actions as a mother would have irrevocably damaged your father and made him unable to live a happy life. But such are the worries of a mother and an old woman.

Know that I have lived a good life. I suspect your father found a few of the journals I kept over the years, though not the ones from the years when I was in active service. I think given your interest in politics, you may well be interested in some of the things I lived through, sweet girl.

I only have one final wish. It is that you live your truly happiest life. Do not settle. Do not break for a man. I know you saw how your Dedushka was acting in his final years, but know he was not always a bad man. I do regret not leaving him when things did get bad. It was a different time, and frankly, I was scared. I do not wish this for you. I want you happy.

When we next meet, I want to hear the tales of children filling your life with happiness, if that is what you wish. I want to hear of adventures that you and your beloved have taken over the years. And most importantly, I do not wish to see you again while you are young.

Live your life, Zaychik. Know that I am watching down with pride and joy, wishing I could be there today of all days. Now fold this letter up and pop it in a special place. Wipe any tears that have escaped and fix up any makeup smears.

And go out there and wow this world.

Until we meet again,

Your Babushka

Acknowledgements

Because it takes a village

Thank you for giving this one a read! I've found writing (while overwhelming) is my happy place.

This couldn't have been done without a incredible team of people so please excuse my self indulgence but I need to thank them.

S. Thank you for being your incredible self and cuddling up to me when I wrote some of the more difficult scenes. Sorry I didn't help around the house in the same way I could have if I wasn't an author, but I hope that seeing this one in print will make all those sacrifices worth it.

My whānau, thank you for being there. Mum for managing my first novels southward bound orders, and for always reading things and giving it a solid go, every author needs a mum like you (but they can't have you, only me right?). Dad, though I know you're unlikely to read this, thank you for being you. Thank you for challenging me and being proud when I manage to do the hard thing.

P&A, I hope you both had a read of the first one and loved it. I hope you love this one too!
Also thank you for all your unwavering support <3

The Richardson's – thank you for every conversation, dinner and piece of advice and encouragement. I hope this novel lives up to the hype! This applies to those in New Zealand and the overseas based contingent.

To my Beta Readers, Hayley, Lauren and Hannah.

Lauren, thank you for every comment, video and taking the time to make sure this novel could be more than a dancing skeleton. The advice you provided has been invaluable. So thank you SO MUCH! You will know just how invaluable good feedback is.

Hayley. Thank you for being a hype queen of the highest order. I'm sorry I caused *emotional damage *, but I hope you can forgive me for that. Thank you for your edits, and threatening the tense/POV baton when I arrive at my day job. Also your incredible art – girl. I cannot. Also please note, I've written you're incredible. Someone can read it so it MUST be true.

Hannah, I'm sorry. But no one can hurt Anna now. Taking the time on your breaks at mahi to read and suggest things. It honestly makes my heart so warm. Thank you for being such an incredible cheerleader <3 And please, consider being an editor. Because this book reads like english not the messed up vernacular in my mind because of you.

My workmates, please excuse the amount I always chat about my writing and editing process. I am sure its a pain but hell, how many people at work can say they have a published author (and now there's a second book it's not just a fluke!) in their team.

About the author

Aimee is a New Zealand–based writer living in the Hutt Valley, near Wellington. She balances writing with full-time work, returning to the page whenever she can to explore stories about with strong female leads, family, and the balance of love and loss.

Outside of writing, she enjoys reading and baking, usually with her cat Asher close by, offering constant company and questionable advice and her partner gaming in the other room.

Connect with Aimee:

http://www.aimeeblanc.com

https://www.instagram.com/aimeeblancauthor

Also by

Classified Hearts, the previous book in the series, tells Misha and Matt's story and how they found themselves in Moscow.

There's more to come.

If you enjoyed this book, leaving a review on Amazon or Goodreads is one of the best ways to support indie authors.

Every review helps more than you might think.

www.ingramcontent.com/pod-product-compliance
Lightning Source LLC
LaVergne TN
LVHW030915080826
845145LV00013B/2908

* 9 7 8 1 0 6 7 0 6 8 0 1 1 *